EVIDENCE OF BETRAYAL

Lila Ferrari

Warm wishes
Lila Ferrari

Paperback ISBN: 978-1-7330210-0-5

For more information on books by Lila Ferrari, or to subscribe to her newsletter, visit her website here:

https://www.lilaferrariwrites.com

EVIDENCE OF BETRAYAL

Betrayal, justice and second chances

A DETECTIVE WHO'S HEARD IT ALL.
A WOMAN WHO'S HAD IT ALL.
A STALKER WHO WANTS IT ALL.
WHAT COULD POSSIBLY GO WRONG?

In this edgy tale of romantic suspense, journalist Grace Winslow is starting over in Black Pointe, Florida, after losing her job, husband and reputation in D.C. She thought she left her stalker behind, but no—he's found her again. And this time, he isn't content with just ruining her life—he wants her dead.

Does Grace have the courage to stop her stalker, recover her reputation, get justice for herself and find love?

Detective Luke McBride is used to liars and doesn't trust women. Especially after his ex-fiancée and partner ran off, leaving him at the altar.

Luke values truth and justice above all. Grace challenges all his tightly held principles. Can he learn to trust her before the madman gets his revenge and destroys his chance at love?

Book 2 of KnightGuard Security, *Evidence of Murder,* tells Ben and Marlee's story. Look for a preview at the end of this book.

As always, reviews are nice. If you enjoy the book, please leave a review.

Follow me on:

Twitter: @lsferrariwrites
Facebook: @lilaferrariauthor
Instagram: @lsferrariwrites
Pinterest: @lsferrariwrites
Goodreads: @lilaferrariwrites
Bookbub: @lilaferrariwrites

For more information on books by Lila Ferrari, visit her website at www.lilaferrariwrites.com, where you can subscribe to her newsletter to get updates on releases, fun facts and enter giveaways.

KNIGHTGUARD SECURITY SERIES

EACH BOOK IN THE SERIES is a stand-alone and can be read in any order.

Evidence of Betrayal — Book 1 (Luke and Grace's story)

Evidence of Murder — Book 2 (Ben and Marlee's story)

Evidence of Lies — Book 3 (Pete and Julie's story)

Evidence of Deceit — Book 4 (Joe and Claire's story)

Evidence of Revenge — Book 5 (Sam and Mark's story)

Evidence of Secrets — Book 6 (Hank and Laura's story) - available soon

Evidence of Evil — Book 7 (Logan and Maddie's story) — available in 2022

ACKNOWLEDGMENTS

A great big thank you to everyone who read my words, made suggestions, and gave me encouragement.

Special thanks go to Cindy Bassuk. Your enthusiasm and belief in my ability to write a novel has been a blessing. The fact that you're my sister—doubly so.

Extra special thanks goes to Ray Ferrari. You have been my rock and best friend. Your suggestions have made this book even better.

And thanks to Lin Huntting Congdon for pointing out areas that needed clarification and to Chris Kridler for editing my rough drafts and keeping my story on track.

Any errors, blunders, or inaccuracies made are all mine.

For Ray,
Always

CHAPTER ONE

Jean Mays labored to breathe, her thigh muscles burning. Soon the Florida humidity would settle on her body like a wet blanket. But for now, it was cool. She knew the trail's end wasn't far and she could get her caffeine fix at the little coffee shop she stopped at every day on her way home. Her mouth salivated anticipating the reward of her favorite blend.

Her run had been uneventful and peaceful. She enjoyed the euphoria of the "runner's high." It helped her make it through the day. This particular path was just the way she liked it—not well-groomed. Very few people jogged here. She'd had her fill of intrusions in every aspect of her life in D.C. Now she was alone and could relax.

A rustle in the woods caused her to turn to see what kind of animal it was. In the past, she had seen squirrels, a deer, the occasional raccoon, even a skunk which she managed to avoid. Today, no animal showed itself. Catching herself as she tripped over some roots, she ran on.

But something wasn't right. There was that prickling on her skin, the goosebumps that unnerved her. A whisper of noise. Jean turned her head. The bushes rustled slightly. It was a windless day which made her suspicious. Was someone watching her? Or was her imagination playing tricks on her again?

Either way, she decided it was safer not to investigate and ran faster even though she was tired. The 11 a.m. meeting at the coffee shop with a man she didn't want to deal with weighed heavy on her mind. She didn't want to be late. He was insistent she meet him there, not at her condo, and he was not a man to cross. She wished she knew why he wanted to meet. Why was he even in Black Pointe? Was he upset because she asked for a little money in exchange for not spilling the extent of their involvement in ruining Grace Winslow's reputation in D.C.? Well, she'd know soon enough.

Thump. Thump. The rhythm of her footsteps lulled her into calmness.

A slight movement from the bushes on her left startled her. She almost tripped over a branch on the path. As she righted herself, a dark form stepped out.

"You!"

CHAPTER TWO

Detectives Luke McBride and his partner Ben Green flashed their badges at the beat cop guarding the entrance to Sexton Park. The tree-lined path was shaded and cool, innocent-looking except for the deceased lying on her side.

The bagel he consumed for breakfast threatened to make an impromptu appearance. Even though he had seen his share of killings for the past eight years, the loss of life still sickened Luke, especially when it involved women or children. They were supposed to be protected and cherished.

The police didn't have any information on the woman yet. No keys. No ID. No cell phone. Nevertheless, she had been someone's someone—a sister, mother, girlfriend, aunt, or daughter.

Right now, she was just another anonymous body heaped on the ground, surrounded by yellow tape, flashing red and blue lights, cops, detectives, curious onlookers and the ubiquitous nosy body trying to sneak under the tape, to get a picture or story to titillate the tabloids.

Shit. Luke shook his head. "Why couldn't it be a drug dealer or a gangbanger lying there? Why an innocent?"

"It's the job, man. Gotta tell you, it's getting to me too," muttered Ben.

The woman's body lay on her side along the dirt trail about twenty feet from the entrance.

Her black shorts had been pulled down around her ankles, followed by pale pink panties. The juxtaposition of the innocent pink playing against the background of black wasn't lost on Luke. Had she been raped before her death? Luke hoped not.

The woman was pretty. But now, she lay there broken and bruised, pretty didn't matter anymore.

Her sleeveless purple top was pulled up around her neck. The perp didn't bother to unsnap her bra, just jerked it up exposing her breasts. A long blond braid full of leaves and debris snaked out from the back of her head, her white sneakers were still on her feet, and her hands were clasped just under her chin as if she were praying. *Posed for sure.* But why?

It was way past dawn. The Florida sun was rising like a giant hot yellow ball on the horizon, and his shirt was starting to cling to his body. Luke hoped to get the body moved before the day got any hotter and decomposition became more of a problem; however, the medical examiner was caught in traffic and running late.

The cop on the scene pointed out a tall, thin man standing at the edge of the path who found the body.

As Ben handed Luke a pair of blue disposable gloves and pulled on a pair himself, he muttered, "I'm so tired of this shit. Why can't a woman be able to take a run without being killed."

Luke looked over at Ben, his partner for the past three years, shook his head. "Tell me about it."

Standing near the bushes behind the body, Luke didn't observe anything out of the ordinary. Nothing screaming, "I'm evidence, pick me up" or broken branches. Nothing showing she died at this location.

Searching for evidence in the bushes, under rocks, in the grass, anywhere that might lead them to her killer didn't yield much. The park was a favorite spot for the homeless because it wasn't used often, and the smell of urine made him gag. They picked up a few empty soda and beer cans; a used condom; an inhaler, some needles, fast-food wrappers and paper. Lots of paper—newspapers, paper napkins—all sorts of paper. God, people were pigs. Bagging and tagging what they found, they set the bags on the ground and walked over to the body.

"Damn. She's the second jogger this month to be killed and exposed like this." Ben rubbed his face and looked quizzically at the body. "Although her hands are posed differently. I wonder if we have a serial killer on the loose?"

Luke stepped closer to the body. "Hope not. We'll find out soon enough."

He and Ben searched the general area but didn't notice any drag marks on the sidewalk or broken branches in the bushes surrounding her body. Luke was perplexed. Bodies didn't just fall from the sky.

"I wonder where she was killed?"

"Could be here in the park. This doesn't make sense. Why place the body here? Does it have some significance or was it just convenient?" asked Ben.

They needed to expand their search so they would walk the park later. *Shit, this was going to be another long day*. Par for the course though.

Did the murderer move the body here? If so, why?

From his vantage point, Luke observed the woman's bloody knuckles and broken fingernails. Good. She put up a struggle. Not that it helped her, but the lab might get the DNA of the murderer. He didn't see any blood on the ground, but that could change when the medical examiner arrived and turned her body over.

A car door slammed shut, and a mumble of voices caused Luke to turn. The crime scene investigators had arrived and were unpacking their equipment. Soon they would take pictures of the body, bag her hands for DNA, diagram the scene and collect more evidence. Following them was the medical examiner.

Luke motioned to Ben. "Why don't you go talk to Wilson, who called it in. I'll talk to the jogger who found her and get his statement. By then the ME should be finished."

Ben nodded and headed over to the officer guarding the entrance.

Luke went over to the twenty-something guy who found the body. He was pacing at the far edge of the sidewalk looking around nervously. He looked a little pale. A lot pale, actually. Pale and greenish. Praying the guy wouldn't lose his cookies on him, Luke took a step back and pulled out his notebook.

The jogger was wiping his hands on his shirt. He stopped when Luke walked over.

"Look, man," he started before Luke even opened his mouth. "I didn't see or hear anyone near the body. I almost didn't see her, and I certainly didn't touch her."

He glanced around the park, ignoring the body and sighed. "I jog in this park every morning, and there has never been any trouble." He shrugged. "I wish I could help, but I don't know anything more."

"OK then," Luke looked at his notes. "Jim?"

The man nodded.

"You didn't touch the body or move anything, did you?"

"No. I told you already I didn't."

"What time did you notice her lying there?"

"Somewhere around 7 a.m."

"Where were you when you first saw her lying there?" *Shit, this case wasn't going to be solved quickly. This guy couldn't add any information.*

The man pointed farther down the path. "I was rounding the corner, looking at the exit when I saw what looked like a heap of clothes on the path. I didn't realize it was a person until I got closer. I called 9-1-1 as soon as I realized she wasn't moving. I definitely didn't go in for a close-up."

Luke rubbed the back of his neck. They hadn't solved the last jogger's murder, and now they had another one on their plate. *Could Ben be right?* Was it possible this was the same killer?

"Did you see anyone else on the path?"

The man thought for a moment. "Hmmm. No. I'm usually one of a few joggers who run here. It's not a popular park. Plus, this isn't the path I normally use. I wanted to spice up my run a little." He grimaced, "I guess I got more than I bargained for."

He glanced at his watch. "Shit, I'm gonna be late for work. Can I go now?"

Disappointed the jogger couldn't give him more information, Luke handed him a pen and paper and took out his card. "Give me your contact information, and you're free to go. Here's my card in case you remember anything."

Luke pocketed the jogger's information and watched as he headed off down the opposite path. Luke turned to see Ben waving him over.

"The ME's done," Ben said.

John Stokes, the ME, motioned Luke and Ben over. John was a tall man who stood out in a crowd, and still trim with a mop of gray hair. He always had a ready smile on his face outside of work. Today his face was grim. They had worked on several cases together, and Luke respected John immensely.

"Luke. Ben." He nodded at them.

"So, what'd you find?" Luke asked.

"Well." John cleared his throat. "It looks like the marks on her throat are consistent with strangling, and her hands staged similarly to that last murdered jogger. I won't know if she was raped until I get her on the table. Hopefully, I'll be able to retrieve some DNA from under her nails and some blood samples."

Pulling off his gloves and throwing them in a bag, John continued, "You boys have your work cut out for you. I don't think her body has been here very long. Rigor hasn't set in. I'm guessing she died within the last couple of hours."

Scowling, John added, "I estimate she's in her late twenties, early thirties and most likely put up a good fight judging from her knuckles."

"Can you tell us anything else?" Luke asked.

"I'll be able to tell more when she's on the table."

John packed up his bag and filled in the body identification sheet to attach it to the body. His technicians gently lifted the woman and placed her in a vinyl body bag.

"I hate this," said John and shook his head. "Damn. Let me know if someone calls in with an identification."

Luke nodded. He and Ben took one last look around before they expanded their search to see if they missed anything. The park was notorious for not having cameras, but they would check near the coffee shop. Maybe they'd get lucky and the camera would be pointing in the right direction.

Luke noticed a police officer interviewing the bystanders. *Yep, been there, done that.* Interviewing people who got facts wrong or the liars who made up information drove him crazy.

Not finding clues drove him crazy. In fact, this job was beginning to drive him crazy.

THE KILLER STOOD toward the back of the bystanders, blending in as much as possible so the police wouldn't notice his glee at their grisly discovery. A small group of about twenty men and women gathered on the sidewalk, all jockeying for a better spot to view the scene. He supposed some were using the park—dog walkers, joggers, etc. He knew he could count on one tabloid reporter in the crowd and probably one pervert hoping for a provocative view.

The smell of coffee wafting from the corner shop was driving him crazy. He desperately needed his shot of caffeine, but that would have to wait.

Suppressing the urge to scream out, *"the bitch deserved it. I did it—me,"* he just sniffed and coughed discreetly into his hand. The humid morning and pollen irritated his allergies, and he desperately needed to use his inhaler, but doing so now might cause the police to notice him.

He knew he was too smart to be caught by these small-town detectives. He watched as the ME arrived and bent over the body. He wondered how many victims the ME processed in a year. Did he ever get bored working on dead bodies? Did he like his job? He speculated about the many ways a person could strangle or kill another. *Hmmm, something else to think about in his spare time. Not!*

With all the police cars, flashing lights, and cops milling around the scene, it almost had the feel of a party, albeit a ghoulish party. *Jean would have loved that description; she loved parties.* He watched as the two detectives leaned over her body, then bagged evidence and wondered if he left any clues.

He had been careful. Oh, so careful. Plastic gloves. Positioning Jean's body just right. Careful not to leave anything that could identify him. Pulling Jean off the running path a distance away was brilliant—there wouldn't be any broken branches or drag marks near the entrance where he repositioned her body, and he could observe the police at work.

Thankfully, she hadn't weighed much, and he had easily thrown her over his shoulder. Although the bitch hadn't gone peacefully. Not like his first victim who gave up almost immediately. Jean viciously fought until the end. *Who knew Jean had it in her?* Tomorrow he would feel the extent of the injuries she inflicted on him.

Even though setting up the meeting with her for later today at the coffee shop had been a ruse, surprising her on the trail was a stroke of genius. How stupid did she think he was that he would meet her somewhere public? *Stupid woman. Didn't she know jogging alone could be dangerous?*

She never knew he had been here on and off a couple of weeks, spying on her and Grace, keeping track of their every move. He had been thankful Jean had led him to Grace. Having lost track of her once and now finding out that she was still a reporter displeased him—a lot. He hadn't been finished with Grace in D.C. before she hightailed it out and moved away.

Having Jean disclose his role in destroying Grace Winslow's reputation was not going to happen. Whether Grace realized it or not, she had already stolen one job from him. The *Chronicle* had been his life. A chance to show dear dad that he could be just as successful as he had been. Then she ruined his life a second time when Senator Irish offed himself. She wouldn't have another chance. He would ruin her reputation for good this time.

Loyalty was all he'd asked of Jean. Rachel, his one and only, would never betray him. His former employer, Senator Irish, never betrayed him. In fact, the senator had rewarded him quite generously for his 'loyalty.' He made substantial amounts of money in kickbacks from that job. That is until Winslow wrote the story exposing the senator and his predilection for extortion and women. Facing ever-mounting pressure from his colleagues and home, the cash cow finally killed himself. And he had lost his job, lost his extra income, his life ruined—again. All because of nosy Grace Winslow.

Over the years, he and Rachel gave Jean enough dirt on people to use in her articles to further her career. Did she think betraying him should be how she thanked him? Or blackmailing him? *Not gonna happen.* Hell, she promised. The man shook his head in disgust. *Water over the dam. Women. Couldn't be trusted to do anything right, except for his Rachel.*

And now, there she was. Fodder for the tabloids. The cops and journalists would have a field day with another half-naked dead woman. They would never know the other woman had only been practice. Practice made perfect so they say.

He had arranged Jean's hands to look as though she was praying—*the right pose for a traitor.* He hoped this would send a message to that bitch Grace Winslow. If not, well, killing Jean satisfied him immensely. Another glance around revealed he was still alone. He scanned the ground not noticing anything to connect him to the murder.

Calmly walking to the coffee shop that had a view of the entrance to the park, he waited for someone to find her body. He wanted to relish the discovery. After all, he would always be a journalist at heart, a spinner of facts, and a teller of tales. Jean's murder would make a great story for someone.

He noticed one of the cops moving toward the onlookers, and he slowly stepped backward. His heart pounded loudly. Could anyone hear it? He hoped not. He couldn't risk someone talking to him, getting his name and perhaps identifying him.

The cop was writing down a woman's name, distracted

while her yapping little dog wound his leash around the officer's feet. The man briskly walked out of the park toward a side street where he'd parked his rental car.

His nose itched, and he pinched back a sneeze. Bad enough the damn pollen was making his eyes water. He wished he had used his inhaler before coming to the park.

Huffing and trying to catch his breath, he needed to use his inhaler now before he had an asthma attack and called attention to himself.

He reached into his pocket to retrieve it and touched—nothing. He tried the other pocket. Nothing. No inhaler.

Shit, shit, shit. Did he lose the inhaler when he confronted Jean?

Did he lose it in the park?

Did he even bring it with him this morning? He couldn't remember.

He debated whether to go back and look for it after the police left the park. Would it be too risky? He didn't know when they would leave the scene. The cops picked up and bagged all sorts of garbage. With any luck, if they found the inhaler, it would only be so much junk to them. Then again, why worry? His fingerprints weren't in any database that he knew of.

God damn. Jean was going to drive him crazy even in death.

CHAPTER THREE

A sliver of pale moon was barely visible as dawn approached. Grace Winslow slowly rounded the trail's corner. The wooden boardwalk was steps away and would get her safely over a swampy area and to her home. Ahead, like giants guarding the path, the lamplights provided enough light for her to feel secure. Pepper spray provided an additional sense of safety. Grace hoped she would never have to use it. Or if she did, she wouldn't spray herself by mistake.

Moving back to her hometown of Black Pointe two years ago where she had grown up had been blissfully uneventful. No stalker. No police. No newspaper articles splashing her name on the front page. None of the hoopla she lived through in D.C. Her life was calm, just the way she liked it, but she still took nothing for granted.

Usually, she met her friend Anne at Riverwalk. They enjoyed the water views while jogging. It was a good spot to meet, halfway between where they lived. But Anne called earlier. She had been sidetracked by a migraine and couldn't run today. Memorial Park was convenient to Grace's condo, so she chose to run here.

A thigh muscle started to cramp; *I must be crazy to do this to my body so early*. Having warmed up earlier, she decided today to run an extra three miles since she didn't have to be at the office until later. Her breath was becoming more labored, but the trail's end was just ahead. Then it was a short walk to her condo.

Although the park was tranquil at 6 a.m., in less than an hour, it would be full of joggers. The quiet early hour gave her time to enjoy nature. The few joggers she encountered didn't talk. They just nodded their hellos. The park, with its two small lakes, babbling brooks, a shady canopy of live oak trees dripping with Spanish moss, palm trees, and the towering but invasive Australian pine trees, made it a peaceful area to run in. The trails were a mixture of flat and slightly hilly—some manmade—perfect for the kind of workout Grace wanted and needed.

A soft wind caused the pine branches to rustle and swish. Occasionally a branch would break or creak as an animal pushed its way through the forest. Realistically she knew that was what it was, but it didn't stop Grace from continually looking around and checking out the noises. Deeply inhaling the musty smell of the rotting leaves and the sweet smell of flowering bushes, she started thinking about her day, concentrating on upcoming events. Thankful those events no longer centered on her.

Slowing down, Grace walked the last few yards to her exit and stretched to cool down her body.

Grace felt a sense of euphoria and accomplishment after her run. In the predawn light, the buildings and trees were backlit, creating an ethereal scene. She knew if she looked to the east, the sky would be streaked with shades of gray and salmon as the sun rose.

Heading towards her condo, Grace saw a few people out and about and waved to a couple she recognized. Traffic was light now, but that wouldn't last long. She could smell coffee, her addiction of choice, drifting from her favorite coffee shop. The city was stirring.

She bounded up the few stairs to her condo building and punched in the building code. Usually, the sea-inspired turquoise and beige foyer was welcoming with its overstuffed chairs, a couple of tables, and her favorite, the bronze wall fountain producing soothing sounds. Right now, however, workers were renovating her building, and the white sheets covering the furniture created a ghostly effect.

Grace glanced around the foyer and stopped at her mailbox. There was an envelope stuffed in it and partially hanging out. *Did I forget to pick up the mail yesterday?* She walked over and opened the box. No mail, just the envelope. She tore it open as she walked toward the stairs that would take her to her third-floor condo. A small pink note fell out.

No. NO. NO. Her mind flashed back to other times when she received the pink notes. The dread returned with a vengeance, the sick feeling she'd had in D.C. whenever the phone rang or when other pink notes arrived with their menacing messages.

With her heart racing a million miles an hour, she forced her body forward, her mind trying to block what her eyes were seeing.

Not happening. Not happening again. Grace repeated the mantra even as she moved to pick up the note. Even though her hands were shaking and clammy and she really didn't want to pick it up and read it.

She picked up the note by a corner and held it as far away from her body as possible. Then she forced herself to focus on the writing. *"Silly Grace, thought you could disappear on me?"* Her legs wobbled. Her hands shook. And she couldn't stop the bile slithering its way up her throat.

Unable to hold back nausea any longer, she ran into the small half bath off the foyer and vomited.

JEAN'S KILLER stepped back into the shadows. Following Grace in the park had been easy. Too easy. He was curious about what happened to Grace's jogging buddy. He had followed the women every day for the past week running at Riverwalk.

His luck was holding out, as the Riverwalk route where Winslow and her friend usually jogged was too out in the open. Memorial Park, however, had lots of places to observe. Although at the moment, it seemed like he was spending more time in the bushes than on the street. That would change soon.

Smiling as he recalled the thrill of killing Jean, he had followed Grace at a respectable distance. He had disguised himself as a jogger this morning, ducking into bushes when he got too close and watching as she continually turned to check out noises. *Again, didn't women know how dangerous running alone could be?* Jean learned that lesson yesterday.

He contemplated his punishment for Grace. She had stuck her nose in his affairs too many times. She didn't even know he existed but still managed to ruin his life. Twice.

He wanted to play his little game with her for a short time before he destroyed her life forever.

He didn't need to follow Grace back to her condo. Thanks to Jean, he knew where Grace lived. Her street was too quiet this early in the morning to confront her. Getting caught on camera was not part of his plan. He had too much to accomplish before he left for D.C. and his Rachel. And he had lots of plans for Grace.

Would Grace appreciate the note he tucked into her mailbox? He hoped so. He loved the juxtaposition of the innocent pink notes and their sinister messages. He was grateful to the real estate agent who had given him a tour of a condo for sale in her building and unknowingly gave him the code to get into it. Smiling to himself, he walked to his car and drove back to his dumpy motel.

While his mind worked overtime thinking up more ways to make Grace pay for ruining his life, he whistled to the radio. Life was good.

CHAPTER FOUR

Grace stared at her cell phone. One call. That's all it would take to get the police to her condo. Her hand uncontrollably trembled as she reached out to pick it up, the numbers blurry. She drew her hand back. Her mouth was so dry. It felt like it was stuffed with cotton balls. Her head throbbed. She needed to call the police.

No. She didn't need to call them.

Needed. Didn't need.

Back and forth. Indecision. *Coward. What is wrong with me?* She gulped in some air and managed to pick up the phone to try one more time.

Dialed 9-1. Stopped. Her heart throbbed with fear and indecision.

She couldn't dial them.

She flung the phone onto the sofa, pulled her hair and screamed into the air. The police in D.C. called her a liar, accused her of making things up, didn't believe a word she told them. Why would this time be any different?

Instead, she called her best friend, Sam.

It was too early to be up, but when Samantha "Sam" Knight received the semi-coherent call from her best friend. She promised to come right over.

Sam sat quietly on the comfortable overstuffed sofa in Grace's condo. After working into the wee hours of the night, she was having a hard time keeping her eyes open. The recent late-night security job her company, KnightGuard Security, had contracted for was taking its toll on her. As she took a sip of coffee, she made a mental note to hire more employees.

Scanning Grace's living area, she could see Grace's personality reflected in soft beige walls, the brown sofa and bright pops of turquoise—cheerful, relaxed and vibrant although the mood in the room right now was tense.

Grace kept pacing the sunlit living room, her jaw clenched, her shoulders hunched, wringing her hands.

Finally, Grace stopped pacing and sat across from Sam, the lively pillow colors in direct contrast to the agony Grace's face exhibited.

"Sam, I'm sorry I called you. I don't want you to get involved," Grace said, her voice cracking, "but I didn't want to be alone."

"Sweetie, I'm glad you called. You know I'm always here to help." Sam paused. "But I can't help if you won't call the police. I agree they were incompetent jerks in D.C.," Sam said vehemently. "But I know a lot of detectives on the force here, and I know they will take you seriously."

Grace ran her hands over her head, closed and opened her eyes. Her lips trembled, and she whispered, "You weren't in D.C. the whole time, but I was persona non grata at the police department. They treated me like shit. I can't go through that again. I hate that I'm in this situation yet again."

Unable to banish Grace's fears, Sam could only console her. It pained her to see her put-together friend so distraught and looking so disheveled. Dried tears on her cheeks. Her auburn hair in disarray. Her body rigid in distress and fear.

"How did he find me? It's been two years," Grace whispered.

A tear dropped from her eye. "Two years since I left D.C., I've stayed under the radar. The events beat barely gets my name in the paper. Why now?"

Sam hated that Grace was reliving the humiliation and fear she thought she left in D.C. Her reputation ruined. Her dream of being an investigative reporter, crushed. The four years she worked at the *Washington Chronicle*—destroyed.

"I don't know, sweetie but we'll find out." Sam reached over and rubbed Grace's shoulder. "You mentioned your boss wants you to take on more responsibility. Where are you with that?"

Grace grimaced and shook her head. "The same place I was when I got this job." She sighed. "I'm still afraid to take on more important work. I want to. Lord, I want to. But I've been humiliated enough. My self-confidence is shot." She inhaled deeply. "And now ... now that crazy person has found me and is going to ruin my life again."

"Goddamn it, I want to kill the son of a bitch." Sam punched her hand into her fist. "However, we are not going to let him ruin your life. We're going to find him and send him back to hell." She paused; her brows furrowed. "I can't believe he found you in Florida. Why now? It doesn't make sense. Thankfully you're here now, and I can help more."

Sam rubbed her forehead in frustration. "Although, I can't provide a bodyguard right now. I'm short-handed and in the process of hiring more people. Honestly, hon, I don't believe you're in any physical danger at this moment. I think this creep is playing games with you."

Sitting on the edge of the chair, Grace said, "Sam, I don't want a bodyguard, and I don't want you to get involved right now. Shit, I ... I don't know what I want." She closed her eyes and opened them. "Yes, I do know. I want this to go away. I want to wake up and be the woman I was before everything happened."

Furious that her self-confident, trusting friend who loved investigative reporting, and was loyal to her friends and family had been reduced to the self-doubting terrified woman standing before her made Sam was ready to punch someone. However, that wasn't going to help. There wasn't anything she could do to help Grace until she was prepared to help herself.

And this was what the stalker had done to her friend. Before the stalker, police, ex-husband, and betrayals, Grace would have stood up and taken charge of her life. She would have fought for herself. But now, beaten down, Grace didn't have the courage or strength to do that. KnightGuard Security could help but Grace didn't want help.

Sam continued her argument, "I know, hon. But remember, you're a stronger person now than when you left D.C."

Grace took several deep breaths. "Riiight. I'm so strong. When things got bad, I up and ran back here with my tail between my legs. I should have stayed in D.C., fought for myself, and regained my reputation. I should have told everyone to go to hell. But I didn't. And I still can't because I am cowardly and weak. I'm still running. I'm afraid to take on more substantial work. I stay under the radar." Grace covered her face with her hands and sighed. "I'm a coward."

"Sweetie, you've done what you needed to do under the circumstances. You were under too much stress, and you made the right decision leaving D.C. Please, please, please." Sam folded her hands in prayer. "I'm begging you if you won't let me help you, call the police."

Silence.

Finally, Grace shook her head emphatically. “No. I can’t make myself do that right now.”

Sighing, Sam said, “OK then.”

Sam hoped someday Grace would find the courage to defend herself, to be the strong woman she had been, to get back into investigative reporting, to find someone to love. All the good things in life Grace had enjoyed. But she realized Grace was still healing, still unsure of herself. It would take time, and Grace’s friends were rooting for her. Grace only had to take that big step herself when she was ready.

Sam reached down for her tote. “Let’s bag up the note.”

Removing a plastic bag, tweezers, and disposable gloves from her tote, Sam put on the gloves and opened the baggie. “I know you’ve touched it but place it in the bag. If you decide to contact the police, they can take it and check for fingerprints. Maybe the slime-ball left some this time.”

GRACE GAVE Sam the note and watched as she inserted it into the plastic bag and sealed it. Sam took off the plastic gloves, balled them up and tossed them in the wastebasket. She handed Grace the plastic bag. “You should call the police and give this to them.”

Grace knew that wouldn’t be happening.

Watching Sam work, she was in awe of her especially when Sam went into her “super sleuth” mode. Protecting the innocent and getting justice had always been Sam’s passion in life, ever since Grace knew her. Especially when Susie, Sam’s good friend from high school, had been murdered after senior prom. It was weeks before her bruised, broken and bloodied body was found. Sam made it her mission after college to find her murderer and put him away. And go on to establish KnightGuard Security.

She looked at her oldest friend whom she met in nursery school. Sam was a small woman with a big attitude. Over the years, the serious rule-following Grace and the scrappy Sam, even then a pint-size terror, became fast friends. As unlikely as their friendship seemed, Sam always told Grace she grounded her. Grace always admired Sam's take-charge, take-no-prisoner attitude. Something Grace wished she had now.

Grace snorted. She liked to mull things over, and words came easily to her; Sam acted first, talked later. They were a perfect twosome.

Sam's business, KnightGuard Security, was growing by leaps and bounds. Her career was going great guns. Grace's, not so much. For a moment, that little green-eyed monster called "envy" made a pass, but she shooed it quickly away.

Her present assignments, while not boring, were unfulfilling, but she was too scared to take a chance on what she loved—investigative reporting. She trusted too many people in D.C. and suffered the consequences. *Oh, let's not forget I had a stalker who tried to ruin my life, and he's found me again.* Crap.

"I need to go," Sam said as she stood and gathered her tote. "I have a meeting in a half hour that I can't be late for." She looked at Grace sitting on the sofa looking dejected. "I hate to leave you. Promise you'll be careful. Be aware of your surroundings, lock your door and call me if you need anything. I'll check in with you tonight."

She gave Grace a quick hug and kiss on the cheek. "Remember, you are a strong woman.".

Alone. Again. Grace looked around her condo, not seeing the comfortable furnishings nor appreciating the life she tried to re-create for herself.

Phony. She was a phony. The event beat was not investigative journalism. It was ... safe. She was just pretending to be a journalist. She knew her stories were fluff compared with investigating corruption. She was playing a role, and unless she took a chance and changed, this would be her life. Maybe at some point in time, she would take a chance on reclaiming herself and her reputation. But not yet. She wasn't ready.

Feeling empty, Grace sat on the sofa staring at the family pictures on the glass coffee table. Picking up the gold-framed picture of the last family vacation with her happy siblings and parents and the ocean in the background, she smiled at the peaceful scene. Her family and friends were her anchors. She didn't want to worry them. She wondered if her life would ever be normal again.

Bzzzzzz. Grace jumped up. Damn. Her phone. Too much time had passed daydreaming. She had only an hour to get to work. She put the picture down. Her position as society editor at the *Black Pointe Journal* meant she spent many nights covering the rich and famous as they partied. It was a minor job; however, Steve, her editor, insisted all the writers attend weekly staff meetings. She needed to be there on time, especially if she ever got the courage or opportunity to do investigative reporting again. *Courage being the keyword.* Grace shook her head. *Coward. That's never going to happen.* Mentally reviewing her schedule, she headed to her shower and hoped she could keep down a cup of coffee before she left for the office.

But first, Grace opened her middle desk drawer. Her "drawer of shame." Just looking at the pink notes reminded her of the betrayals, the injustice she'd endured and her failure to fight her battles and stand up for herself.

She placed the latest pink note on top of the macabre collection.

THANKFULLY THERE WAS no rush-hour traffic to slow her down, and an hour later, Grace strode down the editorial floor of the *Black Pointe Journal*. Walking past tiny cubicles, many of them were overloaded with papers and pictures, except for her co-worker Bryon Hart's desk. His looked so neat, she questioned when he even worked there. Everyone else's space looked like a tornado came through and left all the papers willy-nilly.

The staff meeting was starting in the conference room. The smell of coffee and donuts permeated the air.

Grace still felt emotionally drained after receiving the note and talking with Sam. Would this nightmare ever end? She had been so optimistic about a new start here in Black Pointe. It looked like that wasn't happening now. It had been two years of bliss. Well, maybe not bliss but uneventful.

Hurrying in, she noticed that one empty seat next to her boss that seemed to have her name on it. Talk about being in the hot seat. Grace hated being late.

"Glad you decided to grace us with your presence," her boss Steve Wetherly said sarcastically. "We were going to start without you."

"Sorry." Grace quietly slipped into the empty chair next to Bryon who winked at her. She hated being late for anything and especially being singled out at work.

At the weekly meeting, everyone threw out what they were working on, and Steve decided which project would be front-page news. For the most part, events were always low on the list, so she had to work hard to get her news in the paper. Even though this was an election year, and there was more interest in events.

"Tomorrow night is the big fundraiser for Senator Evans. We should probably include pictures of the event," Grace volunteered.

"Make it happen."

Steve looked around. "OK, people, what else?"

Mary Esposito, who followed the police beat, spoke up. "I

haven't heard anything more about the woman who was murdered in Sexton Park yesterday morning. Another jogger found her body on the path—no witnesses. I don't know the particulars yet, but I'm hoping to receive more information from the detectives by this afternoon. Maybe by then, they'll have a name."

A few reporters mentioned other stories they were working on. Nancy Frey was investigating an environmental spill. There were several stories on the political front. A sappy dog story. The usual day-to-day stuff. Finally, Steve stood up and told them to get back to work, asking Grace to stay behind.

Oh God, she thought, *this is it.* Steve had asked her on and off to take on more responsibility, but she had always declined. *Is this the day Steve fires me for not stepping up?*

Steve sat and motioned her to the chair next to him.

"Grace, I know we agreed when I hired you, you wouldn't take on any investigative reporting until you were ready. I've respected your wishes."

He looked her in the eye. "You're a damn good reporter."

Steve took a deep breath. "Nancy Frey is taking a six-month leave to care for her mother. I want you to step up and take over her beat while she's gone."

Grace's stomach clenched, and her hands started shaking. *OK. He was not firing her. But this is worse.* She prayed Steve wouldn't sense her panic and she hoped the bile forcing its way up her throat wouldn't erupt before she left the room.

She inhaled deeply, let out a long breath. *What could she say that wouldn't get her fired, since Steve had told her he expected her to step up sooner rather than later.* "Steve, please don't ask me to do this. You promised you wouldn't assign me any substantial reporting until I thought I was ready. I'm not ready. And quite frankly, I don't know when I'll ever be."

Steve looked at Grace sympathetically. But she knew he

was not giving in. "You're ready. You can't hide behind what happened in D.C. anymore. You're a good reporter, and investigating is what you do best. We have a couple of weeks before Nancy leaves, and I want you to fill in."

"No." Grace put her hands together in prayer. "Please. I beg you, don't do this. I enjoy my job covering events. I don't have to worry about people pointing fingers at me, questioning my ability, or incriminating me in some way." *Oh Lord, she was afraid*. How could she make Steve understand that she wanted the opportunity but was fearful of stepping out of her comfort zone?

Steve scratched his brow. Concern etched on his face. "I know this will stress you out. I hired you knowing about the fiasco in D.C. I know it ended your career and marriage. But whatever mistakes you've made, I know you've learned from them. I've read your work and consider you one of the best investigative reporters around. You're passionate, fair, persistent, and not afraid to take on the big boys."

Grace felt her face turning red. If only she could believe in herself as Steve did.

"I gotta tell you that ..." Steve squinted, rubbed his forehead trying to remember. "Shit, what was that senator's name?" Steve shook his head. "Ireland?"

He put his fingers up to his chin, tapped them and thought for a moment. "No. It was Irish." He drummed his fingers on the table. "Gotta tell you that bastard got off easy. It certainly wasn't your fault that Irish committed suicide. I've heard rumors that many executives were in the senator's pocket." He looked at her sympathetically. "Grace, you didn't stand a chance to have your career survive in that corrupt hellhole."

So many unpleasant memories flashed through Grace's mind. *What others?* What had she missed?

Steve put his arm on her shoulder. "I promised when I hired you not to pressure you."

He chortled. "Well, not too much. Look, you're a great reporter. You're great at researching and digging deep. What happened in D.C. is water over the dam. Black Pointe isn't D.C. We take care of our own here. People may not forget, but they will forgive. Why can't you do the same for yourself? Give your readers and yourself the benefit of the doubt."

Grace sighed heavily. Steve had given her a huge second chance hiring her. But, stepping up, that was a whole other ball field. She wanted it. She wanted this opportunity desperately. But ... Steve interrupted her thoughts.

"I'll give you a couple of weeks to let me know." Steve patted her arm. "You're ready. You need to take that next step on your own. I'm not going to have you on events forever."

She didn't want to disappoint him, but she was afraid, beaten up, unsure of her abilities. D.C. had taken that from her. She had been an ambitious young reporter. It was the betrayals that came with the mistake—betrayed by her newspaper, betrayed and ignored by her "friends" and the biggest betrayal of all, by her husband.

Grace lowered her eyes. The pudgy gray-haired, balding guy sitting next to her had taken a chance on her when she was down. He was her mentor and friend. He had confidence in her even if she didn't have it in herself.

What if she took the job? *No. Not going there. Yet.* Her heart was beating so loudly she was sure Steve, heck, the whole office could hear it. She was a coward, didn't deserve a second chance.

Oh well, water over the dam. Thinking about the what ifs didn't help her cause now. It would be a long time before she would ever have the confidence in herself to write investigative pieces again despite Steve's offer.

CHAPTER FIVE

Ben and Luke finally had a name, Jean Mays, and were on their way to search the murdered jogger's apartment.

"So, you and Kaylie, huh?"

Luke rolled his eyes. "Really? You want to discuss my love life now?"

Ben nodded and grinned. Luke knew he would have to give Ben a bone or the man would hound him until he did.

"The date was all right."

"Just all right?" Ben grunted. "I need more details. You know I'm living vicariously through you."

Ben fiddled around with the air conditioner. "She was hot at the bar Friday night. So. What happened? Did she have body odor? Dirty dance in the corner with another guy? Spill."

Luke shook his head. He didn't want to talk about his date with Kaylie. She seemed nice enough when they met. But on their date, he sensed she was looking for a forever relationship. That wouldn't happen with him—ever. *Once burned, twice shy.*

Besides, Ben held his own with the female population; he

didn't need any of Luke's details. Luke would never call him a man-whore, but Ben came very close.

His date had gone well considering it had been a while since he'd asked a woman out. They went for a burger and afterward caught a movie. Safe enough for a first date. He liked the way she laughed, and they enjoyed each other's company.

The conversation took a nosedive on the way home when she broached issues dealing with kids. Did he like kids —yes, he did. Did he want kids—not so much and not anytime soon. Did he work all hours of the week—yes. Did he ever think about going into another field of work less dangerous—no, nada, never. Deep subjects but not for a first date.

Driving her home turned awkward. Kaylie kept up the conversation but Luke had tuned her out. Arriving at her door, she invited him in for a drink. After the kid conversation, he knew she wasn't for him. He didn't respond. Knowing she was asking, no, inviting him to spend the night, he couldn't do it even though his cock needed the release. So, he'd given her a chaste kiss goodnight on the cheek and a half promise to see her around—no promise to call the next day or any day. Kaylie heard him loud and clear. The hurt in her eyes said it all. But he couldn't go there especially since Becky's betrayal still hurt.

Slamming the door was her goodbye.

Ben and Luke finally reached May's street and found a parking spot. The victim's eighth-floor apartment was on a quiet tree-lined side street close to Sexton Park, where they'd found her body. There were few cars on the road and fewer people walking around. It was a quiet working-class neighborhood—a couple of quick in/out markets but no chi-chi coffee shops. Several rundown storefronts lined the street but the shops that were open appeared busy—a simple, uncomplicated community. Her red brick apartment building looked well maintained.

"Shit, I need to get to the gym more," Luke moaned as he and Ben huffed their way up eight flights of stairs. "Of all days for maintenance to be working on the elevator."

"Yeah man, you're freaking old and out of shape."

Luke looked over his shoulder at his partner and shook his head.

Reaching Jean's apartment, Luke used the key the super had given him and opened the door.

"Well, it won't take us long to go through this," Luke said as he looked around the cozy, but basic studio apartment.

The apartment was plain except for a few pops of bright pink color on the pillows lining the sofa. He assumed the chocolate brown sofa contained a bed since he didn't see a bedroom. The room also included a small, light brown chair on one side of the couch with a beat-up coffee table in front of it. Papers and magazines were strewn around the coffee table.

A large bookshelf against the opposite wall appeared to take up more space than the other furniture combined. A small wooden desk with a black metal chair pushed under it was covered with papers sat under the one large window letting in the sunshine. A black metal chair was pushed under it. The minuscule kitchen included a two-burner stove and a mini-fridge. A tiny island with two metal chairs tucked beneath it completed the decor. The apartment smelled musty. Luke detected the lingering odor of fried food.

"I'll check out the kitchen," Ben said. He opened the cupboard doors moving food and dishes around. Next, he opened the apartment-size refrigerator, nudging things around. "Not much in here and nothing hidden in the back. It's filled with food chicks like to eat—yogurt, chicken, vegetables. Christ, give me a hamburger or steak any day."

Luke laughed. "I'll start with the desk."

He sat on the small folding chair and poked around the desk. Unfortunately, if Jean used a filing system, he couldn't find it. *Just once, it would be nice to find a neat freak to make his work easier.* "I'm not seeing much here."

He lifted a pile of papers, finding notes on a yellow scratch pad pertaining to work. It included research notes and names and addresses of people Jean checked to follow up with. Then he focused his attention on a padded bulletin board stuffed with pictures. Luke glanced at several images of babies and smiling families. It always bothered him when a young person full of life died.

Luke opened a couple of invitations to wedding and baby showers. He put aside bills requesting payments. Noted a small calendar with dates circled. Saw several notes half stuffed into envelopes, a pink one saying "meet me at 11" mentioning a coffee shop nearby. Picked up a half-written note to a Grace Winslow apologizing for something and what looked like lots of work memos.

He pulled open the center drawer and found a flowered day planner. He never understood why women liked these planners with the flowered covers. Or, God forbid, the ones quoting something from Rumi or whomever. Quickly scanning it, noting names and dates, he placed it in the box with other items to go back to the office. He and Ben could go through everything there.

He placed the half-filled box on the kitchen island. Ben had finished looking in the tiny kitchen.

"Ben, pull out the sofa bed and check under it. I'll pack up her laptop. We'll bring it back to the station and let IT look at it," he said. "The neighbor said Jean was a reporter but I don't see any stories she's working on. I bet if she has any, they're on the laptop."

Ben nodded, walked over, bent down and pulled out the

bed to look under it. Standing up he dusted his hands off. "Nothing but dust bunnies."

Luke pulled over the box they brought with them and finished packing up what they could to look at later. Luke thought about the woman's life and how sad it was that all her personal effects fit into a small box.

"Who called in and reported her missing?"

Luke thumbed through his notes. "A friend from across the hall. Diane Benoit. Said her neighbor was missing."

"Wonder why she thought she was missing? It's only been a couple of days."

Walking out with the box and laptop, they locked Jean's door. Luke placed the yellow police tape over it. Ben knocked on the neighbor's door. No answer.

"What's their relationship? Is she a relative?"

"Don't know. I'll touch base with Benoit tonight," Luke said.

CHAPTER SIX

When Grace finally arrived home, it was after 10 p.m., and she was exhausted from chasing around the chairman of the event for an interview and then trying to avoid his busy hands all night. Thanking the parking gods for the available space at the back of her building, she pulled into a spot close to the door. Unlocking the back door, she walked toward the elevator to go up to her condo. The designers of the building had paid as much attention to the rear of her building as the front, so it had a pleasant, open, safe feel.

Getting off the elevator, she thought about stopping in to say hello to Maggie Evans, her elderly neighbor. She decided it was too late and she was too tired. She could hear little Toto yipping behind Maggie's door and hoped he didn't wake his elderly mistress.

Inserting her key and opening the door, she stopped and stood in the doorway for a moment. Something was off. Grace couldn't put her finger on it. But her condo didn't feel as welcoming as it usually did.

For a moment, Grace thought about walking out and

closing the door. *No, I'm tired and imagining things.* Reaching into her purse, she pulled out her pepper spray. Brushing the moisture from her forehead, she scrutinized the living room. Nope, nothing looked like it had been disturbed. A faint odor she didn't recognize puzzled her. She took a deep sniff—nothing. *Must be my imagination* she thought. *Maybe I picked up a scent from the event or Maggie cooked something new. She does like to try new cuisines.*

Dismissing the odor, Grace walked cautiously toward the bedrooms, her pepper spray in front of her. Reaching the master bedroom, she turned on the lights and looked around. Nothing appeared out of place. Same with the other bedroom and bathroom. Returning to the living room, she turned on the balcony lights and peeked out. Everything seemed just as she left it, and no one hid in the shadows.

Feeling a little silly but more relaxed, Grace returned the pepper spray to her purse. She decided to check her computer for any last-minute updates to her schedule. Sitting at her desk, she opened her laptop and reached over for her pen and pad. Coming back empty-handed, Grace looked at her workspace but didn't see anything else out of place except her pen and notepad which were nowhere to be seen. *Weird. I must have been too tired yesterday to put them back.* The problem was, she was a creature of habit and tired or not she would have put them back in their place.

Focusing on her desk, she looked carefully around again. Nope. Nothing jumped out at her. Grace yawned. It had been an exhausting day, and nothing else seemed out of place. Tomorrow she would look over her condo again, but right now she made one update to her schedule, turned off the light and went into her bedroom to change and read for a while.

THE NEXT MORNING after jogging with her friend Anne at Riverwalk and promising to meet soon for coffee, she went up to her condo to change for the day. Maggie stood outside her condo putting the leash on Toto.

"Grace, dear, how are you?"

"I'm fine Maggie. You're up early." Grace looked at her eccentric neighbor. Today was Maggie's yoga day. Grace took in Maggie's bright pink pants and a purple top which accentuated her white hair. Tomorrow it would be some other activity and an equally colorful outfit.

She and Maggie had become fast friends when Grace moved into her condo two years ago. Maggie didn't have any family nearby, so Grace became her surrogate granddaughter, and Grace loved having the spirited grandma around.

"Well, Toto has some stomach problems and needs to go out."

Grace looked down at the little terror. Thankfully the little beast wasn't feeling well; otherwise, he would be licking or nipping at her ankles depending upon his mood. "I won't keep you then. By any chance, did you see anyone near or in my condo yesterday?"

Maggie thought for a moment. "No dear, but I was out most of the day. I know they painted the lobby and workers were coming and going. Why?"

"Oh, nothing important. I smelled a funny odor when I got home. It's probably nothing."

Toto started jumping around and yipping, so Maggie said a quick goodbye and left.

Grace shook off the unease of the night before. *I need a vacation. My imagination is running wild.*

She opened her door. Stuck her head in first and looked around. Nope, everything looked the same. Receiving the note the other day surprised her and was making her question everything. Shaking her head, she changed her clothes and left to meet Sam.

CHAPTER SEVEN

Luke arrived at the *Black Pointe Journal* a few minutes before noon. Grace Winslow had told him she would be at the paper for an hour or so for a staff meeting and could give him a few minutes. The office was quiet when he walked in, but as he was talking to the receptionist, several women walked out of a conference room. Luke wondered which one was Winslow. An older, attractive woman gave him the once-over and he pretended not to notice. A short, heavy woman was talking to an even shorter woman. Neither paid attention to him.

Another woman walked out behind them, and it was as if the waters had parted and he was seeing perfection for the first time. *Should there be a gong sounding somewhere?* He shook his head. A weird reaction even for him.

He stared as a gorgeous, willowy brunette walked toward the reception desk. Every question he wanted to ask her disappeared. He never thought sexy could be a white blazer covering a white tee and black pants, coupled with heels accentuating long legs. Her hair was in a messy bun that he longed to set free. Shit, big Luke decided just then to stand up and say heeello. He buttoned his jacket to cover his erection.

"Grace Winslow?" he asked.

"Yes." She held out her hand to shake his. "And you must be Detective McBride."

One touch. Electricity zapped through Luke's arm. He knew Grace felt it too. He saw her startled eyes as she dropped his hand. What had just happened?

Whiskey-colored eyes appraised him. *Cool, McBride. Just stand here and stare.* He pulled himself together and asked if there was somewhere to sit where he could ask her some questions. She nodded and told him to follow her to the conference room.

"Detective, what can I do for you?" Her voice had just an edge of ice to it, just enough to freeze his blood. Luke had hoped to charm her—win her trust, have her confess. Or at the very least, acknowledge in some way their attraction. All scenarios a bust. He got the sense she didn't like the police very much. Her lips were tight. Her arms crossed over her body. Legs crossed. The message "*leave me alone*" quite clear.

"Tell me about Jean Mays."

She scrunched her face. "Who?"

"Jean Mays. Your name was on some papers in her apartment."

"I don't know a Jean Mays and I don't know why my name would be on something in her apartment."

A half-hour later he realized Grace didn't know Jean Mays. Never heard her name mentioned and had no idea why her name was in Mays's apartment. He had also been dismissed rather abruptly.

ERIC, the police station's IT guy, was still trying to get into Jean's computer. Ben and Luke hadn't found Jean's cell phone at the crime scene or her apartment, so they hoped her laptop had a "find my phone" app. It would help track where her phone was located and maybe point to her murderer. A long shot for sure, but Luke was staying optimistic.

The frou-frou calendar had highlighted dates. Luke thought they might be personal. He hoped her computer had a business calendar, which would make his job easier. He saw several names listed more than once—Richard, Ken, Hailey—but no last names. He knew Diane, her neighbor, called in the missing person report. Maybe Diane knew these other people. He and Ben had an appointment to meet her the next day; he would ask her then. Touching another person's personal belongings made Luke feel like a voyeur. But if it helped bring her murderer to justice, he'd get over it.

Richard? Ken? Could one be a boyfriend? Did Jean entertain more than one boyfriend? Did she get caught cheating and one killed her? He shook his head. Why those thoughts now? *Shades of Becky. Don't go there. Not every woman is a deceiving, cheating bitch.* Think only good thoughts, that was his mantra now. Well, most of the time. He spent too many days and hours cursing his ex-fiancée and his fucking ex-partner. Of course, he also spent every day wondering which scumbag he arrested was going to lie to him.

He had to stop thinking negative thoughts, concentrate on work. Ben was making calls to everyone with a phone number on Jean's calendar.

"Anything yet?"

Ben ran his hands through his hair. "Not getting many people who are home. I left messages. I'd love to get the last names of those listed on the calendar."

"We have a tentative appointment tomorrow to talk to Diane Benoit; maybe she'll have answers."

Having gone over Jean Mays's items one by one at the precinct, they knew she didn't live extravagantly, nor did she appear to possess a secret life. Everything they saw pointed to a relatively typical life of a 29-year-old woman. Since Jean had been an investigative reporter, could she have gotten too close to the truth, and someone she investigated had it in for her? He made a mental note to contact her employer and coworkers. Because it appeared Jean wrote freelance pieces for different publications, it made it more difficult to track everyone down who had contact with her. Hopefully, there would be more information on her laptop. IT would notify them when they cracked the password.

Ben nodded and walked out of the squad room. Luke called Jean's employer and made an appointment to meet with him at the magazine the next day. Luke hoped someone there would have some additional information on Jean. She hadn't lived in her apartment for long. Without Diane Benoit's help, they were at an impasse.

He also called Grace Winslow again and made another appointment to meet her at her office. When he spoke to her the other day, she didn't know anything about Jean or even who she was.

But there were still so many unanswered questions. Why did Jean have Grace's name listed multiple times on her calendar? He had hoped Grace would have remembered something. Yup, definitely needed to touch base with her again. *Shit. Who was he kidding?* He wanted to see her again. Getting involved with a suspect was a big no-no, but the reaction he had to her surprised him, and he hated surprises. Besides that, she was easy on the eyes. *Boy, what a cliché. Easy on the eyes. What the hell am I thinking?* Luke didn't understand the attraction he felt toward Miss Grace Winslow, but he sure wanted to pursue it.

He just hoped Grace was not involved with Jean Mays's death.

CHAPTER EIGHT

"You know ..." Ben started and then stopped to pull out his phone to read a text, then closed his phone. "I've been wondering about Grace Winslow's name on Jean's calendar. I know she is a reporter here in Black Pointe. Didn't you contact Winslow to see if she knew Jean and she said no?"

"Yeah, I met her briefly at the *Journal* where she works, but she appeared confused as to why Jean had her name at all or why she would write a note apologizing to her. She claims not to know her and was a little testy." The image of him meeting Grace passed quickly through his mind. He remembered stumbling through his questions feeling like a horny teenager and an even bigger jerk. For sure, he didn't need to share that with Ben.

He shrugged. "Maybe she was lying or just doesn't like cops."

Ben thought for a minute. "Find anything out about Richard or Ken?"

"Still working on that. Maybe Richard's a boyfriend or coworker. We need to ask Jean's friend Diane when we meet with her. I'm sure she'll know more."

LUKE AND BEN were just about to knock on Diane Benoit's door when a human dynamo came rushing down the hall and almost knocked them over.

"Oh, my goodness, I had to work late and thought I missed you. Thanks for meeting me here. I didn't want to go to the station." Her words were rushed and sounded like one continuous run-on sentence to Luke.

She unlocked her door and they followed Diane into her apartment. She dropped her purse on a table, turned and asked them to sit. She asked if they wanted coffee, Ben and Luke nodded, and she rushed off to make it.

Luke took in the cozy one-bedroom apartment. It appeared similar to Jean's across the hall, but Diane's was full of color and bigger. Physically the two women also had nothing in common. Diane Benoit was the opposite of Jean Mays. Jean had been tall with blond hair; Diane was pixie-like —small-boned with cropped brown hair.

The sound of a coffee machine broke the silence and a few minutes later, Diane walked back with three cups and the fixings.

"Miss Benoit, why did you report Jean missing?" Luke picked up a cup and stirred in some milk and sugar. "Were you close? Did she have any relatives here?"

"Please, call me Diane." Diane took her time answering. "Jean was an only child. I believe her father died a while ago and her mother has Alzheimer's and is in a facility somewhere in Florida. She didn't talk much about her."

"How did you know Jean didn't go away for the weekend? I'm confused as to why you reported her missing so quickly?"

Shrugging, Diane looked at Ben. "The thing about Jean is, was, she believed in always being prompt, and she liked tradition. We had a long-standing tradition to meet at my place on

Friday nights for dinner and movie when I was home. Since she never called to cancel, I got concerned."

"She had confessed to me someone in D.C. from her past was harassing her and wanted to meet. She seemed nervous about him."

"Did she say who?"

"No. Jean never told me his name, so I stopped asking. I think she was afraid of him. As an investigative reporter who exposed people's secrets, her job didn't make her popular. She used to say threats came with the territory."

"What else can you tell us about her?" Luke watched Diane fiddle with a pillow. Something was off, but he wasn't sure what.

"Did she live here long? Have many friends? Perhaps a boyfriend?"

Diane looked up startled and took her time answering. "We've been friends since college. She only moved to Black Pointe about six months ago. We met almost every week, as I said, for dinner and a movie. Occasionally my fiancé, Richard, would join us."

"And what is Richard's last name?"

"Marsh. Richard Marsh."

Luke penciled in his name. "So, she didn't date anyone here?"

Diane stopped to think about her answer. She tilted her head, tapped her lips with her fingers. "Nobody serious. An occasional date with someone from work or a club. She never went on more than a couple of dates with any one man."

Ben asked her if she knew what Jean was working on. She shook her head. Then Ben asked if she knew a Grace Winslow, Hailey or Ken.

Diane hesitated. "You know, the name Grace Winslow sounds familiar, but I don't know where I would know her from. I introduced Jean to Hailey Marshall, who owns The BookShop downtown. I've never met Ken."

Well, not a lot of information but it was more than they came in with. Getting up to leave, Ben asked for Richard's information and if there might be anything else she could add. She said no. They put their business cards on the table, thanked Diane for her time, and left.

"What'd you think?" Ben asked.

"I think Ms. Benoit is hiding something. She hesitated too long before telling us she didn't think Jean was serious about anyone. As for Grace Winslow, her name is in the paper all the time; she might have recognized her name from that."

Ben nodded. "I picked up on the hesitation too. Maybe we should ask the fiancé if he noticed anything peculiar going on with Jean."

IT WAS Thursday before they touched base with Richard Marsh, Diane's fiancé. He had been out-of-town and was willing to come down to the station.

Ben was at his desk talking to him when Luke arrived.

"Richard, this is my partner, Luke."

They shook hands, and Richard sat down. Luke leaned against Ben's desk while he asked questions.

Ben looked down at his notes, and then up at Richard. "I understand you met Jean at your fiancée's house several times."

"Yeah, they would sometimes invite me over for dinner and a movie. Sometimes I didn't stay for the movie if the girls chose a chick flick. Sometimes we would go out with their friend Hailey."

"Did Jean ever mention a boyfriend?"

"Well ..." Richard paused and rubbed his brow. "She mentioned something about a guy in D.C., no name, and she dated a little, as far as I know."

Ben glanced at Luke. Something was off.

"Did you ever see Jean outside of the dinners?"

"Sometimes. When I was in the neighborhood." Shit, Marsh was looking anywhere but at them. *Guilty some?*

"Had she acting funny in any way?" Ben asked.

Richard shook his head. He was looking around the station and wouldn't meet their eyes.

Luke was sure the guy was guilty of something, but he didn't know what. Yet. His name sounded familiar, so he walked over to his desk to get the list of bystanders at the crime scene. Glancing down the list, lo and behold there was Richard Marsh's name.

Coincidence? He didn't think so.

Walking back to Ben's desk, Luke stared at Richard and asked him what he was doing in the park that day.

Stuttering, Richard said, "I jog there occasionally."

"Occasionally?"

Richard frantically nodded his head.

"So, you're telling me you jog in a park several miles away from your home when there's a park right around the corner from you."

Luke watched as Richard's mind worked over scenarios and wondered which version he was going to get.

Richard leaned forward, blew out a breath and sighed. "Look, I was banging Jean on the side. I'm not proud of that. I love Diane. Jean wanted to confess to Diane, and I only wanted to talk to her with nobody around and convince her not to. I know it doesn't look good, but she was dead when I got to the park. Please believe me."

Riiight, Luke loved it when they said, "please believe me."

"Did Diane know you were cheating on her?"

Richard hesitated. "No. Jean and I were careful."

Luke thought Richard had to be the dumbest guy he'd met recently. Did this jerk think that while he was banging his fiancée's best friend, he could keep his infidelity from her? Richard must have been thinking with his little head. Moreover, what did it say about Jean's values if she would sneak around with her best friend's fiancé?

If her values were that loose, perhaps going one step further, could Jean have had something on Grace? Or the elusive Ken? Was she a blackmailer? They needed to talk to Diane Benoit again and re-question Grace Winslow.

After Richard spilled his story, they let him go with a warning not to leave town. Ben would check the security cameras by Richard's house. They had a lot more searching for the truth to do. As of right now, he was their prime suspect.

JEAN'S EMPLOYER at the weekly magazine had nothing to add except that she was working there on a freelance basis and that she had been excited about a political exposé she was working on. She was going to fill him in but was murdered before she could. Luke and Ben headed over to the *Black Pointe Journal* hoping to catch Grace Winslow.

They were in luck. A guard ushered him and Ben to the main floor reception desk, and the receptionist called her.

Luke looked around the newsroom which was similar to his bullpen at the precinct. The cacophony of noise. Phones ringing. Clicking on the keyboards. People scurrying around or focused on their computer screens. Piles of paper everywhere. He felt at home.

Ben was flirting with the receptionist. Luke shook his head. Yep, Ben's man-whore card was getting a workout. He looked up to watch a distracted Grace walking toward him. She seemed focused on Ben and Luke knew she didn't see him, so he stepped in front of her as she got to the reception desk. She had Ben in her sights and didn't process his presence right away.

"Ms. Winslow?"

Grace stopped short. Her hand covered her mouth. "Oh. You scared me.

"What can I do for you, Detective McBride?"

"Please, call me Luke." He put out his hand to shake hers. Whoa. Electricity, sparks zapped through his arm again. Had she felt it too? He felt it the first time they shook hands also. *What the hell was that about?*

Grace pulled her hand back. Her eyes dilated; her cheeks flushed. *Oh yeah, she felt it too. Good Lord, she was beautiful.*

Ben left the reception desk and walked over. Luke introduced Grace to Ben and asked, "Can we talk somewhere private for a few minutes?"

She nodded her head and told them to follow her. Walking into the chaos, Grace snagged a chair from an unused workstation and moved it to her cubicle motioning them to sit.

Luke watched her bite her lip then rub her tongue over it. His eyes followed every lick. Her eyes flitted around the office. *Did he make her nervous?* "Ms. Winslow."

Grace jerked her eyes back to him. "Sorry. Please call me Grace."

"Grace then. Are you sure you don't you know a Jean Mays?"

Grace took a moment to answer him. She wrinkled her brow, leaned forward, her lips pursed. "Detective, you asked me that already. I told you I didn't recognize the name."

"Why would your name be on her calendar and a letter addressed to you? Did you ever receive something from her?"

Grace thought for a moment and then shook her head. "I don't know why she had my name as I told you before, nor have I ever received any correspondence from her," she replied with a little more snark than Luke liked but he would let it go this time—chalk it up to nerves.

"I come in contact with a lot of people for my job. Maybe that's how she got my name."

"You cover events, right?"

"Yes."

"Do you keep a list of everyone from these events you cover?"

She snorted. "God, no. The list would be enormous. I have the names of people I interviewed or whose pictures I take, but that's all. I'll check the list, but Jean Mays's name doesn't sound familiar."

Luke was puzzled by Grace's name on Jean's calendar. But if Grace didn't know Jean, he would keep digging.

"Well, thanks for your time." Luke stood up. "If anything jogs your memory about Jean Mays, let me know." Handing her his card, he and Ben left.

The humidity soaked Luke's shirt the minute they walked outside. He wiped the sweat dripping down his face. The meeting with Grace didn't satisfy the cop in him but as a man ... whoa.

Ben looked at him. "What'd you think? Do you think she's lying?"

Luke shook his head. Grace seemed genuinely confused by Jean's name.

"What a looker." Ben winked. "I wouldn't mind exchanging information with her."

Luke opened his mouth to respond but closed it. He never ceased to be amazed at Ben's man-whore style. What he knew for sure was that Ben was never getting near her. Luke couldn't put his finger on his reaction to Ms. Grace

Winslow, but he liked what he saw. No way was Ben getting there first.

"She probably meets tons of people in her job. She didn't seem to be hiding anything, so we need to keep looking."

SEEING the detective at her office again confused Grace. On the one hand, Detective Luke McBride with his scruffy beard, strong chin, blond hair, serious gray-blue eyes, and body to die for, was easy to look at. And, oh Lordy, was she looking. On the other hand, he was a detective, a cop. Her history with the police was not a positive one. Plus, men were off her plate. For good. Betrayal was a bitter taste to get rid of.

The other detective, what was his name? Ben. He was handsome too, but she sensed he was a player. She was so not interested in players or men in general, period.

Grace sighed. If only. If only Luke wasn't questioning her about a murder or even assuming she might be a suspect. If only she didn't have a stalker on her back making her suspicious of everyone. If only she could believe the sparks were real when she touched Luke's hand. Damn, she hated the "if only's" in her life.

FINDING a good time to meet again with Diane Benoit turned out to be more difficult than the first. She traveled a lot for her job.

Finally, after a week of calling and rescheduling, Luke had a commitment to meet her again at her apartment. The sun was burning off the overnight mist when they arrived at her building. Ben knocked on the door, and Diane let them in, asking if they wanted coffee. Nodding yes, she invited them into the kitchen and started the machine. Luke and Ben sat at her kitchen table.

"Detectives, I don't know what else I can add to what I've already told you."

Luke decided to dive right in and watch her reaction. "Did you know your fiancé was cheating on you?"

Diane stopped midway reaching for cups in the cabinet. Heavy sigh. "No way."

"Yes, way. He admitted it the other day. He was having an affair with Jean Mays."

She reached again for the cups, her hand shaking. She placed the cup on the counter with a bang, the cup broke. She stood there silent, a tear running down her face.

Huffing out the breath, she barely whispered. "I suspected."

"Did you know it was with Jean?"

She snorted. "Not at first. A while ago, I noticed Richard had a guilty look on his face whenever I saw him. I'm not here all the time, but I noticed a personal item of his in Jean's apartment one day and asked him about it. There were other signs too. I was going to break off the engagement, but Jean got killed."

"Did you ever confront Jean?"

"Yes. She told me he meant nothing to her and not to worry. She was sorry." Diane sniffed. "Sorry. As if a lame apology would make it better."

Luke got a bad feeling about this. "When did you confront Jean?"

Diane hesitated too long and finally gulped before she answered. "The night before she was murdered."

Oh, sweet Jesus. This was getting interesting.

Ben jumped in. "You didn't get angry and decide to kill her? Perhaps blame it on Richard, did you?"

"Holy crap, no. I confronted Jean that night. The next

morning, I was going to give Richard back his ring." Diane squeezed her eyes shut. "I was mad, but a person doesn't kill everyone who betrays them or makes them mad."

Luke rubbed his forehead. Love triangles. Nothing good ever came of them. "Did Richard know you found out about him and Jean?"

"I think he suspected I put two and two together, but I don't think he knew for sure."

Richard was dumb. Diane clueless. Jean, well, she sounded like a woman who didn't care who she hurt. Richard and Diane were both in the running as suspects.

Oh yeah, things were getting "curiouser and curiouser" as Alice said going down the rabbit hole.

CHAPTER NINE

The weather turned hot and sunny. The sky was a robin's-egg blue, and the warmer temperatures felt good after a few cold rainy days. Happy to get out of the office, Grace was meeting with Sam, Hailey, and Anne at Salt & Sea. Their good friend Laura Clark owned the upscale bistro overlooking the river, and their little group got together at least once a month for lunch.

Seeing her friends already seated, Grace hurried over. They had taken the corner booth considered the best spot in the restaurant to see the water yet enjoy the air conditioning on hot days. There were no empty seats at the crowded bar, and most of the tables outside were full. Her friend Laura had created a restaurant that was bright, airy and popular. The exposed brick walls and tall windows reflected its heritage as a warehouse. Boats gently bobbed, stretching their ties on the dock, and the Memorial Bridge soared over sparkling water connecting historic downtown to the mainland.

Air kisses all around.

"I'm sorry I'm running a little late." Grace sat down next to Sam. "There are so many breaking stories we're handling at the office. You know the usual—robberies, murder and mayhem. I'm glad I cover events."

Anne grimaced. "There's enough mayhem going on with my kindergarteners to keep me busy every day. I wouldn't want anymore."

They all laughed.

"Speaking of murder ... "

They all turned toward Hailey, who had spoken. "My friend Diane called to tell me Jean Mays was murdered Monday in Sexton Park."

"Oh my God!" exclaimed Sam. "I saw Jean in town a few days ago, and we spoke for a while. Everything seemed to be OK with her. What happened?"

Hailey opened her mouth to answer, but Grace interrupted her.

"Sam, how did you know Jean Mays?" Grace thought she knew all of Sam's friends but never heard her mention Jean Mays's name.

Sam raised a questioning brow. "Grace, you know her. We met her in D.C. several times. I believe she used the pen name Jan Lawson. She worked at the *D.C. Chatter* when you were at the *Chronicle*. Don't you remember her?"

Grace shook her head. "Not ringing a bell."

"Aggressive, blond hair, about five feet eight inches, always looking for dirt. A real bottom feeder." Sam took a minute. "I'm surprised she didn't contact you down here for some stories or information."

"Oh my God." Grace put her fork down. "That's Jean Mays?" She knew Jean. Boy, did she know her. She wiped the moisture forming over her eyes, and her voice trembled. "I never knew Jan Lawson was a pseudonym. When the detective asked me if I knew a Jean Mays, I told him no."

"I remember her telling me she didn't want to be harassed at home after she did an investigative piece," Sam said. "Hailey introduced her as Jean when I saw her at the BookShop. I recognized her and asked her why she went by Jan."

Grace's stomach was churning. *This couldn't be happening.* She turned to Hailey. "D.C. and Black Pointe aren't exactly close. How did you meet Jan, I mean Jean?"

"Well, my friend Diane Benoit introduced us. She, her fiancé Richard, Jean and I would catch a drink now and then. Jean's only lived in Black Pointe for several months. She stopped by the bookstore occasionally. I liked her." Hailey turned to Sam. "Although as you said, Sam, she could be pushy."

Sam turned to Grace. Her brows knitted together. "Grace, back up. Why were the police asking you if you knew Jean?"

"Oh." Grace gulped. "my name showed up on her calendar. And in a letter Jean was writing."

Grace waved it off. "They questioned me about the connection between us. Since I didn't know a Jean Mays, I told them there wasn't any.

"Wow, I can't believe she's dead. Hailey, do you have any more information?" Grace asked hoping to defuse Sam's interest in her reply.

Although, she wasn't sure if she wanted more information on Jean, but she supposed it couldn't hurt, especially if the detectives came calling again. Damn, who was she kidding? They were definitely calling again.

Hailey said no, and she would keep everyone informed if she heard anything else.

Grace got up to use the restroom. No surprise Sam followed her. Grace knew once her friend had an inkling of trouble, she was like a bulldog with a bone, never letting it go.

Sam's lips pursed as she tugged at Grace's arm. "Spill."

Grace swallowed hard, and whispered, "Sam, if the police come back and ask me about Jan Lawson, I'm in trouble."

Shit, shit, shit. Did she just say that? She didn't want Sam to be involved or worried more than she was.

"What do you mean?" Sam demanded, worry in her eyes.

Grace shook her head. "Forget it. It's nothing. Don't worry about it." She was not above begging. "Please?"

Grace did not want Sam to become involved in the mess Jan Lawson started. Sam squinted at her and pursed her lips. She knew Sam wanted to say something else but thankfully let it go. Grace also knew she would be in for cross-examination by Sam sooner rather than later.

"OK ..." Sam huffed. "For now, but I am so not forgetting it. You may not want to talk about this now, but we are having this discussion." Sam frowned at her as if daring her to disagree.

Grace nodded. Sam turned and went back into the restaurant.

Grace stayed in the restroom longer than she needed to. Splashing water on her face, she stared at the wild-eyed, pale person in the mirror. Why couldn't things be easy? She was a good person, tried to do the right thing but kept getting screwed. She let out a deep moan. Worrying about what could happen wasn't helping. Facing her friends with the knowledge she had of the meeting with Jean/Jan and the fact that the detectives were sniffing around her was embarrassing enough.

Too many questions flooded Grace's mind. Was Jean working on something that could hurt her? What had she hoped to gain by reaching out to Grace now? Would the fact she knew Jean/Jan in D.C. affect her case? Could her murder be related to Grace somehow?

She thought about the cute detective, Luke, who came to her office asking if she knew Jean Mays. Had he believed her? She had told him that she didn't know Jean Mays, but knowing Jan Lawson was another story. Jan had reached out to her a month ago. Grace knew if the detectives found out about their conversation, she was in deep trouble. However, the police weren't helpful in D.C. when she went to them. How could she trust that they would be here? Would they even believe her if she told them she had nothing to do with Jean's death?

Jean's death seemed too much of a coincidence. Jean/Jan had been a bottom feeder in D.C. and from her conversation, she was still up to her old tricks. Jean had also contacted her again. Something important about D.C., she claimed. Grace did not want to have the fiasco that happened in D.C. follow her here. But she was afraid it had. Shit. Could life get any worse?

CHAPTER TEN

"Grace?"

"Ms. Winslow?"

Grace looked over at him. Her eyes wide with shock. Her lips were trembling and for some reason, he wanted to kiss them until the trembling stopped. But the reality was that Grace was a suspect. He needed answers and she could have them.

He continued, "You swore to me you didn't know and had never met Jean Mays."

"Yes. But ..." Grace started.

"And," he interrupted, pointing his finger at her, "I find out not only did you know her, but it turns out you had met with her." He wagged his finger at her. "Lying to the police is not a good thing."

"Please, if you give me a chance, I will answer your questions."

Grace straightened and squared her shoulders. He knew she was surprised when they asked her to come down to the station. He was unhappy Grace lied to him about not knowing Jean Mays and wondered what else she had lied about.

Now he was trying a new tactic by bringing her into an interrogation room. Luke had taken a chance she'd never been in one before. He hoped the reality and grittiness of the process might shock her into confessing. The confessing part was taking a slow turn to nowhere.

When she had walked into the precinct, heads turned. Hadn't his fellow officers ever seen a good-looking woman before? The way they were staring he wasn't sure, and if Grace noticed, she didn't let on. He followed her every movement until he stood up and waved her over.

She had on a pair of loose, gauzy pants emphasizing her long legs. Legs Luke wouldn't mind wrapped around his waist. And that form-fitting white top that accentuated her other assets. Assets he would love to explore. He forced himself to stop staring at her little pink toenails gracefully moving up and down in the sandals she now nervously tapped on the floor. *Mind out of the gutter, boy*. Her hair was tied back in a ponytail. Damn, she looked gorgeous even without makeup on. *Whoa.* Why was he even thinking about that? She was a suspect. Pure and simple.

Grace's confession could be their big break. After all their questioning of witnesses and getting nowhere, his IT guy finally managed to crack the password on Jean's computer. More meetings and notes to go through. Luke found a meeting at a local coffee shop that Jean had scheduled with Grace about a week before her murder. Finally, a solid connection between Grace and Jean. Add in the half-written letter Jean addressed to Grace about a problem in D.C. and Luke had no choice but to call Grace back to the station.

Grace lied.

Luke hated liars.

Grace took a deep breath, let it out slowly. "I did meet

Jean, but I knew her in D.C. under her alias, Jan Lawson. So, when you asked me if I knew Jean Mays, I didn't lie. I didn't realize that was her real name."

"So, Jean asked to meet you. When did you meet her?"

"A week or so before she died."

Luke already had that information. He wanted to see if Grace was going to continue to lie about Jean Mays.

Grace looked uncomfortable. Too bad. *Shit, this is getting better and better.*

"Where did you meet?"

She hesitated. *Oh yeah, like pulling teeth.* "At Cool Beans, the coffee shop across from my office."

"Now here's the big question. What did Jean want to talk to you about?"

Grace hemmed and hawed. He knew he wouldn't like her answer.

"She said she wanted to talk about a piece she needed help with."

"What piece and what kind of help?"

Getting information from Grace was like pulling teeth. Luke tapped his fingers on the table.

"Oh. Something about a politician."

Could she get any more vague?

He slammed his hands down on the table hoping to scare her.

Grace jumped.

Luke stared at her, his patience wearing thin. "Look, Grace. We're not getting anywhere. You're evading my questions."

Grace closed her eyes, leaned over, put her head in her hands and slowly shook her head.

Sitting up, she said in a soft voice, "Look, Jan wanted help with an exclusive on a politician I'm good friends with. She thought she had dug up some dirt on him and wanted to write the story and have me confirm it. I knew the story wasn't true. She had already approached him, and he told her no interview. I explained to her I wouldn't get involved in such cheap tactics. I didn't treat my friends like that.

"She said to me, 'Well, you didn't care about ruining people's lives in D.C. If you don't help me, everyone in Black Pointe will know what a liar you are. A phony. No one will want to talk to you. I bet you'll even lose your precious job."

Luke was stunned. "Are you telling me Jean Mays threatened to blackmail you if you didn't help her?" *Did she understand the implication of what she just said?*

Crossing her arms over her body, Grace looked flustered. "Yes, that's what I'm telling you. A piece I wrote in D.C. caused me all sorts of problems, which is why I left to come live here. Look, I have a good life in Black Pointe now, and if Jan, I mean Jean, blackmailed me, she would have ruined my life."

"Did that make you mad?" Luke paused. "Mad enough to kill?"

Grace looked at him in astonishment and sputtered. "Kill? Not hardly. I lived through hell once before and didn't kill anyone. I ran away like a coward then, and I will never, ever run again. Besides, if I killed everyone who made me mad, it would be a very long list."

"OK, we'll leave that for now. So, what did you say to Jean?"

"I said I would get back to her and I left to prepare myself for whatever she was planning. No way was I going to let her bully me or give in to her demands."

Luke sat back in his chair, steepling his hands. "So why did she write you a letter apologizing and mentioning a problem you had in D.C.?"

"Look, I have no idea. Jean and I didn't work together. I don't believe she knew my co-workers and she didn't help me with anything. We never socialized. I don't know what she thought I knew or even why she thought I would help her." Grace leaned back in the chair.

Luke was perplexed and a little relieved. Her story was weak, but there was a chance she was innocent. However, she was still a liar.

LOOKING AROUND THE SMALL, dismal interrogation room, Grace couldn't believe her life had come to this.

Three beat-up metal chairs surrounded a battered metal table, and a dirty mirror hung on the wall. Grace knew the mirror wasn't there so she could freshen up. She also didn't want to think about the things petrified on the table. Grungy, repulsive, just plain nasty came to mind. She already accidentally touched the used chewing gum under her seat. Yuck. The room smelled like dirty, damp, sweaty socks. She shivered. It was freezing in the room and she was sure they turned the thermostat down to make criminals—her—even more uncomfortable. Wishing she'd remembered to bring a sweater, Grace could only hope the interrogation ended soon before she turned into an icicle.

Ah, maybe the cute detective would have to thaw her out. *Gah, why the hell was she thinking about him?* He thought she murdered Jean. She could go to jail for life, and here she was thinking about a detective thawing her out. Grace could only shake her head. *Not reality-based, Grace.*

Luke's, no, Detective McBride's partner, Ben Green, had stopped in earlier to hand him some papers and left. But not before he scowled at her. She had no idea what his problem was.

Detective. She had come a long way from calling him Luke. Should you call someone who might charge you for murder by his or her first name? She didn't know the answer and frankly, at this point, didn't care to find out.

Learning Jean called herself Jan Lawson in D.C. had thrown her off. Why couldn't Jan have left her alone? They weren't close friends or even friends. She barely saw Jean outside of the few times they crossed paths in D.C, and, she had tried hard to avoid her there. *Crap, what a mess.*

Although as nervous as she was about being questioned, she tried hard not to stare at Luke. There was something about his scruffy beard, defined chin, grayish-blue eyes that appealed to her. She knew he had dimples, only because he had smiled at something his partner had said. And, Lord was he built. Broad shoulders, flat stomach, long legs. A walking, talking piece of eye candy. As before when he met her at her office, he was sharp-looking in a white shirt with its sleeves rolled up and black pants.

"Ms. Winslow?"

Grace returned from her fantasy realizing he had asked her a question. She felt a flush racing up from her throat to her face. *I hope he didn't notice me eyeballing him.*

"I'm sorry, what did you ask?"

A small crinkle at the corner of his eye told her he did.

"I asked where you were. From 4 to 6 a.m. on Friday, the morning Jean Mays was killed?"

"Where I am every morning. I would have been in bed until 5:45 a.m. then gotten up and dressed, ready to run with my friend." *God, did she run with Anne that morning?* She couldn't remember.

"Were you alone?"

"Yes. I was alone." *Ass. What did it matter if I was alone?*

Good. Luke didn't want to think about why Grace sleeping alone was comforting to him. They suspected her of murder, for God's sake. But the sparks he felt when they touched were not his imagination. Were they? No. He knew Grace felt them too. He watched her sneaking glances and blushing when she thought he wasn't looking. Lord, the woman could blush.

"So, what I hear you saying is you met Jean Mays, she threatened to blackmail you, and now she's dead. You have no alibi for the time frame in which Jean was killed. Also, we found a note she wrote that ties her to you again."

Of course, she wouldn't confess. But he didn't know how to get the truth from her. Lucky for her, they outlawed torturing witnesses a long time ago. Why wouldn't she just tell him what happened or confess to killing Jean?

"So, tell me why I shouldn't arrest you right now. So far, I'm hearing you had a motive and means to kill her. Maybe even the opportunity if you're lying about the time. Any witnesses that can confirm you were alone?"

Grace's face turned red. Her lips pressed together. Her arms hugged her waist. She was agitated and scared. Good. Maybe now they could get some more answers.

"Look," she finally spat out. "I told you I met Jean for coffee. You can call Cool Beans. I'm there all the time; they know me. As for the time of death, well, my friend Anne Walker called me at 5:30 that morning to tell me she wasn't feeling well and wouldn't be jogging. You can check with Anne and my phone records. Besides, my condo building has security cameras you can check and see what time I left my home."

Finally, he got a rise out of her. God. She was even more gorgeous spitting fire.

"So, you were ..."

Grace interrupted him. "As for my conversation with Jan,

Jean... shit, whatever her name is, I discussed her allegations with the congressman. I told him how I handled it. He appreciated it and told me not to worry. Jean thrived on digging up dirt. She had nothing on him he couldn't handle. He told me to ignore her."

Grace stood up, placing her hands on her hips. "Look, you have nothing to hold me on. Either charge me or let me go. But I'm telling you right now, I'm not going down without a fight. I'm also going to call a lawyer and Sam Knight of KnightGuard Security. The police aren't helping me. You're looking at the wrong person. I'm sure there's more to this story which doesn't involve me. I don't know what it is yet, but I might, just might, share any information with you when I get it."

Ouch. He wanted to tell Grace the police could help if she told the truth, but he wasn't going there today.

"Why involve Sam Knight?"

Luke knew Sam. Her company KnightGuard Security enjoyed an excellent reputation in the field, and his friend Pete Carson worked there.

"Sam is my best friend. Jean hinted someone she knew from D.C. had hurt me and still wanted to. I want to find out who and why."

"Who?" He was baffled. "Hurt you how?"

"I don't know, but it doesn't matter now, does it?"

He guessed it didn't for the time being. He added the congressman to his list of interviews. Luke hoped he and Ben would be able to get more from him. Maybe a reason why Jean had targeted him and Grace.

Luke let Grace go with the promise that he would be asking more questions and told her not to leave town. As she huffed out, Luke made another note to himself to touch base with Sam or Pete although he didn't see that going anywhere. If they were searching for more information, Sam would consider her friend Grace a client. Would she be willing to share information?

Ben walked in as soon as Grace left.

"What'd you think? Is she looking good for this?"

"As much as I would like to pin this on her, we need more information. Check out her alibies." Luke crushed his empty water bottle and threw it into the wastebasket. A perfect metaphor for this case.

"I'm not sure Winslow knows anything else that can help us. Let's keep a casual look at her movements though, just in case she makes a mistake."

"Who you going to put on her?" Ben blew an air kiss, "I wouldn't mind, she's a looker."

Luke looked over at Ben. *So not going to happen.*

"I'll do it."

CHAPTER ELEVEN

Grace couldn't wait to get out of the police department. Luke and his partner had grilled her about Jean/Jan for what seemed like three hours, but when she looked at her watch, it had been less than an hour. She couldn't tell them anything else because she didn't know anything. She believed the notes she'd been getting were connected to Jean's murder, but didn't understand why as she barely knew the woman.

Freedom. That's all she could think about as she walked down the street. *This must be what it feels like to be released from prison.* After sitting and answering questions for so long, her mind was mush. How could the sun still be shining when it was a black day for her? By the time she got to her car and managed to get the door open, her whole body was shaking. Getting into the seat and fastening her seatbelt, she took a deep breath and debated calling Sam. Damn it. She couldn't do this alone. She needed Sam's help yet again.

She got Sam's voicemail, and left a message.

Turning on her car, Grace thought about leaving Black Pointe and heading to Boston. Maybe hiding out there forever with her family surrounding her wasn't such a bad idea.

No. Not going there. She was tired of running. Besides she had her close friends who had her back and a decent life here in Black Pointe

She was now late for an assignment at the beach, and she couldn't afford to lose her job.

She took a left onto Marshall Boulevard and headed east toward Seaside, on the barrier island. Troubling thoughts invaded the peacefulness she tried to maintain. *Why was this happening to her again? She was being targeted by a stalker and now by the police. Would this harassment ever stop?* She just wanted peace, a quiet life with no controversy and, for sure, no murders.

Her cell phone rang, thankfully interrupting her pessimistic thoughts.

"Grace, It's Sam. You called?"

Knowing Sam was always there for her calmed Grace down. "You're not going to believe this. I just spent an hour downtown at the police station. They're trying to tie me to Jean's murder."

"You're kidding." Sam voiced the anger Grace felt.

"Grace, honey, tell me what happened."

Grace recounted all that had gone on and the questions the detectives asked her. "Sam, they put me in an interrogation room," she whispered. That had been almost as embarrassing as being called to the station.

"I'm so sorry the police are putting you through this. None of this makes sense. How does a note in Jean's apartment with your name on it make you a suspect?"

"Well, it's not just the note. I didn't tell you I met with Jan. Jean. Shit, I can't keep her name straight."

Silence on the other end.

"I didn't want to bother you about it, but she threatened

to blackmail me if I didn't give her access to a politician. The police want to pin the murder on someone, and now I'm looking good for it."

Grace heard Sam blow out a deep breath. "OK, stay calm if you can. Look, I have an appointment this afternoon I can't get out of but why don't I come over tonight? I'll bring dinner. We'll open a bottle of wine, and you can tell me how I can help. In the meantime, I'll try to reach my friend on the police force and find out if he knows what's going on."

Grace sighed. "Great. I have an appointment on the island that will last a couple of hours, and then I'll be home. See you later."

Grace sped along the highway towards the beach. There weren't many cars on the road for which she was grateful. Her mind wandered back to D.C., where the traffic was horrific most of the time. She was thankful she didn't live there anymore for more reasons than just bad traffic. Time and moving back to Black Pointe had soothed some of the horrendous events she had experienced there.

She could see the causeway leading over to the island in the distance. The Intracoastal views always relaxed her but not today.

Her mind was still miles away when she looked ahead and noticed two small brown dogs running into the road, chasing each other around, playing. Grace stomped on the brakes.

Her foot hit the floor. Nothing.

Oh, God. She let her foot up and tried pumping the brakes.

Nothing.

The car was still moving forward, and she had no brakes.

Trying not to panic but losing the battle, she looked for a safe place to steer.

Her choice became the steep embankment by the canal on her left or a stand of palms on her right with the Intracoastal behind them—neither a good choice. The car was slowly moving. The dogs still chasing each other around the road oblivious to the danger.

Again and again, Grace pumped the brakes. Nothing.

Finally, the dogs raced off into the trees, but Grace still needed to stop the car. Her mind was frantic trying to remember how to use the emergency brake in case of emergency. Pull it up? Push down? Or ... or? Shit, she couldn't remember. It was now or never. Easing over to the side of the road with the car still surging forward, she headed for the stand of palms. A safer choice, if there was one, since she could land upside down in the canal and drown. She pulled the emergency brake and braced for impact. It wasn't gentle. But the car stopped. Abruptly.

The right side of the car had hit the palms and the airbags deployed. Grace sat there stunned for a few minutes, trying to catch her breath and assess her injuries. Nothing felt broken. She unhooked her seatbelt, pushed the airbag out of her way, and opened her door. Her legs felt like wet noodles, and she grabbed hold of the door so as not to fall onto the road.

Her body ached. Her wrists hurt where the airbag had blown them off the steering wheel. Her sunglasses were somewhere in the car. She looked around for her phone but couldn't find it.

She stood by her car hyperventilating. A few minutes later she noticed a blue SUV heading her way. She held her hand out and waved. Thankfully, the car stopped, and a man and woman got out and raced over.

"Are you all right, miss?"

Grace mentally checked her body. Her voice was shaking, "My arm hurts, but I'm lucky to be alive."

She couldn't stop trembling. "I'm really scared right now."

A sob escaped. "I don't know what happened to my phone. I need to call a tow truck. I think my brakes failed."

The woman put her arm around her as she led Grace to their car. "Come sit in our car, and we'll call the police."

Thanking the couple, Grace sat in the front seat while the man dialed the police. Within ten minutes, Grace could hear the sirens in the distance. The police arrived at the same time the paramedics did. She sat in the back of the van while the paramedics checked her out. Nothing was broken or needed additional looking after so they released her.

Within the hour, her car was in back of the tow truck. She was in the front seat with the driver who wasn't talkative. He deposited Grace and her car at the garage. She reached Hailey who dropped her off at the car rental office and then left for work.

Grace wanted nothing more than to drive home, take a bath, drink a glass of wine and fall asleep. She didn't care in which order that occurred. She was stressed and tired.

One more thing to do then she was done for the day.

"Sam, we need to reschedule. I've been in a car accident and not feeling up to company. I'll call you tomorrow."

THE SUN CAST a cheery glow on the streets as Grace headed to her office the next morning hoping the beautiful day would help her forget yesterday. She was still achy, bruised and stressed. She barely made it to her desk when her cell phone rang.

"Grace, I'm so glad I caught up with you." Sam sounded breathless.

"What's up?"

"I just got your message. I'm glad you canceled last night. I was at a stakeout and couldn't get back to you. Listen, I want to talk to you about Jean's murder, plus I just talked to George at the garage about your brakes."

Grace was confused. "Why would you call George?"

"Sweetie, I called him because I'm your friend and was concerned. He found your brake line had a slit in it. Luckily, you were on a back road and not going very fast."

"What?" Putting her hand out to steady herself on her desk, Grace slowly lowered her body into her chair.

"Oh my God, I can't believe this. How did that happen?" Grace's voice came out like mouse squeaks. Was this an accident? Or harassment? And why did that thought even cross her mind? *Oh yeah—stalker.* But he had never done anything like this before—just sent threatening notes.

"Grace don't panic. You probably ran over a branch or probably didn't notice fluid leaking. Stay calm."

Saying goodbye, Grace hung up the phone. What else could happen to her? *No. No. No.* Grace prayed she hadn't just jinxed herself.

CHAPTER TWELVE

Adjusting his tux, as he slowly walked toward the altar, Luke was over-the-top-excited. His bride, the love of his life, would be joining him soon. It had taken months of working up the courage to ask Becky to become his wife. They had planned for this day since high school. Today it was finally happening. Luke looked out at the congregation. He saw his father, pleased as could be for him. His friends from work and other family members were there to see him tie the knot. They were all so happy for him.

He stood tall next to his best friend from childhood, Seth Bowman. His three brothers were groomsmen and stood next to Seth. He waited for Becky to walk down the aisle while visions of children laughing in the sunshine with Becky's blue eyes and black hair filled his mind. A white picket fence surrounding a small house with colorful gardens everywhere completed the picture. And there would be sex! Oh yeah, lots of sex!

The music stopped. Wait. What?

Becky was walking toward him down the aisle, but hand in hand with Jason. Jason, his ex-fucking, shithead-partner. She looked adoringly at Jason and laughed at something he said. They never even glanced at him, just walked straight up to the minister who pronounced them husband and wife leaving him to stand there empty-handed.

Betrayed. Yet another woman abandoning him.

Bells were ringing and ringing. Bells?

Luke opened his eyes, his eyelids heavy, and sat up, realizing he had been dreaming. Bells again. Shit, it was the doorbell. Someone was at his front door ringing the doorbell. It had better be important, or he would be pummeling whomever.

He shook his head. His dream turning into a real-life nightmare as it leisurely left his mind. Luke wasn't getting married. His ex-fiancé and his former partner had seen to that.

Betrayal. How had he missed the signs? He was a detective for God's sake. Never again. He would never trust a woman again.

Luke pulled on a pair of jeans and walked barefoot to answer the front door. Darkness surrounded him. Looking at his watch, he realized it was 5 a.m. Damn, he remembered he had promised to go fishing with his buddy, Paul Atwood.

The doorbell stopped ringing. And the banging began.

"Shit," he groaned as he opened the door.

"Good morning, sunshine." Paul stood on the steps with a great big smile on his face. "You still up for fishing?" Paul looked ridiculous with his silly trout hat on. It was too early to watch the multi-colored fish bobbing up and down as Paul talked.

Opening the door wide to let Paul in, Luke growled, "Fuck you."

Paul walked in smirking, leaving his fishing gear and a cooler on the front step.

Luke led him into the kitchen, rummaged through a cabinet and pulled out the can of coffee.

"Make some coffee while I get dressed."

"Rough night?"

"I wish."

He walked back into his bedroom and finished dressing, then joined Paul in the kitchen. The comforting aroma of fresh-perked coffee teased his senses. He grabbed two to-go mugs from the cabinet.

"I think the milk is sour," Paul said, sniffing it.

"What else is new? I haven't been home for a while and haven't picked anything up. You can drink it black."

"That works." Paul shrugged, grabbed his cup and started toward the door. "I have the cooler packed and ready to go, so collect your stuff."

Paul picked up his gear outside. They headed around the house towards the river where Luke docked his twenty-two-foot bay style boat.

Gathering all their gear, they loaded the boat up. The day was shaping up to be a cool one, and Luke hoped the fish were jumping. On days like this, Luke thanked his lucky stars for finding this comfortable ranch overlooking the Banana River.

The sun was high in the sky when they decided to anchor for lunch. Breaking out sandwiches and beer, they relaxed on the boat. Fishing had been great, and they had more than enough for dinner.

"Any more information on the two joggers' who were killed? Off the record, of course," asked Paul. Paul never wanted to take advantage of his position as a journalist to interfere with his friendship with Luke. But Luke didn't talk much about his cases anyway. "I'm hearing people are leery about jogging in the parks until the murders are resolved."

"I don't blame them. We've identified both women. Why one was killed is still a mystery, the other, we have too many people who could have killed her."

Luke thought about Grace. He didn't believe she killed Jean, but it couldn't hurt to find out more about her.

"I'm interested in a couple of people. Especially this one woman."

Luke collected their trash and put it in the cooler. "In fact, she had been a reporter in D.C. She alluded to a problem there when we questioned her. Maybe you could check some of your sources up there and let me know what you hear. Off the record, of course."

"Happy to," said Paul. "What's your interest in her besides being a suspect or not?"

Damn, not going there. Luke shrugged his shoulders.

CHAPTER THIRTEEN

Luke followed Grace on and off for a couple of days. Followed her when she left the office or her condo. He didn't need to. She might have motive and opportunity to kill Jean, but he didn't think she had the means. She was a suspect until her alibies checked out. Plus, it looked like she led a pretty boring life. Work, more work, jogging and an occasional meet up with a friend. No dates that he could tell. Good.

But he was curious about her. Curious about her life. *Stalkerish some?* Nah. Not him.

Today, as she exited the BookShop, Luke watched as Grace walked across the street. The sun backlit her and created a halo around her head. Her auburn hair was hanging loosely around her shoulders today. She walked into a café and sat by a window. She was a smart and beautiful woman. He didn't quite understand this attraction he had with her. Undoubtedly as the lead detective or any law enforcer who was investigating a suspect, he should be running the other way. But not him. Instead, he was following a woman he was in lust with. Yeah, his captain would love that excuse.

He decided to take a chance, go into the coffee shop and talk to her.

"Miss Winslow, happy to see you out and about."

Grace startled. She looked up. Her whiskey-colored eyes widened in recognition, and her mouth twitched. Nerves?

"Detective."

"Luke," he said. "Can I sit for a moment?"

"Help yourself," she said coolly.

Luke pulled out a chair from in front of the window and turned it around, sat down and faced her. Distrust radiating from her face. Had he been too hard on her at the station? He thought not. They were only trying to get to the bottom of this murder. Besides being tough was part of the job.

"Luke, then. What do you want?" she asked rather brusquely.

"I was coming in to get coffee and saw you sit down. Just thought I would say hello and see how you are holding up."

"I'm fine."

Okaaay, short and to the point. Luke wasn't giving up yet. The waitress came over, and Grace placed her order for coffee and a muffin. She looked at Luke, brows raised.

"I'll have coffee," he said. Silence filled the air. Luke knew he could wait out Grace. She was too nice to let the silence go on.

Finally, she asked him about his day.

They talked for a few minutes after the coffee arrived. Nothing serious; mundane things like the weather, the beach. Subjects Luke thought wouldn't get Grace's back up. There was something about this woman that made him want to know more. Was it her vulnerability? Her strength? Her eyes? Shit, maybe it was the freckles on her nose he craved to kiss one by one. *Really?*

Luke took another sip of coffee and then looked at his watch. "Look, I have to go, but I ..." Shit, the words caught in his throat. "I wondered if you want to grab a drink sometime?"

Grace's eyes squinted, her mouth opened slightly, and all Luke could think of was sliding his tongue in and kissing those sweet lips. *What the hell was wrong with him?*

"Ah, no. I don't think so. My calendar is full right now."

Well, he thought, *as letdowns went, this was tame*. He was disappointed, but he would ask again. He wanted to see how far this fascination with Grace could go.

"OK, maybe another time." Leaving money on the table to cover their tab, he walked out.

WHAT WAS THAT ALL ABOUT? Grace was confused. Luke certainly had a look that appealed to her—tall, good-looking, muscles that rippled under his shirt. Arms she wanted around her, holding her tight. Oh, Lord! She had it bad.

On the one hand, she was attracted to him. On the other, he was a cop, for God's sake. A cop who took her to task over notes she didn't know anything about. Over a dead journalist she thought was someone else. He would be dangerous to her well-being as well as to her psyche. She wasn't in a place to handle another man let alone a detective on the police force —a profession that abandoned her in D.C., called her a liar, and did nothing to help her. She couldn't, no, wouldn't, go out with him. Besides, she had a more important appointment to keep.

GRACE WALKED into Jean's apartment building and took the elevator up to the eighth floor. Grace knew she shouldn't be here. She was a suspect although from what she gathered, so was Diane Benoit. But as wrong and deceitful as it might be, she needed to get more information about Jean. So, she was stepping out of her comfort zone, digging deeper, investigating, all things she did best in another life. It was Saturday so she took a chance that Diane would be home.

She knocked lightly on Diane's door. A few seconds later a short, brunette woman opened it a crack.

"Yes?"

Stammering, Grace introduced herself.

Diane looked puzzled

Grace had one chance to get Diane to let her in. Truth or dare? Grace didn't know which would work. "You don't know me. Jean and I knew each other from when we worked in D.C. I was shocked to hear that she was killed and wondered if you could fill me in a little more about what happened? Maybe a little about her life here?"

Diane took a minute to decide.

"Please," Grace said.

Making up her mind, Diane opened the door widely and let Grace in. She motioned to Grace to take one of the chairs flanking the couch.

"I don't know what I can add to what I told the detectives. Jean was a friend and confidant, at least until she betrayed me with my fiancé."

Whoa, Diane was pissed about that. Maybe she could get more information.

"Ouch. That must have hurt a lot," said Grace.

"Yeah, well, water over the dam, blah, blah. So, ask away."

Grace thought for a moment. "Why did Jean move to Black Pointe? Did she have family here?"

"No family. She and I have been friends for years. I moved here for my job a couple of years ago. Jean got tired of the rat race in D.C. When the apartment across the hall opened up, she jumped at the chance to start over."

"Do you know if she was working on anything special here or in D.C.?"

"Not that I know of."

"Did any friends or someone she was dating from D.C. visit, perhaps?"

"No visitors from D.C. that I remember."

Diane looked thoughtful for a moment. "I know she had good friends in D.C. Some woman from the *Washington Chronicle* and a man who worked in government. I don't remember if she mentioned their names. The man had contacted her here, and his call upset her. She told me she never wanted to see him again."

The *Washington Chronicle?* Was it someone she knew? What were the chances?

"Do you have their names?"

Diane shook her head, "I can't remember any, sorry."

There wasn't anything else Diane could add. Grace stood and started to say goodbye when Diane blurted out, "I remember now. The woman's name was Rachel, Rachel Long. No, wait. Rachel Lang.

"Do you know her?"

Grace tripped over the doorsill. *Do I know her? Shit, yes.*

Rachel Lang worked at the Chronicle with her. Rachel helped her with her story on the senator and then betrayed her. Rachel Lang was her nemesis.

GRACE LEFT Diane's apartment and walked down the street towards her car. *Rachel Lang.* A name she hoped never to hear again. Grace shook her head. The betrayals were staggering. Rachel betrayed her by denying she had the names of the sources to back up Grace's allegations that the senator was taking kickbacks; then removed her name and left only

Grace's on the exposé. The whistleblower who was instrumental in the initial version of the exposé betrayed her by disappearing when she needed his backup. The newspaper's publisher betrayed her by believing Rachel's lies just because she was a seasoned journalist and Grace wasn't.

Betrayals. And, they all added up to disaster.

She didn't want to relive the betrayals—there were too many. It was time to put them out of her mind. The bile gurgled up her throat. *Please don't let me hurl here on the street.*

She raced toward her car, opened the door and got in, trying hard to control her breath. Would this nightmare ever end? Grace had left D.C. in disgrace because she couldn't fight anymore. She thought she was safe in Florida. She wasn't.

First, the stalker had found her, then Jean/Jan and now hearing Rachel Lang's name brought up bitter memories. But she wouldn't run anymore. *What can I do? Certainly not ignore the problems.* She was tired of running.

She needed to contact Rachel and find out what she knew about Jean. Maybe Rachel knew what Jean was working on that might have gotten her killed. Would Rachel even talk to her? She remembered Rachel had moved elsewhere, but she wasn't sure where. Did Rachel know this guy who had the government job?

I'll think about that tomorrow. Good Lord, why did that quote pop into her mind? She had to stop thinking of quotes from *'Gone with the Wind.'* Although, at the moment, she wished she had Scarlet O'Hara's optimistic outlook on life.

IT WAS another day before Grace thought about tracking down Rachel. She had put in a call to Karen St. Clair, a coworker at the *Chronicle* with whom she always got along well with.

"Grace." Karen's calming voice sounded welcoming. "It's been too long since I've heard your voice. How are you?"

Grace told her a little of her new life and asked about Rachel.

"Gosh, I haven't thought about Rachel in a while. The powers that be fired her shortly after you left. She moved away, and rumors are she recently came back to D.C."

"I didn't know the paper fired her." *Wow, that was news.* Why did they fire her? "Who is she writing for now?"

"No one in particular. I believe Rachel managed a political blog. I haven't seen it in a while, so maybe she's doing something else."

Grace sighed. She had hoped it would be easy finding Rachel but talking to Karen and getting nowhere was stressing her out. It wasn't Karen per se. It was the notion she would have to keep exposing herself to everyone in D.C. who had witnessed her demise.

"Did you know any of her friends outside the office?"

"No." Karen paused. "There were rumors Rachel had dated someone from the office. But I don't know who. She never talked about him and I don't remember her mentioning anyone else."

Grace said goodbye after promising to keep in touch with Karen.

It was now or never. Grace Googled Rachel's name and got the name of her blog and contact information. Sending her an email, Grace could only wait, and hope Rachel would respond. And if she did, would Grace like Rachel's answers?

CHAPTER FOURTEEN

Jean's killer watched as Grace left her condo for work. *Sharp dresser, pretty in an innocent way.* Not his type though. He liked full-figured ballsy women like his Rachel.

He knew Grace would be at the paper for at least a couple of hours waiting for her eleven o'clock appointment. He made sure when he called to make the appointment to tell her that he might be late. Late indeed. He would be very, very late.

He nursed a coffee at the shop across the street from her condo for over an hour watching her doorway. It was a dreary, rainy day, perfect for the workmen in the building to be indoors and to implement his plan. He wouldn't stand out.

A couple of weeks ago, anticipating that getting into Grace's building would be difficult, he had a real estate agent show him an empty condo on the fourth floor. It was easy enough to give her his award-winning smile and flirt with her to get information.

Luckily for him, the building was being renovated. Using the agent's code and "borrowing" a painter's uniform, padding it, and gluing on a false mustache, he had knocked on the super's door. After he explained that he was there to paint, the stupid man had let him into Grace's condo. They ought to fire the dunce.

Today was going to be just as much fun. For him, anyhow.

Today, he dressed up as an installer for the glass company. It had been a piece of cake. *So easy. You can get anything printed on a shirt these days.* The hard part would be getting into Grace's condo. He couldn't ask the super to let him in again; he would be suspicious—or not. But he wasn't taking any chances. His lockpicking skills were mediocre, at best, plus, he didn't want to break down the door. There were too many people working today, unlike the last time he was here. However, he had a backup plan.

Pulling his cap down low to avoid the security cameras, he walked up the stairs, knocked on Grace's door and waited. He knocked again a little louder and yelled "Hello!"

Then he waited. The condo door across from Grace's opened. Sure enough, a nosy neighbor.

"She's not home."

"Shi ... ugar," he said. "I'm from the glass company, and we're measuring her windows today. If I don't do it now, it will hold up the entire project."

"Nobody said anything about that to me."

The man scrutinized the old woman, who looked about his grandma's age, that is, if Grandma were still alive. He tried to avoid the nips her stupid dog was aiming at his ankles.

"Cute dog." He leaned down to pet the tiny monster who promptly swallowed his fingers.

The old lady nodded. "Toto seems to like you."

Retrieving his fingers from the mutt's mouth, he said, "Well, I had a cute little doggy just like him when I was a kid. He was my best friend next to my grandma. Miss him a lot."

That was a joke. He was too busy avoiding being beaten up by bullies to worry about a pet. That is until he smartened up and realized you didn't need physical strength to bully. He had years of fun getting even. And boy, did he get even. Plus, his grandma hated dogs.

The old woman smiled. "Yes, all children should have pets, especially if they are as sweet as little Toto here." She bent down to pat the sadistic beast who wagged his tail and jumped around even more enthusiastically.

"Listen, I had made an appointment with Ms. Winslow, but I guess she forgot. Can you contact her, or do you have a key? The super isn't around to ask. I know they're anxious to get the measurements and install the windows."

The old woman hesitated. "Well, I'm not sure I should let you in. But I know Grace is anxious to get the renovations over with. It's been very disrupting."

"Thank you, ma'am, appreciate it. My boss would be furious if I don't do this today. We're overbooked, and I don't know when we can come back. Plus, I just got married, and I'm trying to impress him."

The man watched as emotions flooded the old woman's face. He knew he passed her scrutiny when he told her he used to have a dog like the sadistic monster now chewing on his shoe. Throwing in the fact that he was a newlywed was icing on the cake.

"Wait here. I'll get the key."

The old woman shuffled back to her apartment but didn't take the nipper with her. *God, he hated dogs, especially small yappers.*

By the time she came back, he was ready to throttle the dog who was now chewing on his shoelaces.

"When will the installation take place?" the woman asked as she opened Grace's condo for him.

"Next week."

The old woman chatted a few more minutes with him,

but she didn't seem anxious to leave. Thankfully, the beast wiggled around as if he was going to pee any second.

"There, there, Toto. We're going." She bent down to pick up the rat.

"Toto's waited long enough for his walk. Please close the door on your way out. It will lock automatically. Just leave the key under my mat."

He thanked her, walked in, pulled out his measuring tape, and started recording measurements. Hearing the elevator door open and close, he shut and locked Grace's door and looked around.

He remembered how nice her condo was from the last time he was in it. The bitch did well for herself while he was scrounging for work. She had taken everything from him, his job at the newspaper, and then exposing the senator who had been his meal ticket. He worked harder than the bitch did and what did he get? Thrown out on the street—twice—because of her.

Pulling on latex gloves, he placed several listening devices around, ones he hadn't had with him when he installed the spy cameras.

Then he went into Grace's bedroom and started pulling out drawers, admiring her lingerie. *I love a woman in matching underwear*. He slashed her mattress, pulled clothes down from the closet and finally, dumped the chicken blood he brought with him on the bedspread.

Leaving the note, he checked around for anything he might have dropped. The anticipation of finally hearing Grace's surprise had him salivating. He didn't have that opportunity before when he slit her brakes.

He closed her door, deposited the key under the old woman's mat and left.

It had been a frustrating and tiring day. Grace was exhausted. The day couldn't have gotten any worse. She had been stood up for an interview and was late for another appointment. Then she lost her umbrella when a gust of wind blew it out of her hand causing her to get a good soaking.

Thinking a nice cup of tea and a bath would soothe her, she inserted her key into the lock.

Opening her door, she stepped into her living room and stopped. Something was off. Focusing on what was wrong, she realized her living room was messy. Not just messy but torn apart.

No. This couldn't be happening to her. Perspiration ran down her face. Her hands were shaking. She pulled out her pepper spray from her purse. Cap off, Grace walked around the strewn papers and furniture to check the kitchen. Nothing was out of place there. Slowly walking down the hall and opening her bedroom door, she felt her legs buckle.

It looked like a tornado had blitzed through her bedroom. The bureau drawers were emptied and dumped all over the floor. The duvet was covered in something Grace hoped wasn't blood but probably was. Everything in her closet was now on the floor in a ragged heap. Furniture was tipped over but not broken. Bile formed deep in her stomach. *This losing my cookies is getting old.* Taking deep controlling breaths, Grace turned and walked out of her bedroom. She checked the guest room, which looked untouched.

She trudged out of her condo and knocked on her neighbor's door.

"Grace dear, how are you? Maggie stood in her doorway while her little toy poodle, Toto, sniffed at Grace's ankles. It was always a toss-up as to whether he would lick or nip. Today it was a lick. Thank goodness.

Maggie tugged on Grace's arm. "Come in and have some tea. I made chocolate cookies today." Maggie was always baking, and her condo always smelled like warm cookies. Today Grace was not in the mood to enjoy them.

Grace held back the scream she wanted to let out.

"Maggie, did you see anyone today in the building who was unfamiliar?" asked Grace as she moved slowly into the living room.

Maggie was in her early 80s but looked 70ish. Her white hair was in a bun on top of her head, and she had on her bright red skirt, cowgirl top and boots. Today was Thursday, so Grace knew Maggie had her weekly line dancing lesson. Her blue eyes crinkled as she smiled at Grace.

"You know, dear, there were a lot of workers around today. They're hurrying to get the building done before hurricane season. The window man measured for the new hurricane-resistant glass. Lovely man. Dog lover on top of it all. He loved Toto."

Maggie winked. "I must say, they are making them cuter and cuter these days."

Grace tried hard to keep the frustration out of her voice and took a deep breath. "How did he get into my condo?"

"I hope you don't mind, I used your spare key to let him in. He was only here for the day, and I know you want your place done as soon as possible. The super wasn't around, and the man said he wouldn't be able to come back for several weeks if he couldn't get it done today. I told him the door would automatically lock when he left and to leave the key. I hope that was all right?" Maggie looked worried. "Is everything OK? I had to leave and walk little Toto before the installer finished and he did put the key back under the mat."

"Maggie, he wasn't a contractor." Grace's voice cracked. "He vandalized my condo."

"Oh my!" Maggie covered her mouth with her hands. "Oh Grace, I'm so sorry. I didn't know. Did you call the police?"

Maggie's voice quavered, and she looked like she was going to cry.

Grace patted her on the arm, told Maggie she was going to call them and that everything would be all right

Grace went back to her condo, closed and locked the door. Déjà vu. Wasn't it just a couple of weeks ago she sensed someone had been in her condo and she attempted to call the police? Couldn't do it then, can't do it now. She sat on her couch. Despair filled her mind. Anxiety took over her body; her heart was pounding, her hands trembling.

Calling the police meant going through all the distrust and agony she went through in D.C. The cops didn't believe her then. Why would they now? They could say she trashed the condo herself to distract from the murder investigation.

Call. Not call.

Damn it. This was the last straw. Her personal space had been invaded for the last time.

She wasn't going to be a victim anymore.

Grace didn't care if the cops believed her or not, she was calling them. She was taking her life back.

The dispatcher told her the police would be there as soon as possible.

HER CONDO COULDN'T FIT in another person if it tried. The police sent two officers. The two detectives from Jean's case also came, although she had no idea why they would be interested in a break-in. Maggie was there holding the high-strung Toto who had been trying to attack everyone's ankles and shrilly yapping. The super came up and was less than thrilled about the distraction and destruction.

Grace was asked to make a list of missing items. She didn't think anything was missing, just thrown around. The officers took fingerprints from the door although considering how many people had touched the door, Grace didn't think they would find anything. They bagged a sample of the blood from the duvet to be analyzed. The detectives questioned the super and Maggie. Toto was whining. Police radios squawked. So much noise. People were everywhere. There was no placc to sit down. No room to escape to. Grace had the beginnings of a mega headache.

The officers had questioned her *ad nauseam* about who she thought would do this and why. Grace told them she had no idea specifically who, but if she were guessing, it would be her stalker.

The cops were interested now. "How long have you had this stalker?"

"Well, it's been a couple of years. I thought I got rid of him in D.C."

"Why haven't you reported it?"

"I don't know." *Oh yeah, that was lame*. The cop just gave her a look and shook his head. Grace had no idea how to explain to him why she didn't report it.

"Any guesses as to who it might be?"

"No idea."

They were throwing so many questions at her, she didn't have time to answer one before the other one came.

Grace's nerves were raw. She wanted to vomit. As she went to her desk to get the box with the notes, she noticed that detective, Luke McBride, who accused her of murdering Jean, walking toward her. What did he want now? Had he heard the exchange with the cop? Maybe to accuse her of trashing her condo. Of lying?

He stopped in front of her. He tilted his head, paused for a moment. "A stalker, huh? Anything you'd like to add to that? This is the first time I've heard you had a stalker. Why you? Why now?"

"I had a problem in D.C. with notes and weird things happening. When I left, I thought I left all the crazy stuff behind." It had been two years of semi-bliss. Why had the stalker surfaced now? She opened the drawer and pulled out the box. "No fingerprints according to the police in D.C.," she said sarcastically.

Luke shook his head. "Call me curious, but why didn't you think this was important enough to report to the police or tell me about it when we spoke?"

"Look, the police in D.C. never took my reports seriously. I got tired of reporting the notes and nothing being done. I moved here and thought the stalking was over."

"Apparently not," said Luke. He took the box from her hands and opened it, read several of the pink notes and handed the box back to her. "This doesn't sound like a person who is going away. I need a list of names of people who might have a grudge against you."

"Well, that might take more than a few minutes. I was an investigative reporter, and lots of people had grudges against me in D.C. Here, not so much since I handle events."

After what seemed like a nightmare marathon, everyone had left. Grace felt drained. She couldn't stay here. What if the stalker came back? Sam insisted she stay at her place. Grace didn't want to take anything from her condo that the creep had touched. She picked up her laptop and would stop at the store for some clothes and personal items.

There wasn't anything else she could do tonight but tomorrow...tomorrow was another day.

CHAPTER FIFTEEN

An hour later, Grace rang the buzzer to KnightGuard Security, and the door clicked open. Waving to the guard who was staffing the night desk, she took the open elevator up to the second floor.

KnightGuard Security took up all of the downstairs of the old warehouse. But Sam had converted the upstairs space for herself. Getting out of the elevator Grace stepped into the living room of Sam's loft.

Grace loved what Sam had done with the previously cold, open space. The main floor with its tall ceilings and exposed brick was now calm and understated. Browns, grays, and pinks dominated the expansive living room. Mammoth multi-paned windows let in tons of light. A guest bedroom and bath were behind a wooden wall, and exposed stairs went to the upstairs master bedroom and master bath. Sam didn't cook much, but she had a big industrial kitchen a professional chef would covet.

Settling into the comfy gray sofa, Grace took the glass of wine Sam handed her and gulped it down.

"How are you doing?" Sam's face showed nothing but concern for Grace.

"I feel violated. I'm upset that someone could get in my condo so easily plus I feel bad for Maggie. She didn't know the installer was an impostor and felt guilty about letting the creep in."

"I'm so sorry this happened to you. It makes me so angry that this bastard has violated your space. But I'm glad you brought in the police this time."

Grace thought about it for a minute. "That was the hardest call I've made in a while. I'm still not sure if they are going to be helpful or if they even believe me. But I'm not letting this go anymore."

Leaning forward, Grace took a sip of wine and said, "I'm not going to be a victim anymore." She rubbed her forehead, "If the cops don't help, I want to hire you to find this bastard and stop him."

"You got it, sweetie. I'll do anything to help, you know it. Just tell me when you're ready. In the meantime, I'll keep in touch with my source at the station for any updates." Sam's nostrils flared, her hands clenched, she hissed, "I'm so disgusted by this. I can't imagine how you feel."

"More than disgusted. I'm drained and afraid. I don't understand what is happening."

"Oh hon, we'll get to the bottom of this. I promise."

Grace smoothed her pants and looked over at her best friend. "Sam, I can't thank you enough for everything you do. I really appreciate it."

"Grace, you don't ever have to thank me. I've got your back. I've made up the guest room. Do you want to freshen up?"

Grace shook her head. "Nah, I'm going to sit here and drink until I'm numb."

Hugging Grace, Sam laughed. She got up and returned

with a bottle of white wine and filled Grace's glass. "I'm with you, girlfriend."

It was still early, but as the evening wore on, Grace was feeling more than a slight buzz.

"I can get the cleaning crew we use out there tomorrow if you want, and I have time to help put things back together. Do you want to stay here for a while?" asked Sam.

"Yes, to the cleaning crew. Yes, to you helping. No, to staying here. I'll go back tomorrow and sort through the mess. The bastard is not forcing me out of my home, or my life, not again. I do want to talk to you about security though."

It was getting late, and Grace was too hyped-up to sleep. This invasion of her privacy wasn't the worst thing that had ever happened to her, but it was the worst thing to happen to her in Florida. Maybe not the worst, if she were honest with herself. She could add in the notes she received, her brakes slashed, becoming a suspect in a murder. *Shit, the list kept growing.*

"Sooo, changing the subject. How's your love life?"

Grace looked at her quizzingly. "Sam, are you living vicariously through me?"

Sam laughed. "Why not? I'm not getting any."

"That's because you won't give Mark the time of day." Mark Stone was Sam's on/off "special friend." Grace knew he wanted more from Sam. He had asked Sam to marry him once. But Sam claimed she wasn't ready to commit to anyone until she built her business up. Grace suspected that Sam was afraid of personal commitment, even though she loved Mark.

"Plus," Grace continued, "you can't compare your love life to mine; at least you have a man who cares about you. Besides, I'm not looking for a man. One betrayal at a time is enough. I'm sure at some point in time, I'll want it all—kids, the house, the hunka hunka."

Sam looked at her, crossed her eyes and fell over laughing, "Hunka hunka? Seriously?"

Grace smirked. "Yeah, as long as I've waited this long, I want a hunka hunka."

They both raised their wine glasses and toasted the "hunka hunka."

"Although," Grace said, "one of the detectives who's investigating Jean's murder is very handsome and sexy."

"Hmmm, which one, Ben or Luke? Wait." Sam held up her hand, "Don't tell me. It's Luke, isn't it?"

Grace nodded.

"I should have known."

"Do you know him well?"

"A little. One of Luke's best friends, Pete Carson, works for me, so we see each other occasionally. Actually...," she stopped, tilted her head, nodded. "You two have a lot in common. You're both conscientious workers, value justice, loyal to friends. But Luke's a black-and-white kind of guy, not so much gray if you know what I mean. Doesn't suffer liars or trusts people much. That might be because of his job."

Sam took another sip of wine. "I remember hearing he was engaged once. Right before the wedding, his fiancée ran off with his partner, well, ex-partner. I don't think he's ever gotten over the betrayal."

Grace thought about what Sam said. She could tell Luke didn't take any bull. However, in her experience as a reporter, everything wasn't black and white; there were always shades of gray. Nevertheless, betrayal by a loved one or anyone was something she was intimately familiar with.

"Does he date?"

"I think so but not anyone serious."

Having been on more disappointing dates than she could count since moving back to Black Pointe, Grace could relate. The men had been pleasant enough. But no one made her palms sweat, her heart race, and could kiss as if they might send her body up in flames. Besides, she had the husband and career. Look where that got her—betrayed by the very man who promised to watch her back and love her no matter what.

Sam continued, "I think Luke's married to his career. Something that I can relate to. The problem is that your career can consume you. There's more to life than just work."

Sam and Grace said at the same time, "Says the workaholic." They both giggled.

Changing subjects, Sam said, "I'm sorry I'm going to miss Nate's concert on Friday."

Grace, Sam and Danny had grown up with Nate Hayes, who had made it big on the country charts. Nate always gave them backstage passes and front-row seats to his concerts when he came to town.

Grace nodded. "It'll be fun, and it's for a charity in town, so I have to do double duty and write something for the paper. I know Danny wanted to take Hailey. But she had an event at the bookstore she couldn't get out of."

She took another sip of wine. "I meant to call her. But I'm concerned about Hailey. Lately, she seems so distracted."

She looked at Sam. "Has she said anything to you?"

Sam shook her head.

"Hopefully she'll tell us when she's ready." Sam yawned. "Listen, I'm exhausted. Everything you need is in the guest room."

Rubbing her forehead, Sam stood up. "I wish I could go with you to the concert. I'm thrilled that KnightGuard Security is getting so busy. But sometimes I wish for more downtime. It's a double-edged sword. I have several more people starting in a month or so. Danny's been working twenty-four seven, so I'm glad he's able to go."

Hugging Grace, she went upstairs, calling out. "Don't stay

up too late thinking about your condo. Tomorrow, I'll get the security updated, your condo cleaned and anything else you need. Get some rest."

Sleep didn't come easily to Grace. She tossed and turned. Names and faces from her previous life kept flashing through her dreams. Notes from her stalker floated out of nowhere. Luke's blue eyes and dimpled chin flickered in between.

CHAPTER SIXTEEN

The thunder roared and multiple bolts of lightening streaked across the sky. It wasn't raining yet but it would. Luke was glad to be inside. He and his father were sitting at a corner table at the Salt & Sea Bistro. The bistro was a good halfway point for the two of them to meet and reconnect.

Hearing loud laughing near the bar, Luke glanced over at the lively group and saw Sam Knight and others huddled around a table drinking. He didn't know Sam well but ran across her a couple of times when cases they were investigating crossed. He admired her ability to get things done. His noticed his best friend Pete was at the table.

Pete had his back to him and was talking to Sam. Grace Winslow sat next to her and had her hand covering her mouth, holding in a laugh. It was good to see her laughing. She had to be the prettiest woman in the bistro.

He started to get up to go over and say hello when, whoa. Who the hell was that dark-haired guy with his hands all over Grace? Luke sat back down and watched as the guy put his arm around the back of Grace's chair and lean in toward her, laughing. Were they dating? It sure looked like the guy was very familiar with Grace. It shouldn't bother him, but it did. He had no claim on Grace. Moreover, he wasn't comfortable with the feelings of jealousy that were eroding his calm façade.

Pete had gotten up and was walking back from the men's room when he spotted Luke and his dad. He made a beeline over to them.

"Hey man, how are you?"

Luke stood. He and Pete did the handshake and half hug.

Turning to Luke's father, Pete held out his hand, "Mr. McBride, I haven't seen you in a while."

Luke's father and Pete shook hands and exchanged pleasantries for a few minutes. Luke couldn't hold back and asked Pete what he was celebrating.

"No celebration. I was having lunch with a co-worker when Sam and her friends came in, and we asked them to join us."

"I know Sam. Smart woman, good business sense. Who else is with you?"

Pete looked over at the table and told Luke the blond woman was Hailey Marshall, who owned the BookShop in town. Hailey Marshall? She was Jean's friend. *I've got to ask Ben if he had interviewed her.* Pete pointed to the brunette. "That smoking hot one is Grace Winslow."

"I've met Grace. Who's the guy with his hands all over her? Boyfriend?" Luke was having a moment. *Jealous, me? Not much.*

"Oh, that's Danny Knight. He co-owns KnightGuard Security with Sam. They grew up with Grace right here in Black Pointe."

"Hmmm, I don't remember ever meeting him. Is he dating Grace?"

Pete looked at Luke and smirked. "Right to the point, huh? Why do you want to know?"

Play it cool, Luke. "Nah, just curious. I'm on a case that she's involved in."

They talked a little more until Pete had to get back to the table. He leaned over to say something to Grace who stopped talking to Hailey and turned to look at Luke.

Thanks, Pete. Luke did the chin-up thing and turned to talk to his father.

It was always special when he could get together with his dad and brothers. They were all so busy with careers and life. Ever since their mother died, his father had tried hard to take on both parental roles.

"If I didn't know better, one could say you have an interest in that young lady," his dad teased.

"There's something about her that I'm attracted to." Luke paused. "Saying that, she might be a suspect in a murder. I can't let my feelings about her get in the way of this case. I sure hope she's not involved though. I'd love to ask her out."

"Do you have any other suspects?"

"Possibly a neighbor or her neighbor's fiancé or rather ex-fiancé. The dead woman was cheating with the fiancé."

"Ouch. What is wrong with young people today? When you find your true love, it should be easy to be faithful."

Luke looked at his dad. His brown eyes held a world of pain. It hurt Luke to realize his father still missed his wife after twenty-some years. Luke still felt guilty about why.

"Yeah, I still miss Mom too." They both sighed at the same time.

Would he ever have a love like that? He thought he would with Becky and look how that turned out? Love was for suckers. He was way past that. *Liar.*

Luke said goodbye to his dad and walked to his car. He couldn't stop thinking about Grace and Sam's brother with his fucking arm around her. She didn't seem to mind. Did she have feelings for this guy? Shit! She was getting under his skin. He wanted her.

Grace had made it clear she wouldn't go out with him. He hoped it wasn't because of his profession—the profession that came between Becky and him. Since Grace was a journalist, she was aware of the long hours involved in a career. Maybe if he were dating Grace, he could put some hours aside for a relationship? After all, no one ever said on their deathbed, "I wish I had worked more." If he hadn't been so obsessed with his career, he might be married to Becky now.

Although, maybe not.

He had loved Becky. They had been together since high school. After the first rush of young love, he was comfortable being with her and wanted to get married. In retrospect, maybe he was in love with the idea of being married and having a soft, warm body to come home to. If he were truthful with himself, he had never given her his whole heart like he had the service or police force. She wasn't afraid of being a cop's wife. She understood the danger. Becky just wanted someone who would love her more than the job and Luke knew he hadn't been ready to do that. He loved her, just not enough. Becky realized that after a while and Luke knew it bothered her great deal. There was that disparity between them regarding what love meant.

Maybe that's why she ran off with Jason, his fucking, ex-partner. Jason wanted a committed relationship like the one his parents had. The woman, the children, the white picket fence. *God, that's so not me.* That was all Jason talked about when they were on duty together, and Jason was willing to make compromises in his career.

So how did he feel? Betrayed? Oh yeah, that was a given.

Angry? Definitely.

Relieved? Yes. Ah! Never thought about it that way.

He had never wanted it all, the career, the woman, the kids. But he definitely wanted the sex that came with it. However, it had always been his career that he put first. Would he ever find a woman that he would place first?

And why was he thinking about all this now? If he was being honest with himself, he wanted Grace. She fascinated him. There was more to her than a pretty face, and he wanted her more in his life. Somehow, she slipped into his mind and under his skin. *Under my skin? Isn't that a Sinatra song? Yes, she's gotten under my skin.* He wanted to be near her all the time. *Is that what love is? What about my career?* What about it?

Plus, he hated liars, and Grace had lied to him. Well, not actually to him. The Mays case was confusing at best. Was there a lot more to her story than what he knew or what she had told him?

Was there a gray area he could embrace? Could he?

Not everything had to be in black and white. Did it?

It was way after dark when Luke got home. He was exhausted mentally and physically. The afternoon had been busy. They were still looking at alibies for Richard, Diane, and Grace. Ben was checking her security tapes.

Luke hoped Grace didn't have anything to do with Jean's murder. But the one thing he learned early on in his career was that you couldn't trust anyone. People cheated. People lied. In fact, they lied straight to your face.

He pulled a beer out from the fridge, got comfortable on the couch, and turned on the TV, hoping to catch up on sports. After nodding off several times, he looked at his watch and saw it was later than he thought. He had to be at the precinct first thing. Brushing his teeth, pulling off his clothes, not bothering to put them in the hamper, he pulled down the bedcovers and slid in.

"Mom, pleeeeease. I need that new laser power blaster. Me and Frank are going to play against two popular older boys tomorrow. Pleeease." Luke didn't really have a game the next day. He just wanted the new power blaster. Now.

"Luke, honey, it's nasty out there. I don't have time to go and shop."

"Pleeease, it's only a short distance. If I don't get this today, my life is ruined."

His mom gave out a short huff. Luke didn't ask for much, and this seemed important. "OK, but you will stay here and listen to your brothers. Your father will be home any minute."

"Thankyouthankyouthankyou." He hugged his mom.

Getting her raincoat and keys, his mom went out to the garage. He was ecstatic. In a short time, he would have the latest and greatest laser power blaster. Better than Frank's. He couldn't wait to show him.

His dad came home a little later, and Luke told him mom had gone to the store. He didn't want to mention the power blaster because dad would get mad that she went out on a rainy night for that. An hour passed and Luke was getting impatient. Did the store have them? Did she stop to pick up groceries? That's what she usually did. He was hungry, and his three brothers were complaining too. He hoped she would get home soon. He couldn't wait to get his hands on the blaster.

Another hour passed. It was dinner time and still no Mom. Dad asked him if he knew where she was going, but he lied and said he didn't know. He and his brothers were hungry, so Dad made them some sandwiches. Dad called his mom on her cell phone but no answer.

Luke and his brothers had homework to do, but they were all getting worried. Where was Mom? Dad called her cell phone again.

Another hour passed. dad was getting ready to go out to look for her when the doorbell rang. His dad opened the door, and a policeman stood on the step with his hat in his hands. Thunder was booming behind him—it was raining so hard. Luke and his brothers stood behind his dad.

"Mr. McBride?"

"Yes."

"May I come in?"

The policeman came in and proceeded to tell them how a drunk driver hit his mom's car broadside and, and ....

Mom was dead.

His dad stood there silently. His brothers cried, and Luke knew it was his fault.

Two years later, when the case finally went to court, the drunken kid lied about what happened. Having a rich family that had a lot of pull in the town helped him. The kid only got a slap on the wrist and some community service. Luke's family never got the justice they deserved.

Luke shook himself awake. God, it had been a long time since he thought about his mom's death. Seeing his dad today had awakened the memories for some reason.

Her death and the leniency of the court toward the drunk driver were part of why he became a cop. His lying to his dad about why mom was at the store was the other.

No lies. Never again.

Luke finally confessed to his dad what had happened that night. Dad was sad but told him it wasn't his fault, mom could have said no and not gone out, but that didn't mean she was safe forever.

However, Luke knew it was his lies that got her killed.

CHAPTER SEVENTEEN

Grace sat at her desk, head in her hands. The stalker was wearing her down. Nothing had come up about him or her—no cameras catching a face, no fingerprints, no phone records. She was afraid and discouraged.

She had seen Luke a couple of times to go over the case. But she needed closure. Now. She wanted to find out if her attraction to Luke was real and if it might go somewhere. She wanted a life.

Grace sat upright, pulling herself together, and took a deep breath. Well, maybe three deep breaths. The detectives and Sam were stumped. Grace didn't think she was still a suspect in Jean's murder. Or was she? The police hadn't specifically told her she wasn't.

Grace was deep in thought when a shadow bent over her desk. She jumped.

Mary Esposito stood in front of her desk. While they weren't close friends, they did enjoy a good working relationship. Having Mary on the police beat was sometimes helpful.

"Oh Grace, I didn't mean to startle you. I thought I'd pass

along some new information from the police department on the jogger's death, in case you hadn't heard."

"Have they found the killer?" Grace's voice sounded doubtful even to herself.

"No." Mary leaned in closer. "Listen, keep this to yourself. It's not public knowledge, but my source at the station told me they found similar pink notes in the victim's apartment like the ones you've received. They think there might be a connection between her murder and your stalker."

Well, it wasn't precisely what Grace wanted to hear, but it wasn't bad news. At least the police hadn't dismissed her claims entirely. Strange Luke hadn't mentioned that Jean had received the same pink notes. Why not?

Mary continued, "I didn't betray any confidences, but I pulled a hypothetical case with Ken."

Grace was confused.

"You remember him? My new boyfriend," Mary said.

Grace nodded. She had met him once at the office and decided right then that he gave her the creeps. He was good-looking enough, seemed smart and savvy, but there was something off about him. Could it be the way he smirked or was so smug around her as if he knew a secret she didn't? She didn't know. Nevertheless, Mary was happy with him so who was she to complain?

"So, Ken suggested researching where the pink paper for the notes came from. It's a long shot, but who knows, maybe you'll find an obscure manufacturer or a name on an order somewhere."

Grace pondered that thought. She had the time so why not research where the notepaper came from or who might have bought it? A long shot for sure. How many companies sold that style?

Thanking Mary, Grace put aside her project and started researching pink notepaper.

Hours later, it turned out dozens of companies sold the pink notecards, including some from overseas. It was a standard pattern. Moreover, millions had been sold, so it would be impossible to get a name since Grace didn't know where or when the cards were purchased.

It was another dead end. She was still in deep shit.

CHAPTER EIGHTEEN

Nate Hayes's concert was everything a performance should be—lots of great music, lots of cheering and applause, energy, excitement. Luke hated for it to end. It had been a crappy week, and he was finally relaxing.

Hordes of people spilled out of the stadium doors, and Luke and Pete got caught up in the middle of the mass exodus. It took a little time, but they were finally able to walk around the corner to their favorite bar, the Hungry Pelican. Opening the door, Luke saw the bar already packed with what looked like half the concertgoers, but the music was loud, and a cold beer was in his future.

He was at the bar getting drinks and turned to look for Pete. Pete had grabbed a table by the front door and was talking to some women at the next table. The entrance was like a revolving door, people in, people out, in, out. The crowds of people were never-ending. By the time he got to the table, Luke was exhausted. Pete was engrossed in a conversation with a blonde. Sitting down to take that first sip of beer, he looked over at the door and noticed Grace Winslow walking in. Good timing.

He stood up to say hello but not before he noticed a tall, dark-haired man putting his arm around Grace's waist and leading her to a table that had just been cleared. *What the fuck?* Who the hell was this guy?

Wait. He remembered seeing him with Grace when he and his father were having lunch at Salt & Sea. Wasn't that Sam's brother? What was his name again? He couldn't remember.

Not one to let things go, he decided he would walk over and say hello. Working his way through the crowd and only spilling his beer on a woman once, he managed to get to their table.

"Grace."

"Grace." Louder because she wasn't looking his way and didn't hear him. He reached out to touch her shoulder.

Startled, she turned, almost knocking the beer out of his hand.

"Luke." She gave him one of her big welcoming smiles. "Hey. Were you at the concert too?"

"Yeah, it was great." Luke stood there wondering if Grace was going to introduce him to the guy or if this was going to get even more awkward.

"Oh." Grace turned toward the guy. "Luke, this is Danny Knight, a childhood friend and Sam's brother."

Luke breathed a mental sigh of relief. He reached over to shake hands with Danny, giving his hand an extra hard squeeze. He thought Danny smirked, but it was gone quickly.

Danny invited Luke to join them. Luke looked back at Pete who was neck deep in the blonde. He wouldn't be missing Luke anytime soon.

They ordered more beer. Luke wasn't surprised he and Danny had much in common with their jobs.

After an hour, Danny stood up and asked if Grace wanted to go home or stay.

Grace shot a questioning look at Luke.

"I'm here for a while if you want to stay." *Say yes.*

Grace nodded yes.

"Did you drive?"

Grace shook her head no.

"I'll drive you home then." Saying goodbye to Danny, Luke turned to look at Grace.

She was gorgeous, no doubt about it. Grace had slicked her hair back in a ponytail. She wore a white button-down man's shirt paired with belted jeans and had on a pair of red leather-tooled cowboy boots. A cowboy's wet dream, for sure. Well, at least his.

"Have you gone to other Nate Hayes concerts?" he asked.

"Oh yes. Nate is a hometown boy, and he always gives us tickets and backstage passes when he's in town."

"Were you able to get backstage?" he asked.

"We were, but Nate was busy. There were so many excited fans anxious to meet him and get autographs that we didn't want to wait. So, we left early to come here."

Luke and Grace sat there talking about everything for another hour. Ever so slowly they moved their chairs closer to each other since it was difficult to speak over the rowdy crowd. Tonight was the first chance he had to talk with Grace without the case getting in the way.

"So how long have you known Sam?" He asked.

"Oh, gosh. We go back to nursery school. My family moved away when I was in high school but then we were roommates in college. I moved back here after D.C. and ..." She opened her hands and smiled.

"What about you? Had you always wanted to be a cop?"

"Well, no. When I was five, I wanted to rule the universe."

Grace laughed. "And now?"

"Still would like to rule the universe but I love being a detective. Hate the crime and lying but it's part of the job."

"I hear you on that. Part of writing researching a piece is getting to the truth. So, I guess our professions are more alike than not."

She took a sip of beer and Luke reached over and began rubbing the back of her hand. "I'm glad we could spend some time tonight getting to know each other. I've wanted that since I met you."

Grace's eyes widened. A little smile crossed her face. "Me too."

The bar was quieting down. Grace brushed a piece of hair from her forehead and tucked it behind her ear. "Luke, I'm exhausted. Would you mind very much driving me home?"

"Come on. Grab your purse, and I'll get you home."

They walked out to Luke's truck. "Well, this is awkward. I don't know where you're staying right now. Are you back at your condo or elsewhere?" he asked.

"I'm back at my condo. It's all cleaned and painted."

Stopping in front of her condo, he turned the truck off and turned to look at her. "This has been fun. Can I see you again?"

It took her a moment. "I'd like that," she said finally.

Yes! Luke did a mental high five. But as much as he wanted to ask her out for the next night, he didn't want to push things.

Getting out of the truck and opening her door, he walked her up to her building. She pressed the code, and he followed her into the lobby.

"Thank you for driving me home. I had a good time getting to know you better."

Grace licked her lips. Luke wanted nothing more than to kiss them. Then throw her over his shoulder, walk upstairs to her condo, get lost in her body and not come down for at least a week. Getting control of himself, Luke stepped forward, put a finger under her chin lifting her face and gave her a chaste kiss. He prayed the whole time that certain parts of his body wouldn't betray him. He stepped back, and if she was disappointed, he didn't take the kiss further, he couldn't tell. They took the elevator up to her floor over Grace's objections.

No way was he letting her go in to find someone standing outside her door or in her condo. She opened the door, turned off the alarm and let Luke check out her condo.

No one was there. Nothing was disturbed. Grace stood in the doorway staring at him. Little Luke was demanding he take her into the bedroom and get naked and sweaty. But he was more mature than that. *Riiight!*

He pulled her into his chest and inhaled her sweet scent. He lightly kissed her on the lips and then again.

"I wish I could hold you all night, but it's too soon."

She held him tighter and sighed.

Pulling away was difficult. Luke turned and heard the door click. He couldn't wait to see her again.

GRACE LOCKED the door and hugged herself. There was some fine muscle on that man's body, and he had the softest lips. She wanted more from him, but it was early in their relationship. *Did they have a relationship?* She thought so. At least the beginning of one. They were both attracted to each other for sure.

The innocent kisses were sweet but what she really wanted was a kiss that would rock her world. It was only a feeling, but if Grace were a betting woman, she would bet money on Luke rocking her world. She was attracted to him like a moth to fire. And Lord, did she want to burn.

But she couldn't forget he was a cop who was still investigating a murder that concerned her.

Nevertheless, the evening had been fun. Luke's light touches to her arm, her thigh, her lips, ignited intimate feelings she wanted to explore with him.

Good Lord, she wanted more. More with Detective Luke McBride.

She set the alarm and walked into the bathroom to take a shower. It had been a long night. She was sexually frustrated. Grace only hoped Luke would call and they would go out again. She hadn't missed the bulge in his pants, and she truly wanted to explore that too.

CHAPTER NINETEEN

Grace finally talked to Steve about accepting the temporary investigative beat. He was thrilled. Grace not so much. However, this was another step in reclaiming her life.

She was excited but still not feeling the self-confidence she had started her career with. While she loved the investigative aspect of journalism, the events in D.C. continued to leave a bitter taste in her mouth.

The Thursday staff meeting had just finished. Steve had asked everyone to sit for another minute and then announced that Grace would be filling in immediately while Nancy Frey dealt with her mother. Grace sat there in shock. All eyes were on her. Were they surprised? Pleased? Upset? She couldn't tell. There was a moment of silence, then clapping and congratulations. Grace let out the breath that she had been holding. *That went over well.*

"OK, people, settle down," Steve said. "We have a lot on our plates especially with elections coming up and I need everyone to do their job." He and the paper loved election time. All the promises made; all the dirt dug up. More ads. Good stuff!

Bryon raised his hand. "Steve, I didn't want to bring this up now, but in light of Grace taking Nancy's position, it's important."

Oh, my God. No. What had Bryon heard? Grace would bet her life the problems she had in DC were coming back to haunt her just as she feared. Her face flushed, she couldn't meet anyone's eyes. Didn't matter that everyone had stopped talking and were all staring expectantly at Bryon and her. Her throat constricted and she was gulping in air.

He continued, "Recently some information has come to my attention that might affect Grace's ability to do fair and unbiased coverage of the election or any investigative writing."

Grace hoped Steve would step in and say something. However, he just sat there and looked expectantly at her and Bryon.

Resuming as if nothing happened, as if Grace's psyche wasn't on the verge of breaking, Bryon said, "I have a friend who is a journalist in D.C. He mentioned rumors about Grace's alleged bad exposé on a senator. He told me that she was fired from the *Chronicle* and couldn't get another job in the field."

The quiet was audible. Could she crawl under the table? Would anyone notice? *What to do?*

"Are you sure she's the right person to be interviewing candidates? They're going to find out about this, and the paper might not get the story, or our reputation will be damaged."

Steve looked unconcerned. "Why is this coming out now?"

Everyone looked at Bryon.

"Whaaat?" He shrugged his shoulders. "I was in D.C. for

the weekend visiting a friend. We started talking about the elections and how we were handling everything down here. He mentioned a problem a journalist had a couple of years ago not getting facts straight, destroying a senator. He mentioned Grace Winslow-Moore, and I put two and two together."

Grace's mind was blank, her body immobilized. Disbelief, anger, and betrayal washed over her. *I'm not going through this again. I'm not putting myself in the line of fire to be consumed by it.*

She collected her notebook and slowly stood up.

GRACE STOOD BEHIND HER CHAIR, palms sweating, bile roller-coasting in her stomach. However, she wasn't going to let this information set her back. She made the decision to take Nancy's place, and consequences be damned. She pulled herself together, straightened her shoulders and stood tall. She turned to look at Bryon.

"Bryon, your source is right. I did have a problem in D.C. I couldn't fact-check the sources a co-worker had quoted for my piece. I depended upon her too much and let myself be hyped up about the story I wrote. The paper had already printed it by the time I found out the problem. Since we couldn't corroborate the sources, the paper was forced to run a retraction. They fired me, and as you know, no one would take a chance on hiring me. I came back to Black Pointe."

She had been called into the publisher's office. Shit, not even into her editor's office. She knew this was not going to end well. They had exchanged pleasantries. John was Southern enough that good manners were ingrained in him, but there were no smiles, grins or showing of teeth. Not good.

"Grace, we had high hopes for you. You came in here first in your class, guns-a-blazing, wrote some damn good pieces. But your exposé

on a fine senator was too much. I've known Warren Irish for years. He's brought good legislation to the Senate, and now he'll never be able to get a fair trial in the Senate or the public. His reputation is ruined. His family is ruined. All because you didn't fact-check or prove beyond a doubt that what you wrote was true."

Grace started to explain, but John put his hand up. "Enough. I can't let you ruin any more lives. You're fired. The guard will meet you at your desk. Clean it out and leave."

Grace got up, pushed down the bile and the urge to hurl. She would not cry. She would not let John see her cry. As she turned to leave, John said, "And by the way, please don't ask for a reference. You won't get one."

Grace sat down before she passed out. She wasn't running anymore. Bad enough her D.C. reputation was tarnished. She also lost her husband. And her stalker found her again. She was not going to let anything else get in her way.

"Steve knew what had happened and had faith in my abilities as a reporter to hire me. I take full responsibility for what happened. I have no intention of letting it happen again. I feel I've been punished enough and will deal with whatever comes along."

Grace looked around the table. Everyone was looking at Bryon and Steve.

Bryon spoke first. "Grace, I've known you for two years now, and you are a good reporter. Fair to everyone. I'm not questioning your ability to do the job but know that if I found out about this, other people will find out also. It might affect your ability to get a story."

Grace nodded. "I know that and can accept the consequences."

Steve piped up and said, "People, discussion over. I know a little bit more than you about the politics at the D.C. office, and Grace wrote a damn good story that was truthful. She didn't get a fair chance. I'm sticking by my decision to have Grace fill in."

He glanced around the room. "Does anyone have any objections or questions for Grace? Now is the time to spit them out."

The group looked around and at each other. Mary stood up and said, "Nope, I'm good."

Everyone stood up to leave. Bryon patted her on the shoulder and gave her a thumbs-up on the way out. That left Grace and Steve.

"Don't." Steve put up his hand.

"I know what you're going to say. Just don't. You are the best and most capable person for this position. There were no objections. Bryon was right to bring this up, so we are prepared for any blowback."

Tears rolled down Grace's cheek. "You know I hate you right now. But thank you for standing up and believing in me."

Steve winked, picked up his papers and left.

CHAPTER TWENTY

Sam hated doing surveillance. She hated patiently sitting waiting for something to happen. Give her someone's butt to kick or any action, and she was happy.

However, she was grateful that KnightGuard Security was so busy. Since she was down a few employees, it was up to her to take up the slack—*the perks of being the owner*. The irony of the situation was not lost on her.

It was 2 a.m. and still hot and humid. Tonight was her fourth night of purgatory, and she was sweating profusely but couldn't turn on the car's a/c. Plus, she was tired. Actually, way beyond tired. Tired of sitting in her parked car. Tired of surveillance. Tired of not having a life. Just. Plain. Tired.

Parked on a deserted access road, she had a clear view of the electronics store that had hired her company to find the thieves that were stealing goods and supplies. Its parking lot was empty now except for two van delivery trucks and four metal rubbish bins by the back door.

Whoever was stealing the electronics was shrewd. The thieves hadn't been caught on camera. That meant, in addition to security cameras in and around the building, someone had to be physically there to watch the building. Tonight, as well as the past few nights, that someone was her.

The past couple of nights had yielded no activity except for a couple of early deliveries and the cleaning crew. They had vetted the cleaning crew as well as the delivery drivers, so it had to be someone else who was stealing. She was confident they would catch the thief.

Spending all night in her car gave her lots of time to think and Grace was on her mind. It didn't make sense to her how the stalker knew where to find Grace or knew when she wasn't in her condo. Security cameras in Grace's building hadn't picked up any strangers or people lurking in the shadows. There were no new tenants, so there had to be something they had missed.

The renovation workers had been vetted except for that one glass worker whom nobody knew. However, the super confessed to giving him a key without asking for ID. Sam shook her head. How stupid. The guy had disguised himself and was smart enough to get in and fool everyone into thinking he worked there. Her conversation with the super wasn't pleasant. He had been mortified that he made a mistake and was taking measures not to let it happen again.

The stalker appeared to know where all the building's cameras were located and managed to avoid looking directly at any of them. With everyone going in and out of the building, it was difficult to know exactly who was harassing Grace.

A slight noise from the woods behind her made her pause. Leisurely looking around, she didn't see anything.

A scritch. A scratch. Then rustling in the bushes behind her car.

She pulled her gun out keeping the safety on, her heart pounding. A fleeting thought of this recon ending soon had her excited. Getting ready to exit the car, she turned the flashlight on her gun on. She had her hand on the door handle when she looked over to see a deer casually stroll out of the bush. False alarm. Damn. Almost captured a deer. Her employees would have a good laugh over that and never let her live it down if she stalked and apprehended Bambi.

Sam started thinking about cameras. Cameras and Grace's condo. What if someone somehow got in and hid a camera? It could have happened when they trashed Grace's condo. She was curious if the police even checked. Would that even cross their minds? No one even thought about that at the time. But now it made perfect sense. Making up her mind, she decided she would go over tomorrow and check Grace's condo and computer. Spy programs were so easy to get and install. All a person had to do was Google it or go to YouTube. Everything was on the internet. It made crime so much easier to get away with.

How else would the stalker know when Grace was out? Or where she was going?

First thing tomorrow, she would touch base with Grace. Asking Luke if he could meet her at Grace's condo to check her theory out was a good idea also. Having the police on Grace's side was a positive thing.

CHAPTER TWENTY-ONE

Grace drove along Duval Street singing with the radio. She was excited. It was Thursday afternoon, and she didn't have to work. She had an obligation to fulfill to six little girls. Thursdays Grace tutored at the local girls' club, and it always made her week. She was lucky she had the flexibility in her schedule to volunteer there. Knowing she was going today made a shitty week less shitty.

Grace parked in the already crowded parking lot and got out of her car. Retrieving the freshly baked cookies from the passenger side, she closed and locked the door. It was a chilly afternoon, chilly for Florida anyhow.

An uncomfortable sensation of being watched gave her shivers. Placing the cookies on the hood of the car, she pulled her wrap around her shoulders. However, when Grace looked around, she didn't see anyone. Well, not that she would.

Shaking off the feeling of being watched, she quickly walked up the path to the weather-beaten brown double front doors, to enter the red brick building. Greeting Alice, the grandmotherly volunteer at the front desk, she could already hear the squeals of laughter and smell the remnants of sandwiches and fruit from lunch.

"Miss Grace, Miss Grace," screeched a skinny little girl who ran over to her. Her multiple pigtails tied with brightly colored elastic balls created a whirlwind around her face. "You came."

As Grace hugged one of her favorite girls, she said, "Jacqui, would I ever give up the privilege to be with you girls? Don't I come every week?"

The little girl nodded her head vigorously, the balls clicking with abandon as she did.

"I've been waiting forever for you. What are you going to read today? Do you like my hair? What color do you like best? Did you bring cookies?"

"Whoa, honey. One question at a time."

Grace took Jacqui's hand and answered her questions as they walked over to a large room filled with desks where five other little girls waited impatiently. *Probably for the cookies she brought.* It was reading time, and the tension of the day was melting from her body. Spending time with the girls was the best time of the week.

Two hours quickly passed by with lots of questions from the girls, lots of laughing. Grace helped them with their homework and topped the afternoon off with a cookie treat.

After giving many hugs, saying goodbye multiple times and promising to see them next week, Grace left the building. As she walked toward her car, she couldn't shake the uneasy feeling she was still being watched. Upon looking around, she didn't see anyone lurking. The parking lot was full of cars, but no one was out there except for her. It was too quiet, especially after the noise in the club. The feeling of being watched unsettled Grace. Was she paranoid? Or just going crazy? She started walking faster to her car, keys in hand.

Passing the car parked next to her, she was relieved to reach her car. That is until she looked down—a flat rear tire.

Damn. I don't need this right now. I'll be late for work tonight if Triple-A can't get to me quickly. She pushed the button on her fob to open the door, then glanced around the parking lot one more time. No one around. Hand on the door handle, she looked at the front of her car and noticed that tire was flat also.

Her hands were shaking. Gasping for air, she stopped and took a deep breath. It couldn't be her imagination. She could feel someone watching her. And now, two flat tires? Not her imagination. She glanced around the parking lot, again. No one else's car had a flat tire.

Afraid of what she would find, she walked around to the passenger side and sure enough, the other two tires were flat.

She couldn't stop trembling. She swiped at sweat rolling over her eyelids. Was this the action of her stalker or a mean-spirited neighborhood kid? She did have words with a teenager who was harassing Jackie weeks ago. But she thought that had blown over. Maybe it wasn't a kid. Maybe it was her stalker. However, unless he followed her, how would he know she was here?

The surrounding area was a little rough. She knew there were lots of drugs busts and shootings, but she had been coming here for over a year without incident.

Slashing her tires was no accident. Could her stalker be following her? Fear climbed up her throat step by step. *Would this nightmare ever end?*

She thought about asking someone in the club for help changing the tires but realized she didn't have enough spares. She would need to call for a flatbed to tow the car to the garage.

Well, that was stupid.

What she needed to do first was call the police.

The nagging feeling someone was watching her wouldn't go away, so she ran back into the building. She asked Alice if anyone else had a problem with flat tires. Alice shook her head and told her it happened occasionally, usually kids thinking they were funny.

It was almost closing time at the club. She made small talk with the receptionist while she waited for the police to arrive. Next, she called Sam at her office, and couldn't reach her but got Danny who promised to come right away.

The police hadn't arrived yet when Danny called and told her he was in front of the building, as was the tow truck.

She opened the club's door, looked around, didn't see anyone lurking, ran to the car and jumped in.

"Never had anyone that eager to get in my car before," joked Danny.

"Never had anyone slash all four of my tires before either. Thanks for coming. I was going to call a cab if I couldn't reach anyone," Grace said.

"Grace," Danny growled. "What the hell is going on?"

"Have you talked to the police yet?" Danny was livid. Grace knew Sam had filled him in on the details of the notes and condo break-in. He also knew the circumstances of her leaving D.C.

"Yes." She sighed. It seemed like everyone was afraid for her. "They should be here any minute."

He patted her hand. "I'm sorry I know this is difficult for you."

"Thanks. Anyhow, the tow company doesn't have four of the same tires. They had to order them. They'll have the tires by tomorrow." A sob escaped. "Damn, this is a pain in the ass and plain scary. I don't understand why this is happening to me."

Danny hugged her and lightly kissed her cheek. "We are going to get to the bottom of it, I promise."

Grace nodded. "I hope so. I can't take much more."

THE NEXT MORNING Grace got a call from the garage. Her car was ready. They had replaced all four tires and asked if she had any idea how they got slashed.

"Probably some jerk playing games." Grace didn't want to admit that this could be an act of violence by her stalker. He seemed to know more about her than where she lived and that frightened her. Noticing a voice mail from Sam, she returned the call.

"Grace, Danny just told me about your tires. Are you all right? Is the car fixed yet?"

"Yes, to both," Grace replied. Closing her eyes and smoothing her hair helped her focus.

"Sam, I've been trying to stay calm but between the notes, the brakes, trashing my condo and now the tires, it's beyond difficult." *Would this harassment ever end?*

She gulped and confessed, "I was feeling so strong for a time, but not anymore. I think I would be better off in Boston by my parents. I can't handle any more of this."

There was silence on the other end. "Grace, I know this has been a lot to handle. You're not alone here. You have your friends, real friends who will stand behind you. You have Luke who wants to help. We'll figure this out."

Grace was shaking uncontrollably. Tears formed and fell down her cheeks. "I'm so afraid. I'm so tired of running from this problem. But every time, I think I'm getting ahead, something else happens."

"Stay strong. I'll be there in a few. We're going to catch this creep." Sam hung up.

Grace sat down, suppressing the urge to cry until she had no more tears left to shed. She stood and walked over to the window. The stalker had to be found. Her friends were staying strong for her, encouraging her to do the same but it was getting more and more difficult.

CHAPTER TWENTY-TWO

The stalker stood under the meager water supply, scrubbing the grease off his hands. The shower was minuscule. So small, he couldn't easily move around, plus his head just about touched the shower head. The tiny bar of soap they gave him wasn't enough to wash his whole body let alone get the grease off.

However, it had been a fruitful day. He managed to slice Grace's tires without anyone spotting him. The bushes had covered him and watching as Grace continually searched for something, anything, him perhaps, made him laugh. He was scaring her big time. It was the little things in life that were now making him happy.

Since the senator cowardly took his own life, and he had lost his lucrative job, finding another with the extra "benefits" he required was difficult. He craved the prestige he had, much more than his father ever achieved. Now that it was gone, revenge was all he had left.

The good ol' days of hobnobbing with the movers and shakers of Washington had been quashed, erased, destroyed —take your pick—when Grace wrote that exposé about

Senator Irish taking kickbacks. The stupid man should have let the scandal wash over him. He would have beat it. But did he? Nooo.

Damn! The hot water was running out, and he hadn't rinsed off. He was down to his last few expendable dollars. This flea-ridden roach motel was all he could afford at the moment. He was grateful the rental car had another week on it, but he was going to have to watch his money.

Maybe the bitch at the newspaper would invite him over for dinner again. It was amazing to him how desperate some women were to have a man in their lives. He pretended he was fucking his Rachel and the bitch at the paper got a good deal more than she was entitled to. He got to have sex for a meal and information— a good bargain, as far as he was concerned. The sex took the edge off his anger, and this new squeeze liked a little pain with her sex. He got hard thinking about spanking her rather ample ass.

The water had turned ice-cold, but his cock was rock-hard. He wrapped his hand around his dick and pumped. He thought about harassing Grace as he jacked himself off. Up and down. Up and down. It felt really good. Not as good as Rachel's mouth sucking it, but she wasn't here. He stroked harder and harder. *Aaah*. As he shot his wad at the shower wall, he had the perfect idea for Miss Winslow. Win, win.

Maybe tomorrow he would meet, *Marcy? Mercy? What the hell was her name?* Mary, that's it, at the office and say hello to Grace. She didn't recognize him the last time he was there.

It was so much fun spying on Grace, and right in front of her too.

CHAPTER TWENTY-THREE

Ever since Becky's betrayal, Luke had dated some, but there was no one he was attracted to until now. Grace hadn't said anything to him, but he knew Grace sensed the attraction too. She was always giving him the once over when she thought he didn't see her. Of course, the reverse was also true.

Usually, he preferred more curvy women. If they had big breasts, those were always a bonus. But Grace was willowy, small-breasted, perfect. *Perfect?* Grace? A perfect woman? Wow, he had it bad when he thought that about a woman.

He liked the way she laughed and the easy way she talked to people. He admired the way she was inquisitive but kind. She was smart and brave, even if she didn't think she was. He liked the smile that lit up her face when she saw him. He liked the way her nose crinkled when she smiled. He liked how she fit in his arms. He liked the perfume she wore—Chanel No.5. In fact, he liked everything about her.

After an exhausting week, Grace finally had an afternoon free and met Luke at Salt & Sea. They were sitting at a corner table, and she had told him her good friend, Laura Clark, owned the restaurant. Laura had come over to say hi and take their drink order, and Luke had done a double take when she had walked over. He couldn't remember seeing her here before because he sure would have remembered her. Laura was gorgeous, with her long brown hair pulled up in a ponytail, she had wide sultry eyes and a killer smile. Luke could appreciate the smart, pretty, woman but Grace was it for him, hands down.

"How long have you known Laura?" he asked.

"Gosh." Grace crinkled her eyes, thought for a moment. "Sam introduced us at college. They had known each other since high school when Laura moved to Black Pointe with her family. My family had already moved to Boston."

Grace brought her hand up to her mouth and nibbled on a fingernail while looking at him all wide-eyed.

Luke smiled inwardly. *Oh, yeah.* That was her tell that she was uncomfortable about something.

"So." She licked her lips and hemmed and hawed for a moment. "I've meaning to ask you if you have any new information on my stalker."

Ah, how did he know that was coming? Grace wasn't going to like his answer though. They didn't have any leads. Clues they had plenty of. Results, zip.

"Well, I can't say much, but no surprise, there were no prints on the notes or in your condo. The creep was smart enough to use gloves. Nobody stood out on camera. With all the workers, residents and guests walking in and out, it's hard to tell who he might be."

"Darn." She let out a heavy breath. "That wasn't the news I was hoping for."

"I know, hon, I'm sorry I don't have better news for you.

However, it's only a matter of time before this fucker makes a mistake and then we've got him."

Grace reached for Luke's hand, worry furrowed on her brow. "Thanks for that. Listen, Sam is meeting me at my condo later. She wants to check something out. Do you want to join us?"

"Way ahead of you, babe. Sam also asked me to meet her. She mentioned something about cameras." And a whole lot more that he wasn't sharing right now. Grace was worried enough.

"Cameras? Sam didn't mention cameras to me."

"Don't know any more about them. Sam just gave me the basics." He rubbed the back of her hand. "I hope it's all right with you. I told Sam we were having lunch and would be over after."

Chewing on her bottom lip, and twisting a ring on her finger, Grace looked at him, nodded but didn't say anything.

GRACE WAS DEVOURING her Niçoise salad. The background noise of the busy bar livened the bustling atmosphere of the bistro. Conversation was light, and she enjoyed watching Luke relax and then sneak a forkful of her salad. She lightly slapped his hand. He wiped his face with a napkin, his baby blues crinkling as he grinned at her.

"So," Luke asked, "tell me how you got interested in journalism."

"Hmmm. Good question. Let me think." Grace tapped her fingers on the table. "I guess it was in middle school. I have to say I was clueless about life. I hung out with my girlfriends, was on the cheerleading squad, was just having fun. But one afternoon after class, I was jogging on the athletic field when I heard laughter and heckling and taunts coming from under the bleachers and someone yelling 'No, stop." When I ran over, these boys were bullying a boy from my class." A flashback from that day almost overwhelmed her. She had been living in a make-believe world.

"Boys who were friends of mine had surrounded this kid. Guys who had everything going for them—football players—popular kids. Dylan was lying on the ground, his pants pulled down, crying. I screamed at the other boys, and they ran away. It disgusted me, and I decided I had to do something, so I wrote a piece on bullying for the local newspaper. It was well received, and the school made changes." She hesitated. "I think that was the first time I realized how powerful words could be. It inspired me to continue writing and go to J-school."

LUKE WAS STARING AT GRACE. He couldn't help admiring the bravery it took to stand up to your friends and defend another person, especially in middle school. Moreover, she didn't recognize it yet, but that's what she was doing for herself right now.

After paying the bill, Luke walked her to her car and told her he would meet her at the condo. Grace nodded.

Luke hadn't wanted to talk about what Sam told him and upset Grace at lunch. But he knew whatever was going on in her condo was going to be bad and Grace was going to freak out.

Finding parking on Grace's street was a bitch this time of the day. Luke managed to find a spot about a block down and spotted Sam walking towards Grace's condo. Catching up with her before she reached the door, he asked what she discovered.

She filled him in.

Luke closed his eyes and shook his head. "Can this get any worse? Grace has been through so much already."

"I know. She can't catch a break. Grace never used to give up so easily. But she had been attacked and betrayed in D.C. by so many people, moving back had been good for her but now?" Sam shrugged her shoulders. "I don't know."

She rang the bell, and the door buzzed open. They took the elevator to the third floor. Grace stood in the open doorway. As they walked in, Luke could smell coffee. Coffee. He desperately needed a cup or a stiff drink.

Sam walked over to Grace and hugged her. They grabbed mugs of coffee, sat down and Sam asked her to tell Luke about the incident with her tires. Something she apparently forgot to tell him. Luke closed his eyes and shook his head. Then Sam explained her theory of the spy cameras.

"Hidden cameras, microphones?" Grace squeaked. Her eyes widened, and she covered her mouth. Bending forward and clenching her stomach, she moaned. "This is getting worse."

Grace looked frantically around the condo. "I don't see anything out of the ordinary. Where the cameras or mics would be hidden?"

Sam reached into her bag and removed a small device, pulled out its antenna and held it up.

"This is a radio frequency signal detector. First, we look behind pictures, under lamps, flowerpots, outlets. These are tiny devices; you wouldn't even notice them when cleaning. I also want to see if a wireless router has been connected to your laptop."

"Wow. I'm impressed," said Grace. Watching Sam in full protection mode fascinated her. She knew Sam had gadgets but never asked her about them because she never needed to. Her mind worked overtime. She thought the devices would make a great story. *NO! Not going there. Just keep it simple, she had enough to do for the paper.*

"I'm embarrassed we didn't think of this, although I can't remember an instance where cameras were installed in a victim's home. I gotta tell you I'm jealous of your toys. The Department doesn't have extra money for all the updated technology on the market," said Luke.

"Stick with me, and you'll learn something," Sam replied and smiled.

Luke began manually searching and found a microphone under the sofa, so tiny he almost missed it. Taking off all the outlet covers, Luke discovered two cameras. He couldn't believe someone would stoop this low to harass one woman. It disgusted him that someone would do this and couldn't imagine how Grace was feeling. She didn't deserve someone invading her privacy. The fact he and Ben missed the cameras and mics when her condo was trashed weighed heavily on his conscience.

The bedrooms, bath, and kitchen were next. Sam found a couple more cameras and microphones. "I'm ready to skin this jerk alive," she said. "Who does this?"

Grace had been screwing outlets back in and stood up. "I can't believe this is my life. What did I ever do to this person?"

"Do you think this is the same stalker from D.C.?" Luke asked.

"Luke, I don't know. He sent pink notes, ordered stupid things like ten pizzas, but nothing like this. However, I left before it could get any worse."

"This," Grace motioned around, "is so personal, so invasive, so creepy and to think he watched me undress." She shivered. "Ugh. How did the creep find me here?"

Grace sighed, "I want this to be over. I want my life back. Then I can seriously think about hurting the bastard."

Luke smiled, drew her into his arms and kissed her forehead, "Hold that thought. I'm sure we're going to find him soon."

Sam picked up the tiny cameras and put them in a container. "I have feelers out at the D.C. police station, but the detectives won't talk to me. The detective who originally investigated has retired, and I couldn't reach him. I couldn't get information from anyone. It's as if D.C. totally erased Grace's case," Sam said.

Sam placed Grace's laptop on the table and opened it up. "I'm going to check your IP address and see if there are any attached devices." Luke watched as Sam logged in and went into settings.

"Shit, I was afraid of this," she said. "Someone installed a wireless router."

She pointed out a device name "Spy on you." Sam asked Grace if it sounded familiar. Grace shook her head. Sam blocked the router and set it up so Grace would receive emails if anyone tried to access the blocked logs.

"I can't believe the trouble someone took to spy on you." Sam was incensed. "No wonder the asshole knew when you were home and where you were going."

They completed their inspection finding nothing else and collected the cameras and mics for Luke to bring back to the precinct. Sam was late for work. She hugged Grace goodbye and left.

Grace sat on the sofa looking stunned. Luke felt sorry that Grace had to go through this invasion of privacy yet again. The thought of this fucker watching her as she undressed boiled his blood and he was glad the pervert wasn't around.

"This person knows way too much about you. You're in danger living here." Luke said. A nagging suspicion that Grace's stalker, and Jean Mays's murder had something to do with D.C. He needed to concentrate on a connection if any. Could be just a coincidence but he didn't believe in coincidences.

She nodded her head. "I hate to admit it, but I think you're right. I'll see if I can crash at a friend's house for a while until you find this jackass."

Crouching down in front of her, he said gently, "Grace, you don't want to put your friends in danger. By now this person probably knows all about them and where they live." He took her hand. "They don't know me or where I live. I have a guest room. You can stay there until this case is solved." *Whoa.* Did he just issue an invitation? To a potential suspect? This was such a blatant disregard for rules, but he couldn't stop himself. He didn't quite understand why he felt this need to protect Grace.

Grace looked surprised and started shaking her head no.

Luke was not above pleading. He wanted Grace to be safe, but he also wanted ... her.

And there it was. He wanted Grace. Period. He wanted her in his house, in his kitchen, in his living room, in his bed. Definitely in his bed. Preferably naked. Although that part would have to wait, she hadn't said yes to staying there. Yet.

"Hmmm, I don't know." She thought about it for a moment. "We've only known each other a short time and had a couple of dates. I should stay at a hotel. It might be safer."

"You would be too exposed staying at a hotel. Too many strangers coming and going."

"But ..."

Luke shook his head back and forth. "No buts. How about I take you into protective custody?"

Grace rolled her eyes.

He could see Grace working out the logistics in her mind and noted the second she mentally agreed.

"You're right. It might be a safer place for me to stay. Let me pack a bag, and I'll follow you over."

Oh my God, what have I gotten myself into?

The whole day had turned Grace's world into a place she didn't know anymore. Trashing her condo, cutting her brakes, puncturing her tires, putting microphones and cameras in her condo—who does those things? What more could this creep do to her? *No, wait. She didn't want an answer to that question.*

Moving temporarily into Luke's house both excited and scared her. She was attracted to him and wanted to take their relationship to the next level. But was she ready? She hadn't slept with anyone since her divorce, not that he asked her to sleep with him. It could happen though. They were both attracted to each other, and they both knew it. Maybe it was time to act upon those feelings. But. The big but. Was she still a suspect? Luke could lose his job asking her to stay with him. Well, that wasn't her problem. Hopefully, he had thought this out before asking her.

Packing up a few clothes, her laptop and toiletries into a small bag, she followed Luke through the rear alleyway to her car. He checked underneath her car for tracking devices. After discovering the cameras and mics in her condo, she was relieved he didn't find any. He opened her door and let her in, waited until she put her seatbelt on and started her car. Then, he walked around to the front where he parked, and she followed his car.

The drive to his house took about twenty minutes, and she relished the change of scenery. While she was used to the ocean or downtown where she lived, Luke's small ranch was in what could only be called "old Florida." She saw several horse and cattle farms and a few fixer-uppers. A feeling of peacefulness came over her. There were no sidewalks, and nobody was walking on the streets. Cars were few and far between. Palm trees competed for space with pine trees, and bushes, vines took over anything in between. She thought about what the explorers must have felt seeing the wildness of Florida for the first time.

Luke opened the garage and motioned to Grace to park in it while he parked in the open spot outside. She shut off the engine and got out. He grabbed her bag and opened the door to the house.

Remembering how messy her two brothers were growing up, she was surprised at how clean his house was. There were a couple of pieces of clothing strewn around the living room and an empty beer can on a table, but it wasn't untidy. The light-colored living room had an enormous TV mounted on a wall, a comfortable black leather sofa, and aside chair.

"Welcome. It's not much, but it's mine."

LUKE CARRIED Grace's bag down the hall. "Here, I'll put this in the guest room. The bathroom is across the hall. I have my own, so it's all yours. Unpack, get comfortable, come out and have a beer or soda, whatever. Make yourself at home."

Grace followed Luke as he dropped her suitcase in the guest room. He turned quickly and bumped into her. *Soft.* "Whoops." Rubbing his arms, Luke stepped away from her. She sure didn't need a horn dog hitting on her when she was traumatized.

"Look, I have to call Ben and get back to the station. Are you all right here until I get back?"

Grace looked over at him and sighed. "I'm fine. I promised to call Sam with your address. She mentioned she might stop by tomorrow."

"If you need anything, call my cell. Come with me while I set the alarm, so you know how to do it."

Luke showed her how the alarm worked and gave her the code, reminding her to set it whether she was home or not. He hugged her and promised everything would be OK. Hating to leave her alone but feeling Grace was as safe as possible, Luke headed back to the station.

The drive to work allowed him time to think about what to say to Ben. Shit, Ben was going to be pissed no matter what. Although Luke didn't consider Grace a suspect anymore, he needed to convince Ben. As for the captain, maybe he could hold off that chat until Grace wasn't officially a suspect anymore. No way Grace killed Jean within the timeframe they established.

Luke pulled out his phone.

This was a conversation he couldn't avoid. He dialed Ben's phone.

CHAPTER TWENTY-FOUR

Luke no sooner pulled into a parking space at the station when Ben came stalking over.

Ben started beating on his window and yelling at him even before he turned off the car. Luke opened the window.

"You did what? Damn it. Luke, are you fucking crazy?" Ben's voice got louder. "When we decided to keep an eye on Winslow, nobody said anything about inviting her to stay at your home."

Luke didn't need great detective skills to determine Ben was upset with him. He opened his mouth to reply, but Ben interrupted him. "What part of keeping your distance from a potential suspect don't you understand?"

Wow, he was getting it with both barrels. Opening the car door, he got out.

He put his hands up in surrender. "I understand what you're saying. But hear me out. Grace's condo's has been trashed. Don't know who did it. Her tires were slashed. Don't know who did it. Cameras and microphones were hidden around her condo, and her computer's been compromised.

Don't know who did it. I would say that at this point she is not a suspect."

To soften the blow, he added, "Besides, it wasn't safe for her to be in her condo or at her friends."

Ben was not entirely convinced, but Luke got a begrudging grunt from him.

"What better place to keep an eye on her and provide safety?" Luke was not above throwing in "keeping an eye on her." Truth be told, having Grace in his house was right where he wanted to keep an eye on her.

"We need to solve this case. If the captain finds out about this, she'll have your head or worse." Ben's eyes were glaring. He crossed his arms. "You better make this right, bro."

That was something Luke could agree with, having no intention of telling the captain. Yet. Grace was under his watch. Oh yeah, under his watch all right.

As they walked into the station, Luke brought Ben up to date about the cameras, and mics they found at Grace's condo.

Luke told Ben that he planned to spend the day looking at clips on security cameras from around the girls' club and Grace's condo building. Ben was still checking out alibis for Diane Benoit and Richard Marsh. They would touch base with each other later.

He hoped he would find something on the cameras, but this asshole was smart. He also hoped Ben would get positive proof Grace wasn't still a suspect. He didn't know how he was going to handle it if she was. Luke wanted her. He wanted to believe her. Shit, he did believe her. But it wouldn't look good for his career shacking up with a suspect—time to get to work to clear Grace's name.

CHAPTER TWENTY-FIVE

Luke and Grace danced around each other all week. It was nice having her in his home. Luckily both their schedules were light, so they were able to take turns cooking and talking—lots of talking and stimulating conversation.

Luke felt comfortable enough to tell her about Becky, his ex-partner, their lies, and subsequent betrayal. Although Grace didn't talk much about her life in D.C., he knew she would when she was ready.

By Wednesday the weather had cooled slightly, and they were outside. Listening to the soft lapping of the river against its bank, and the croaking of frogs made for a relaxing evening. They were grilling and Grace was setting the table and asked him to hand her a glass. When Grace reached for it, their hands touched, and although it was a light touch, it hit Luke like a lightning bolt. Zap! Her body had stilled. He quickly removed his hand and asked if she needed anything from the kitchen. She shook her head no. OK then.

"So, tell me about your family?' she asked as he handed her a glass of wine.

Luke spent a few minutes telling her about his father and brothers.

Grace covertly stared at him, thinking he didn't notice. He winked. She blushed. He caught her inhaling his scent, licking her lips. God, he wanted her, and from what he deduced, being the detective and all, she wanted him too.

Steaks done, they sat down to eat. The conversation consisted mostly about the perfect night and the food. After they finished dinner, Grace told him to relax. Since he cooked, she would load the dishwasher.

Luke followed her into the kitchen, sat and took a chug of beer. He watched her fiddle around with plate organization on the dishwasher racks. For some reason, it pleased him that she was comfortable in his house. He got up, turned the coffee on and took out two mugs. When the coffee was ready, he filled them, handed a mug to Grace. They brought the coffee outside and sat on the bench overlooking the river.

"It's beautiful here," said Grace. "What made you decide to buy on the river?"

"The boat, of course. I grew up by a river, and my brothers, dad and I went fishing all the time."

"Do you get time now to fish?"

Luke took a minute to answer. "Not as often as I would like. When my friends have free time, we go out on the boat. Plus, my friend, Seth Bowman owns a fishing camp not far from here. We go fishing quite a bit. He hesitated. "Well, as much as we both can get away."

"Must be nice. I've never been fishing even though I grew up by the ocean. My dad didn't fish, and my siblings and I were into other watersports like ocean kayaking and paddle-boarding."

Ah, two different worlds. Luke's family could never imagine paddle-boarding or ocean kayaking. Fishing from a small boat or the shore was more his style growing up. Somehow, he thought Grace would be comfortable in both worlds. "We'll go out sometime. I think you'll enjoy it."

Grace nodded and yawned. Luke stood and offered her a hand up. "You must be exhausted. Let's go to bed."

She cocked her head. "Whaaat?"

Luke realized what he'd said and amended that to, "let's get you to bed." Her eyes widened.

Wrong again. "No, damn it. I mean, go to bed."

Jesus, could he get any more suave? He wanted her in his bed naked, her hair spread out on the pillow, moaning his name while they made wild, passionate love but she wasn't ready, and he wasn't going to force the issue.

Grace slyly looked at him and laughed. "I know what you meant."

LUKE HAD THE WEEKEND OFF. Grace had a small event Friday afternoon, and he wanted to do something special for her. They had been openly flirting all week. His body was so tense, he thought he might explode—at least, a certain part of him.

Unpacking the string lights he bought, he draped them around the trees and bushes on the patio. He had fat white candles set around, and the fire pit was ready to light. Earlier he had connected the iPod to speakers and checked the playlist. The menu was set—grilled shrimp, salad, and potatoes; the wine was chilling in the fridge along with the pie he bought especially for Grace.

Grace loved pie, especially Key lime pie. She was due home any minute, and he was sweating like crazy. Luke felt this was a giant step for him. For them. What if she didn't like what he had done? Or thought him too forward? Or ...

Too late. The sliding door opened, and he smelled her scent before she walked out.

Grace looked surprised. "Wow, what's this? Are you having a party?"

"A party for two," he teased. "I thought you might like a relaxing night at home with nothing to do."

She sighed and smiled. "What a great thought. Thank you."

Luke indicated she should sit on the bench. "Can I get you a glass of wine?"

"Yes, I desperately need something. It's been a crazy week."

He poured a glass for her and a beer for himself. Turning the music on low, they talked about their day.

Hearing Grace's stomach rumble, Luke pulled the shrimp off the grill. The side dishes were on the table. "Come on and eat. Can't have you passing out and missing the meal."

"Great. I'm starving."

Luke pulled out a chair for Grace.

GRACE LOVED THE COLD, crisp wine and the mellow feeling it gave her. Luke put a lot of thought into this evening to make it special for her. The candles flickered in the breeze. Soft music played in the background. The string lights twinkled casting a soft glow over Luke, who looked so handsome sitting there. His eyes were heavy-lidded, pupils dark, the candlelight projecting sexy promises. He wanted her.

She knew she had a slight buzz going, but it was nothing compared to the electricity between the two of them.

She loved the many different facets this tough guy presented. Luke was loyal to friends and family; easy on the eyes; a great detective, and a romantic. He sat there with a slight smile on his face staring at her looking like a little kid who won the jackpot. So sweet. So sexy.

She wanted to lean over and kiss him, but she didn't want to appear too forward. She thought he was attracted to her. Heck, she knew he was attracted to her, and she was definitely attracted to him. It would be just a kiss. But what if he rejected her? Could she handle that?

Dinner was delicious. Luke wouldn't let her help clear the table. Like a kid at a surprise party, he was so excited when he told her he picked up her favorite pie. Then asked if she wanted coffee with the pie. She said yes to both, and he brought out a slice and a mug of coffee for each of them.

They sat side by side on the bench. Grace started to take a bite of pie and looked over at Luke. He stared back at her with such longing in his eyes.

Oh, please, please kiss me—the words she wanted to say but was afraid to. As if reading her mind, Luke gently removed her plate from her hand and placed it on the table. He put his hands on either side of her face and brought her in closer.

"If you don't want this, tell me now because once I kiss you, I'm not sure I'll be able to stop," he whispered.

In response, Grace moved closer and placed her lips on his, kissing him softly. She was surprised when he clasped her more tightly and sought refuge in her mouth. Opening to allow him in, she placed her arms around his neck.

Holy crap! His tongue was demanding and tender. Asking of her everything he was giving, and she was reciprocating. He tasted of hot coffee and sweet pie. Wow, could he kiss. Grace didn't want him to stop. Ever.

Tentatively reaching under her blouse, he rubbed her nipples through her bra. She moaned. He pulled her top up and pulled her bra down exposing her breasts. He dipped his head, sucked one then the other, running his tongue over her turgid peaks.

"Perfect, just perfect," he murmured as he gently sucked one nipple then the other. Replacing his mouth with nimble fingers, he tweaked and pulled until Grace moaned and bucked against his hand.

"Please," she huffed, "God, please."

Luke's voice came out labored. "Grace, I don't want to make love to you here. I want you in my bed."

It was hard to stop kissing her, but he managed. He stood up and put out his hand. He knew Grace wanted him, needed him, and with one movement, she gave him her hand and stood up.

Luke was about to enter heaven. He hadn't known if Grace would be willing to make love to him, but when she took his hand and stood, he almost howled.

Walking into the house toward his bedroom with Grace in front of him, he gently pulled off her blouse leaving her in a pink satin bra. He decided on the spot that pink was his new favorite color.

Grace turned and unbuttoned his shirt with trembling fingers. He took it off and dropped it in the hall. She started walking towards the bedroom, and he took a moment to unsnap her bra, turning her again to face him.

My God, she's beautiful, and her breasts, well they were luscious looking. Puckered pink nipples, small areolas, full breasts, not big but full. He stopped again to taste. Just taste. Would a taste be enough? He had to stop, or they would never make it to the bedroom. He would end up taking her in the hall, and that wasn't what he wanted for her the first time they made love.

He hurried her into his room, ripped down the bedcovers and looked at her. Grace's eyes were hooded, her lips slightly open, and her breasts—beautiful. *Oh, God.* He had always been a breast man, and he was looking at perfection.

Kissing her. Sucking her breasts. Desiring more. Luke stepped closer and unzipped the skirt she wore. And, surprise. A matching pair of bikini panties in his new favorite color. Gently lowering her to the bed, he slowly removed her panties. While he was there, he leaned over to smell her, inhaling deeply. Womanly. Sexy.

Luke moved his hand to her mound and rubbed her clit gently. Grace moaned softly. Inserting one finger into her folds, he found her wet but not wet enough. Besides he wasn't ready to make love to her yet. Moving up to her breasts again, he tasted one, then the other while rubbing the opposite one with his fingers. Grace moaned louder, moved her body closer, and tried to wrap her legs around his waist.

"Oh no, you don't. I want to touch every inch of your lovely body and hear you scream my name before I enter you. I've waited long enough for this."

Grace begged softly, "Please, please," writhing again when his fingers entered her while he rubbed his thumb around her clit. He paused.

She whimpered, rubbing her body against his. He kissed her face, her arms, her stomach and all the way down one leg and up the other. Grace was going wild. He inserted his fingers into her folds again while he sucked each perfect nipple, now hardened to even tighter peaks.

Luke worked his way down her stomach and lower. Moving his body between her legs, he looked up from her pussy and told her to open wide. Grace gasped.

He licked his lips. His tongue replaced his busy fingers, rubbing harder over her clit. His fingers scissored in her pussy. Oh God, she was so wet. She moaned, groaned, called Luke's name, and begged him for release.

"Come for me, Grace. Come on baby, let go."

With that, Grace bucked and screamed his name.

WHAT JUST HAPPENED? Grace had never screamed anyone's name when she came. In fact, she'd never orgasmed this hard in her life.

Luke was on his side and looking deep into her eyes. His blue eyes darkened with lust. "Wow, you're beautiful when you come."

Grace thought she should be embarrassed, but she wasn't. *Was this how making love should be?* Oh, she had orgasms with her ex-husband, but he never put in the effort Luke just did. James never liked going down on her. He occasionally did but thought it disgusting and dirty.

James would have considered it undignified if she screamed his name or even screamed during sex. He had been too uptight. James had been her first sexual experience, and she hadn't known any better.

Sex with Luke was an entirely new experience, and she liked it. A lot

---

LUKE THOUGHT he had never seen anything as beautiful as Grace having an orgasm. When she finally stopped shaking, she looked him up and down, and smirked. "Someone's over-dressed."

Luke chuckled. He still had on his pants. Standing up, he remedied that, then opened his side table, and pulled out a string of condoms.

Laughing, Grace looked at the condoms and then at him. "Wow, talk about being prepared and hopeful."

"Boy Scout's creed, 'Be prepared and hopeful,'" he said

with a smile. He had to smile. He was always prepared, and now he was very hopeful.

His cock led the way toward Grace. She reached out and gently caressed it—his cock trembled at her touch.

"I'm not going to last long if you keep touching me like that."

Grace ran her fingers down its length and clasped it in her hand, moving up and down. Luke moaned and tried to remove her hand—it felt so good, but he wasn't going to last if she didn't stop. She held on tight. Grace moved so that her mouth was positioned over the tip. She went in deep and slowly licked him. Her warm mouth surrounded his cock which was now rock-hard.

"Minx. I'll get you for that later." Luke could barely talk. All he could do was stand there and enjoy.

She hummed over the tip. Oh, God. He wasn't not going to last if she continued this. He wanted to be inside her. She hummed again, licked the precum and took him back in her mouth. Sucked deep and hard. He moaned. He was in heaven.

Up and down, around, humming, lightly blowing at the tip, and licking.

Heaven.

His balls tightened up. His body tensed. He started to say, "Stop. I'm coming." But he was too late. He exploded. Exploded into Grace's mouth. Exploded as if he hadn't had sex in a year—which he hadn't.

When he finally could focus on Grace, she grinned at him like the Cheshire Cat.

"Devil woman. Be afraid. Very afraid." With that, he tore open a condom, wrapped himself, opened her legs and positioned himself to go home.

CHAPTER TWENTY-SIX

Luke felt light-headed. His heart was racing. He didn't want to believe what Paul had told him. But the truth was there. He was livid. Beyond livid, if that was possible. And so disappointed.

Grace had lied to him.

Didn't she understand how he felt about liars? He had told her enough.

What was she thinking? He was a detective for God's sake. Did she think he'd give her a pass just because they were making love? To make matters worse, she lied in front of his friends and colleagues.

His week had been brutal. Jean's death was still unsolved. He and Ben had two other cases they were investigating. The only redeeming thing was he was spending his spare time with Grace. They no longer considered her a suspect. She had been cleared of Jean Mays's murder.

His captain was not pleased to hear Luke was "guarding" Grace at his home. Grace's stalker was still on the loose. He and Ben had nothing on that front.

Even Sam was striking out.

Paul had texted him yesterday that he had received information on Grace from his sources in D.C. They agreed to meet for lunch today. Paul was already seated when Luke arrived. Ordering beers and burgers, Paul seemed hesitant to give Luke the information.

"Spit it out, man. You're killing me hemming and hawing."

Paul prefaced all the information he gave Luke by saying he hadn't talked to anyone directly involved with Grace. What he heard was after the fact and might be rumors.

It wasn't a pleasant conversation. Paul told him he spoke to his sources in D.C. They had done some checking, and the rumors were that Grace had fabricated her story and tried to blame it on another journalist. Her in-depth piece ruined the reputation of a senator. She claimed to have corroborating notes and sources, but she couldn't produce them. After the publication, she was fired and couldn't get another job. Then, the senator killed himself. His death was blamed on Grace's false reporting.

Paul said he heard the police didn't believe Grace's story about a stalker and dismissed it as sour grapes. She left D.C. for Black Pointe. Rumors had also been flying that her parents were wealthy and helped her get out of the mess.

Shit. Luke couldn't help thinking about his mom's death. How similar the stories were—not taking responsibility for your actions, lying, the wealthy parents ready to step up for their kids, and the privilege.

It wasn't the story he wanted nor expected to hear. Luke's heart was pounding. He didn't want to believe Grace lied, ruined a man's life and let her parents get her out of a jam.

Lunch was ruined. Paul was apologetic. Luke told him not to worry about it; he had asked for the information. They said goodbye and Luke left for the station.

Luke had one more thing to do. That was to contact the

D.C. detective who had investigated her case. Something he should have paid more attention to at the beginning.

Late in the day, he was finally able to reach a Detective Emery. Emery wasn't familiar with the case as he hadn't caught it but remembered a little about Grace's police report. He told Luke the detective who had investigated Grace's allegations had retired a year ago and moved away. Emery told him there was little information in the record. It stated they had found no prints, no records of calls—nothing to support Grace's claims of being stalked. He remembered it was the investigating detective's opinion Grace was looking for public sympathy. He thought she wrote the notes herself, ordered pizzas to be delivered, yadda, yadda, yadda. They closed the case.

The burning in Luke's throat matched the acid churning in his stomach. Betrayal—this couldn't be happening to him again. He had trusted Grace to tell him the truth. Yes, she had told him the D.C. police didn't believe her.

But she "forgot" to tell him the police closed the case because they couldn't find any evidence of a stalker and thought she'd lied. She also "forgot" to tell him she had been blamed for the senator's killing himself because of her exposé, and she "forgot" to tell him she had been run out of town. And, Grace definitely "forgot" to tell him her wealthy parents got her out the mess. It seemed she left out and "forgot" a lot.

Luke was angry—beyond angry. He couldn't go home yet, so he went to the corner bar for a beer. There were a few people at the bar or playing pool. He was thankful that the noise distracted him because he didn't want to think about this mess. He had to confront Grace.

The lies. The betrayal. It was all happening again. Grace probably concocted the whole situation, so her name wasn't associated with Jean Mays. How could he be so dense? So gullible? He thought he had the relationship he wanted with Grace, but she was no different from Becky.

Knowing Grace would be at the house early, he drove home to get the whole sordid story from her.

Why didn't she tell him the whole truth about what had happened? He thought back to the original break-in at Grace's condo. Maybe she trashed her condo for sympathy. Although, why now? He would have to check his notes, but now thinking about it, he realized Grace only skimmed over the facts. She had shown him the notes. Notes she could have written herself or sent to Jean. As he remembered it, she hadn't mentioned harassing phone calls or the D.C. police closing the case because they thought she was lying.

Why not? Why did she lie? What did she gain by lying?

No doubt about it, he had to break off with her. After telling her about Becky and her betrayal with his asshole ex-partner—especially after telling her he hated liars and dealt with them day in and day out—how could she think he would let this go and forgive her?

GRACE WAS STANDING at the counter humming and making a salad when he got home. He couldn't look her in the face. He was done with her. No excuse she could make would ease his mind.

She looked up and gave him that little welcoming smile. At any other time, it would have melted him. Realizing something was wrong, she stopped what she was doing and walked around the counter.

She walked toward him with open arms, worry in her eyes. "Luke, what's wrong?"

It was hard for him to speak. He held up his hand and hissed, "Stop. Just stop there."

Grace put her arms down and stopped. Her mouth open. “What?”

“Stay right there. Don’t move.”

Luke swallowed hard, drew in a deep breath trying to control his beating heart. “Let me tell you about my day. I wanted to check out what happened to you in D.C. to see how it could be connected to your problems here. Asked my friend Paul to speak with his contacts in D.C. They were more than happy to give him your whole sleazy story.”

“Whaat?” Grace’s face turned deep red. “Luke, I’m not understanding. What sleazy story?”

Luke took a deep breath. “You lied. You lied to the newspaper. You lied to me. And, if that isn’t enough, I called the D.C. police who told me they didn’t believe your story either. They said you were lying.”

She put her hands out, reaching for him. “Luke?” Stopped, brought them back to her sides. Tears dripped from her eyes.

Luke didn’t care. He just continued.

“No, I don’t want to hear anything from you. You know how I feel about liars. You lied to me repeatedly. I can’t do this again especially with you. Becky’s betrayal was enough. I told you I deal with liars every day. I don’t want a liar in my house.”

Grace tried to reach out to him again, but he pulled away. She brought her hands to her side. Tears were spilling down her cheeks. “I never lied to you.”

“Well, sugar,” he spat out, “I’ve heard too many stories from D.C. that point to the liar I see in front of me. Pack your bag and find somewhere else to stay. You need to get out. If I never see or hear from you again, I will thank my lucky stars.”

Grace gasped. Her face turned pale.

Luke couldn’t stop himself from asking, “So Grace, did

Daddy really step in and pull strings to get you out of your problems?"

Confusion flashed across her face. "My father?"

It took her a moment to understand what he was saying.

"You bastard." Luke was unprepared for the slap across his face. It stung but not as much as her betrayal.

Grace's eyes formed slits. "I would never ask my parents to step in the middle of any problems I might have. I have too much respect for them and myself."

If the looks Grace was aiming at him were daggers, Luke thought he would be skewered royally. Right now, he didn't care. He was appalled by her lies and could barely look at her.

RIPPING OFF HER APRON, Grace spun around and stomped to Luke's bedroom. Hot tears stung her face. The pain in her heart threatened to shut down her body. *Oh my God.* Had she really slapped him? She had never hit a person in her life. Never even thought it. Luke had been as stunned as she.

Bile crept up her throat. She barely made it to the toilet before losing what little was in her stomach. Wiping her mouth with a towel smelling of the soap and the cologne Luke wore, she clasped it to her face and let the tears fall. She took a couple of minutes to compose herself and splash water on her face. No time, though, to have a pity party. She would never let Luke see how much his accusations hurt her. He wanted her out. She was out.

Grabbing her bag out of the closet, she threw all her clothes and toiletries in it. Making her way back to the kitchen with her suitcase in hand, Grace looked at Luke. He stood there. Fury emanated off his body.

God, he was handsome even mad, and she still wanted his arms around her. She wanted his lips on hers. She wanted him to tell her she was his and for him to say to her that he would always be on her side. *What the hell, Grace. He called you a liar. He's kicking you out. Get over him.*

Her voice broke when she said, "I never lied to you, and if you think I did, I'm sorry."

Luke stood there woodenly, looking everywhere but not at her.

That's it. Grace had enough. *How dare he?*

Putting her suitcase on the floor, the passive good girl in Grace threw off her cloak of invisibility and screamed at him, "You have a nerve condemning me."

She got right up in Luke's face, shook her finger at him. "You lie to yourself every day. You want a relationship, but if the woman has expectations from you, you run away and blame her. You can't compromise or commit. You draw a line in the sand of what you consider a lie or not, and you never cross it. Let me tell you something. You can't love someone if you can't imagine life without them. If you don't have their back. If you wouldn't do everything in your power to keep them in your life. If you don't cherish them."

She poked him hard in the chest. "You're a liar. A sanctimonious hypocrite." Grace took a deep breath. "And I'm glad I found out before giving you my heart."

Grace picked up her bag and stormed out the door.

CHAPTER TWENTY-SEVEN

Grace sat in her car and tried to process what just happened. She had heard a door slamming and lots of bumping and cursing coming from the living room as she was cooking. For some silly reason, Grace thought Luke had bought her a surprise.

When he finally stomped into the kitchen, she hadn't counted on the look of disgust and anger on his face. She couldn't imagine what had happened. Then listening to him spew venom towards her was a knife to her gut.

She hadn't lied.

Grace thought back to her conversation in her condo. She remembered telling Luke the D.C. police were not helpful and didn't believe her. She didn't think she had to tell him the D.C. police dismissed her claims of being stalked as lies to protect herself. And she hadn't known they closed her case. While it embarrassed her, the police looked at her as the culprit, but that was on them. She also suspected something funky was going on with the detective who investigated her case. He never followed any of the clues she gave him, and she thought he didn't even believe her.

As for the senator, well, her story was true even if she couldn't back it up with facts. When he killed himself, she did feel some responsibility, but he had brought his bad luck on himself. As for her not being able to get a job, that was a tough one but true. No one wanted to take a chance on her, and she was too beaten down to defend herself. However, she certainly wasn't run out of town. She left for her own sanity.

For that matter, why would Luke think she wrote the notes to herself? Slashed her tires? Cut her brakes? Ruined her condo? What the hell? Why would she do that? She had a quiet life here. She kept a low profile. Her reporting of events was not controversial.

When her D.C. editor asked her to provide backup sources for her exposé, she couldn't. Jim Harrison, the whistleblower she interviewed, the whistleblower who started her journey down the rabbit hole, had disappeared off the map. The sources Rachel Lang had given her were "lost." While Grace could justify some accusations against the good senator, she wasn't able to defend them all. The newspaper had to do a retraction. *Let's talk lies and betrayal, Luke.*

Packing her things and leaving Luke's house was the hardest thing she had ever done. Even harder than losing everything in D.C. She was in love with him. She had given him her trust. She assumed he had her back and stand by her. *Betrayed by love again*. Why didn't he believe her? She hadn't lied to him. It wasn't fair, damn it.

Driving away from Luke's house, she called Sam, who insisted she come right over.

This altercation with Luke was too much. Grace couldn't stop the flow of tears, so she finally pulled over to the side of the road before she got into an accident. The radio was playing love songs, and she sat on the side of the road sobbing. It was a while before she could control the great sobs consuming her body. Many tissues later, she was still sniffling and hiccupping. The enormous pain in her heart hadn't gone away, but the tears were cathartic.

Pulling into a parking space in front of Sam's building, she gathered her things and walked up the sidewalk.

SAM WAS WAITING at the back door for her. It pained her to see her best friend's shoulders slumped over, dried tears clinging to her cheeks and Grace's face so sad. Sam pulled her in for a hug. Luke was dead meat. It was a good thing he wasn't around right now because she wanted to hurt him badly and it wouldn't matter to her that he was a cop.

"Oh sweetie, I'm so sorry."

Sam closed the door keeping her arm around Grace. "Let's get you upstairs, and you can tell me all about it."

A bottle of wine later, Grace finished telling Sam the whole story.

"That son of a bitch. When I see him again, I'm going to pummel him. I'm gonna kick his ass into the next county. I'm gonna rip out his balls and, and ..."

Sam stood up and clenched her fists. "How dare he call you a liar based solely upon talking to one crooked detective and believing whatever rumors Paul heard?"

OH, Lord. Sam was a force to be reckoned with when she got mad, Grace thought. If her friends were wronged, watch out. Visions of a younger, angrier Sam flitted through her memory. Years of martial arts had helped control Sam's instinct to fight first and talk later. As small and as innocent as Sam looked, Grace never wanted to be on her bad side. She had heard rumors about how badass Sam could be. However, she didn't believe they were just rumors. Sam's feisty attitude would have made her smile if Grace didn't feel so crappy. Sam always took her role as a protector seriously. Always had from a young age, especially after her and Danny's parents had been killed in a home invasion gone wrong.

Gathering her bag, Grace stood up and said she was tired and would see Sam in the morning. Getting ready for bed, Grace went over everything that had happened. She loved Luke.

However, a man who didn't trust her or stand behind her was not worth her effort. It would be difficult for a while, well, probably horrendous, but she landed on her feet after she fled D.C. This time she was staying in Black Pointe and standing tall.

Well, maybe tomorrow. Tonight, though, she pulled her pillow tight to her chest and sobbed.

BEN HAD STOPPED by Luke's to go fishing. He found Luke sitting, no, leaning on the edge of the bench overlooking the dock. Drunk. Drunk as a skunk drunk.

"Shit, man, what the hell is going on?"

Slurring his words, Luke said, "Grace. Liar. Sent her packing."

The effort to talk had Luke leaning further on the bench. Ben went over and pushed him back up before he fell over.

"Man, you have it bad. Don't move. I'm making coffee, and we'll talk. I found out some details about the case I want to go over with you when you're sober."

Ben walked into the kitchen to make coffee. Jesus, Luke must have started drinking hours ago. There was already a pile of beer bottles on the floor. A partially cooked dinner now burned to a crisp was on the stove. The place looked like hell. Pulling the coffee out and filling the pot with water gave him a moment to think about what to say. Ben knew how devastated Luke was by his ex-fiancé and ex-partner's betrayal, although Luke didn't talk much about either of them.

Ben loved women and dated a lot. He didn't feel like he had to settle down anytime soon especially when there were so many beautiful women out there to give pleasure to. But Luke, Luke was a one-woman man. The fact that he gave his heart to one, only to have it ripped out hadn't stopped him from secretly hoping someone special would come along he could trust. Ben thought Grace was it for Luke. Apparently not.

It took a couple of hours and almost a whole pot of coffee to get Luke sober. Ben managed to get him in the lounge chair where Luke held his head and moaned.

"Shit. I can't remember the last time I got roaring drunk. Now I remember why I don't. I have a mega headache and feel like shit."

Ben laughed. "Well, if you consumed the number of bottles on the floor, you deserve it. Want to tell me what happened?"

Luke's tale of woe was upsetting at the least. Ben knew he was a horndog but Luke ... Luke wanted to fall in love. He couldn't believe Luke confided to him what Grace said as she left. If he knew anything about Luke, Grace was spot-on about him. It had to hurt, though.

LUKE'S HEAD WAS POUNDING. Part of it he could blame on the alcohol, but his heart felt like it was being squeezed making the headache worse. Every muscle in his body ached, and he felt a part of him had died. Sure, Luke had a mega headache and wanted to park himself in front of a toilet until his stomach settled, but that wasn't the only reason he was feeling so miserable. He was ashamed of himself for insinuating Grace's father had gotten her out of an awkward situation. He deserved the slap, although he'd been surprised. She sure looked surprised after slapping him. Grace had never even hinted she had asked her father to step in and help her. Just because it had happened to his family didn't mean Grace would take advantage of her father's position.

Why had Grace lied?

Grace was funny, sweet and kind. Not Luke's typical type, which was feisty, hot, and charitable. Charitable with her body, that is. And he was not one who wanted a commitment. But Grace had changed that. He felt at home with her and could see himself making a future with her.

It had been a roller coaster of emotions with him. At first, he hadn't believed Grace's story. As more weird things happened to her, he became convinced Grace was a victim. But Paul supported what Luke thought when he first heard Grace's stalker story. Lies. Luke didn't want to presume Grace was involved in Jean's murder, but this bullshit she was pulling hadn't convinced him.

He needed to talk to Sam Knight. Sam believed Grace. She was Grace's best friend, but she also knew what happened to Grace in D.C. Plus, he respected Sam's opinion. Could Paul be wrong? Could Paul have misunderstood what he heard? Did Paul get all the facts straight? Paul did tell him it was second-hand information. The people initially involved were no longer around. Luke wondered if he jumped the gun and assumed too much.

Was Grace right? That he was lying to himself? Sure, Becky betrayed him and married Jason. In all fairness, she only wanted to be number one in someone's life. She never asked him to give up his job. Was he the selfish, black-and-white only guy Grace accused him of being? His head hurt. What did she say about her heart? Damn, he couldn't remember. But these were all things to think about when he was sober.

Coming back to reality, Luke looked at Ben and asked, "What did you find out?"

"Riiight. Marsh and Benoit alibied. It took a while, but Diane's friend Sue confirmed Diane was crying in her ear all night, at least until 7 a.m. Richard Marsh was seen on camera leaving his apartment that morning around 6:30. It takes about a half hour to get to the park, so he's out too."

Ben checked the notebook he pulled from his pocket. "I've checked with the ME. Jean was definitely strangled. However, the blood on her knuckles didn't match anyone on record. You know Grace has been cleared. I've double-checked all the security cameras around Grace's building, and with her running partner who reconfirmed she called Grace that morning to tell her she was sick."

Ben rubbed his brow and exhaled loudly. "We know there's no way Grace would be able to get over to Sexton Park early enough to kill Jean. You know the captain wasn't happy about you harboring a suspect but with Grace cleared of any wrongdoing, it's not a problem anymore."

Ben sat back in the chair. "Except you seem to have driven Grace away and are drowning your sorrows in beer." He looked at Luke. "And for sure, I'm not getting involved in your love life."

"SMART. I can make a mess of things all by myself." Luke grimaced. He didn't need anyone else involved in his love life.

Though right now, it appeared he didn't have a love life.

Ben took a sip of coffee. "Also, we still don't know who

killed that other jogger. I'm betting it was Mays's killer. Too similar to be anything else. But they had nothing in common except for jogging in a park. We need to find the connection."

Luke sighed. "Damn, we've got to find that killer before he strikes again. I think there's a connection between Grace, Jean, and D.C. We just haven't found it yet."

What a mess. A killer was on the loose, they had no clues, and now he'd chased away with vile words and accusations, the best thing that had ever happened to him. He needed a clear mind to sort out the many conflicting stories about Grace from D.C. He needed to get on with his life. He also needed to find a stalker and find a killer. Damn, the list was getting longer.

Truth be told, he was in love with her not that he would tell Ben. Come to think of it, he never told Grace. Too late now.

He felt betrayed when Paul gave him his information. He acted before he had all the facts. *Guilty until proven innocent.* Some detective he was.

As he told Ben, there were too many questions. Too many screw-ups happened in D.C. He needed to get to the bottom of this situation and satisfy himself Grace either lied or told the truth.

Whatever he did, it was going to hurt. Hurt him. Hurt Grace. Either way, Grace would probably never speak to him again.

CHAPTER TWENTY-EIGHT

As he rushed to Jacksonville Airport, Ken mentally went over all the fun he'd had tormenting Grace. From installing cameras, trashing her condo, sending her notes, to slashing her tires and brakes, Ken was still amazed he hadn't been caught on any of the security cameras.

But then, he was careful and so much smarter than the "average bear." Yogi Bear aside, fake mustaches, hats pulled low, phony uniforms—God, he should write a book on how to avoid being caught. Maybe he would.

He hadn't had this much fun since junior year in high school when Frank Connolly claimed he cheated on an exam. So, what if he had? It was none of Frank's business. But he couldn't go on the New York City trip he had been looking forward to. Plus, his father had grounded him for a month, but not before telling him he was a disappointment as usual.

Good ole Frankie never knew it was Ken who spread the rumors that Frank liked little kids—a lot. Frank was never able to get into college or even have a good career. Ken bet Frank was sorry now that he tattled. People always made the mistake of dismissing him. Too bad for them, he always got even.

Right now, Grace was getting her confidence back. Mary had told him how Grace would be doing major pieces from now on. He couldn't, no, wouldn't allow that to happen. She ruined his life, plain and simple. He had to be more vigilant from now on.

The thrill he got from harassing Grace was nothing compared with seeing Rachel again. They had been apart three weeks since he was last in D.C. and he could only stay for two days. His liquid cash was tight, so he had to be frugal. Rachel understood it took time interviewing for a new position and setting up a household. Of course, it was all lies. He hated telling her lies about his time in Black Pointe.

If she knew he was harassing Grace again, she wouldn't be happy. After she "lost" the contact information on the senator and pretended she fact-checked Grace's article when she hadn't, he knew he had asked her for enough. She loved her job, but that damn editor who had fired Rachel—he was next on the list.

Things were looking up for him. He had interviewed with a lobbying firm in D.C., albeit not a first or even second-tier one. However, they did like his style and knew his reputation from the senator's office. He would tell Rachel the job in Florida fell through, and he had one in D.C. She would be happy.

Arriving at the airport, he parked his car, picked up his carry-on bag and went into the terminal. After going through security, he didn't have long to wait before they called his row number.

It was less than a two-hour flight. Ken saw Rachel waving to him when he walked down the terminal. God, it was good to see her. Her long blond hair was loose, just the way he liked it. The tight, sweater dipping down to her breasts had him thinking all the men in the terminal would be jealous looking at those babies. Add in her long legs and her very short skirt. Shit, he was hot already, and little Ken was coming out of hibernation. He couldn't wait to get her into bed. The bitch in Florida? Mary? Yes, Mary. God, he wished he could remember her name; she only took the edge off.

"Sweetie, I'm so glad to see you," Rachel said as she gave him a big kiss.

She took his hand, and they walked to the parking lot. Driving the half hour to her condo, they caught up on their lives.

"When are we moving to Florida? I'm anxious to pack."

Oh boy! Think fast. "Soon sweetheart. I'm working things out with the editor."

"Did they ask you anything about your past? Did you mention Senator Irish or the *Chronicle*?"

"A little. I told them I worked with Senator Irish. I left the *Chronicle* out. I didn't think being let go from the newspaper, even if it was a lie, would be a positive thing."

"Ken, you are a terrific journalist. It wasn't your fault Mitch found out that bitch gave you a false story. Mitch was too harsh on you. You would have won a Pulitzer for sure with that one." *God bless Rachel, she believed the good in him.* Although he had needed a good story to stay at the paper and had paid the woman to lie, he never thought Mitch would find out. He would never tell Rachel that.

He couldn't remember how or when he and Rachel hooked up with Jean Mays. However, she had been a loose cannon from the start. Happy to dish dirt and always collecting it. It wouldn't have mattered if they were friends; everyone was fair game to her.

The paper fired him anyhow and hired Grace to take his place. The Senator liked his style, hired him and rewarded him well from his kickbacks. They were good together. Too bad Irish had to off himself, and Ken lost his lucrative job again. Thank you again, Grace Winslow. Water over the dam. You win some. You lose some. *OK, time to stop with the damn adages.*

Grace had disappeared from D.C. before he could complete his harassment of her. Seeing the picture of Grace in the magazine standing next to the new senator from Black Pointe had been sheer luck. Then discovering Jean was living in Black Pointe, as was Grace, was serendipity. When Ken had contacted Jean, she originally wanted to help. Then Jean tried to blackmail him. When blackmailing didn't work, she threatened to tell Grace Winslow the truth—to betray him.

The truth about his stalking Grace, ruining her career.

The truth about the disappearing whistleblower. The threats to hurt his damn family, that had been fun, and Jim and his family hightailed it out of D.C. fast, to God knows where. Him again.

As for the sources, Rachel helped Grace and then conveniently lost the names and interviews. All him.

No way was Jean ruining his life. He had to stop her. And, he had.

The two days with Rachel went fast. They had a lot of catching up to do, which they did in bed. Rachel was always up for anything he suggested, and he suggested a lot. She was so beautiful naked. Legs spread apart. He loved going down on her. He loved the way she moaned his name. And he loved when she came on his fingers, and then went down on him.

Over breakfast, they talked about what they were doing. Rachel was excited about her new blog, writing under the name Rachel Peterson, digging up dirt on congressmen, lobbyists—anyone. He was proud of her.

The weekend was over. The plane ride back was uneventful, and Ken was tired but in a pleasurable way. Fucking had its benefits.

The drive back to his shitty home away from home gave him time to think about Grace. He needed to step it up. What to do?

Yes! Ken got so excited about his idea he almost crashed the car into a barrier.

He smiled all the way home.

CHAPTER TWENTY-NINE

Grace hadn't seen or heard from Luke in over two weeks, not that she was expecting to. She had too many events to go to, and when she wasn't working, her friends called to say hello or to take her out for dinner or drinks. They made sure she wasn't alone to reflect on her non-relationship with Luke. So, she had no spare time to think about him.

Well, that was a lie. Everywhere Grace turned, there were reminders of him. The coffee shop where he first asked her out, and she refused. The Italian restaurant they ate many meals at. Who knew the scent of basil or garlic could cause such pain? The way he smiled his little smile when she kissed him. Making love all over the house. Nah, she had no time to think of him at all.

She had spent two nights at Sam's condo. Sam had given her the space to sob, curse and sob some more until she was cried out. *Another lie*. The tears flowed every day. She had moved back to her condo even though Sam pressed Grace to stay longer at her place, but she craved the comfort of her own home.

Sam had made good on her word to install more security. Grace felt safer in her home, but she knew her heart wasn't safe from Luke McBride. She missed him so much. It hurt not to see his sexy smile or have his warm arms around her. Grace had hoped Luke was the one. Apparently not. How could she be so unlucky in love?

She still didn't understand what his problem was with her. She hadn't lied to him. He never questioned her in depth about D.C. so why did he think she had lied about it. What had happened in D.C. was on her, not him.

Grace hated that his view of the world was either black or white. In her profession, black and white were the extremes; gray was the color of choice for journalists. You got all sides before you wrote your piece. Sometimes, the story went to a place you couldn't have foreseen, as was the case of their relationship.

Oh well. Luke was out. She was hurting. Grace only hoped it would get better sooner rather than later. She could only hope she would find someone like Luke, but someone would stand by her no matter what, and apparently, that wasn't Luke.

Grace yawned again. This was her fifth event of the week in addition to reporting on a piece on opioids. She loved attending these events and talking to the guests. However, five affairs in a week were too much. Waving goodbye to friends, she and Evelyn, a fellow guest, walked out of the convention center into the attached garage. She had stayed later than expected to interview Black Pointe's new state representative. Glad to have the company, she and Evelyn chatted about the event and friends in common.

Since the affair was just starting to wind down, the garage was still deserted. Empty garages made her uncomfortable, and she wished there were more people around. But she was exhausted and hadn't wanted to stay another hour for the event to end. Knowing the garage would be filling up soon didn't ease her anxiety though.

Summer evenings in Black Pointe were usually warm and humid. However, it had rained earlier, and the garage was damp, chilly and smelled like wet dog. Grace pulled her shawl up to cover her shoulders. Her feet were complaining about the high heels she was wearing. What she wanted to do more than anything was take them off. How some women wore them all the time was a mystery to her. She kept a pair of flats in her car to change into for just this reason.

Evelyn's car was on the second floor also. They debated whether it was safer to take the stairs or elevator. The elevator probably had cameras. They agreed they didn't want to be stuck running up or down stairs in high heels if something happened.

Getting into the empty elevator, Grace pressed the second-floor button. They got out when the doors opened. Saying goodnight to Evelyn who had parked her car by the elevator, Grace quipped, "Guess it pays to get here early."

Evelyn laughed, got into her car and started it. Rolling down her window, she asked if Grace wanted her to wait until she got to her car. Shaking her head, no, Grace watched Evelyn wave and take off.

Silence.

Grace saw her car at the end of the row. She regretted saying no to Evelyn, but it was too late now.

She heard only the click-clack of her high heels and felt very much alone. The darkness and shadows created a scary scene causing her to keep looking over her shoulders—the thought she might be starring in her movie scene of "too dumb to live" passed briefly through her mind. *My imagination is in overdrive.*

Reaching into her purse, she pulled out her pepper spray and keys. The overhead lights provided very little light. Grace wished it were earlier, brighter and busier. Unfortunately, she parked in a far corner because she had been running late this evening. It had been the only space left.

Click-clack, click-clack.

The echoes from her heels were driving her crazy, but she hurried on.

Click-clack, click-clack

Clunk!

Grace jumped.

What the heck was that? Probably an animal. Hopefully, an animal.

Her imagination created all sorts of crazy scenarios. Her heart pumped wildly. She looked around. Nothing. As she hurried down the aisle, she pulled her phone out hoping to use the flashlight app. Dead. *Are you kidding me?* Placing it back in her purse, she opened her car door with the remote. As she reached the car to open the door, a car came around the corner.

CHAPTER THIRTY

"Grace."

Grace glanced over at the driver who rolled down the window. *Evelyn!* "Evelyn, I thought you left."

"I did. I went down to pay but thought about you up here all alone and turned around."

Grace let out a long sigh of relief. "Thank you. I was scaring the bejesus out of myself imagining all sorts of weird sounds."

"You're welcome. Get in your car and follow me down."

Minutes later, Grace was in her car following Evelyn's lights. She made a promise to herself not to do something like this again. She had been too scared.

KEN PUNCHED the cement block wall. *Goddamn bitch. She just never did what she was supposed to do. What a damn waste of time.* He wiped his bloody knuckles on his pants and pulled off his mask. He had been all set to taser Grace until that bitch in the car showed up. He needed a plan B right now. The room was rented. He was hyped. Everything was ready. He just needed his victim.

Think. He groaned. He was tired of this shit, tired of making plans, tired of missing Rachel and tired of not getting on with his life. What to do?

He snapped his fingers, decision made.

Ken scurried to his car. Initially, he was going to follow Grace home and kidnap her. But when he heard about the event tonight, he assumed she would be covering it like she had all the others. He had come here early to get a good parking space, hunkered down with water and sandwiches and waited.

Grace probably thought she was lucky to get the last spot on the second floor. He chuckled over that. She was lucky, all right. His luck had held out until it didn't. It was serendipity she left the event early and walked alone to her car. He had been all set to sneak behind her until that other bitch drove back. Oh well.

GRACE DRAGGED herself out of her car. What was it with parking spaces tonight? She had to take a spot further away than she wanted at her condo. She opened the car door and put her feet on the ground and groaned. *That's it. The heels come off.* She checked the front seat but no flats. *Must have forgotten them. Damn.* No way in hell was she putting her heels back on.

She gathered her bag, locked the door and started walking to the back entrance. The asphalt was slick with rain. She stepped on something sharp. The pain shot up her leg. *Damn. Perfect ending to a perfect night.* She wanted a cup of hot tea and a bath.

She was close to the back door, keys in hand, when she

was pushed from behind. When she looked over her shoulder, she saw that a man with a black mask had somehow snuck up behind her and was holding what looked like a gun. He hauled back and punched her in the face. Her scream was pitiful, and she tried to scream again. *Didn't anyone hear her?* Panic gripped her. She scrambled up, reaching into her purse to grasp her pepper spray, but before she could reach it, ZAP.

Her body stiffened. Intense pain incapacitated her. She fell hard, hitting the cold cement floor. Someone screamed. Was it her? The pain was agonizing and seemed to go on forever. Lying on the sidewalk and unable to control her body, she saw the man was smiling and talking to her, but everything was fuzzy. And the pain. God, it hurt.

She didn't think she had been shot. *I've been Tasered.* She could do nothing as she watched the man bend over her, pull out the barbs and jab her with a needle. Was he laughing?

Blackness surrounded her, then nothing.

CHAPTER THIRTY-ONE

Grace woke up groggy. She was sweating, and the sun's heat burned her eyes. Her eyes felt like they had been used to sift sand.

Rolling away from the intense brightness, she realized she was on a bed. Swallowing hurt and she realized her mouth was taped, her hands wouldn't move, and she hurt all over, especially the back of her head.

Slowly looking around the room, Grace didn't recognize where she was, but she knew she wasn't home. Home wasn't a shabby room reeking of cigarette smoke, with unknown stains on the carpet, a mini TV with rabbit ears and double beds. Ugh, she didn't want to know what was on the bedspread.

Going over the previous night's events, she thought she had been tasered and then doped before waking up in hell this morning. Gradually moving, while mentally checking her body, she tried to sit up. But she couldn't use her hands or open her mouth. Trying not to panic, she glanced down and saw the ties on her wrists. *Not good, not good at all.* Rolling around and backing up to the headboard, she managed to stand up and look around. The blood drained from her head. She was dizzy. She sat down on the bed. She was alone. Good. *Well, hopefully good.*

The situation was overwhelming, and she wondered how she was going to escape. *This just couldn't be her life*. An image of Sam flitted across her mind. Sluggishly she remembered the self-defense class she and Sam had taken in D.C. God, her mind was in a fog. What was that move again? Grace wished she'd paid more attention in the class when they dealt with getting out of zip ties. She had been naïve to think she would never become a victim and need to use self-defense moves. Stupid.

First things first, tape off mouth. Grace brought her hands up and ripped off the duct tape from her mouth taking a generous layer of skin with it. A small moan escaped—no time to feel sorry for herself.

Recalling the self-defense moves she and Sam learned, Grace brought her hands up over her head. Quickly brought her hands down spreading them apart as she did. Nothing happened.

She tried again.

And again.

Salty tears leaked out of her eyes. She brought her tied hands up to brush them away.

Panic set in. She was frantic that she wouldn't break the zip ties before the kidnapper returned. *Where was he, anyway? And for that matter, who was he? Was he the stalker or a random kidnapper?*

Grace hadn't experienced despair this deep since she left D.C. She felt powerless. *Why can't I do this?* The skin on her wrists was raw, red and bleeding. She wiped the tears from her face again with her hands and took a deep breath. *If I can't do this, he wins. That's not going to happen.*

Visualizing the technique again, she brought her hands

down abruptly. Her hands flew apart. The ties snapped. Finally. Thank the gods in heaven, the kidnapper had zip-tied her hands in front of her and not in the back. Rubbing her arms to get the circulation going, she was still woozy but put the feeling aside. The smell of stale cigarettes and sex made her gag. *Oh, God. Had she been raped? She concentrated on aches and pains, anything abnormal, but nothing down there hurt or felt different. OK then.* No time to get sick. She had to get out of this room. Now.

Tiptoeing around the bed, she pulled back a corner of the drape and peeked out to see where she was. She was in a motel for sure but where was it located? She couldn't see the main road. There were a couple of people walking in the parking lot. Could one be her kidnapper? She closed the drapes.

At least the room was on the ground floor. Grace searched the grungy room—nothing here to help her. Walking toward the back of the room into the bathroom, she closed and locked the thin, cheap door. It would only stop someone for a couple of seconds, but it was better than nothing. She ripped open the doors to the sink cabinet—just toilet paper. She supposed she could throw it at someone, like that would stop them. Holding back the hysterical giggle, she glanced around the tiny room, but there was nothing she could use to help defend herself. She peered behind the tub's shower curtain.

Halleluiah!

There was a small window on the wall. It would be a tight, but Grace figured she could squeeze through. She had to. Plus being on the first floor would make her escape easier.

Working quickly, she struggled to open the window. It didn't budge. Guessing it had never been opened, Grace pushed harder, her fingers drenched in sweat. One more time —eureka! It moved painfully upward a couple of inches. She took a lungful of air and using strength she gathered from deep inside her, she pushed one more time. The window grudgingly opened. Grace pushed the screen out and looked down. It was only about six feet to the ground, and there were a few bushes up close to the building. They would break her fall. It was now or never.

Blowing out a deep breath, she stepped up and balanced on the edge of the tub then pulled herself up the windowsill. Pain. *God, my wrists hurt.* She managed to get one leg over the sill and grab the sides of the window. Shit, she so did not want to do this. But she also didn't want to die. Without hesitation and giving herself one good push, her body whooshed through the window, and she landed in the bushes. OOOFF!

Untangling herself, she scanned the area and didn't see anyone. Her body hurt everywhere. She wanted to cry in pain. *No time to coddle yourself, Grace*.

The motel backed up to a wooded area and Grace started running. A rock embedded itself in her foot. She screamed. Shit. She forgot her shoes, although she didn't recall seeing them in the room. Probably lost them the night before. The forest floor was not kind to her bare feet. But she was alive, and that was a good thing.

"Hey!"

Grace turned towards the motel and saw a man's head in the window yelling at her. *Oh my God! Oh my God! This can't be happening.*

The ground was full of sharp rocks and prickly things. Grace's sensitive soles were hurt and bleeding. No time to stop. She ran faster.

Grace swiped at a thorny branch that had attached itself to her leg and dress, pulling fabric and skin from her body. More blood. Thrashing through bushes, she continued running down the narrow path. Her breathing labored. She looked behind her again.

Nothing. Good so far. There was no one following her.

Turning and facing forward, she tripped over something and fell flat on her face.

"Ouch," a gravelly voice beside her yelled. *Oh my God. Had the kidnapper gotten ahead of her?* She assumed she had tripped on a tree trunk, so the voice surprised her. She noticed a man half hidden in the bushes with his legs straight out over the path—the legs she tripped over. Dirt covered his legs and face. His hair was tangled and wild. Was he homeless? Why else would he be sitting in the woods?

"Oh, my goodness. Are you all right?"

He waved his hand yes. Grace turned and ran. *Seriously? Did she just ask a man she tripped over in the woods if he was OK while running for her life?*

Perspiration clouded her eyes. Her heart couldn't keep pace with her breathing. Her face hurt where she landed on sharp pebbles. Was the kidnapper chasing her? Was he close? She didn't hear any footsteps. She sprinted on.

It seemed like she had been running for hours through the woods. Her body ached. She wiped away the moisture dripping into her eyes. Would this nightmare ever end? Bugs were attacking her bloody legs and feet, but there was no time to stop and scratch.

Stumbling along, she got the impression the narrow, uneven path was getting wider. Over her heavy breathing, she could hear voices ahead. She noticed flashes of color through the bushes. People were moving around. *People. Talking. Laughing. Normal things. Thank God.* She reached the end of the woods and saw that she was on a busy street.

A street.

People.

Help.

She ran toward a shopping center and spotted a patrol car parked in front of a store. But the patrol car was empty. She took a chance and darted into the small grocery store and saw a cop paying at the register. The cashier and cop looked over at her as she raced in. She prayed she wouldn't pass out before she could say anything but managed a deep breath.

Her mouth dry, she screamed, "Help me!"

Grace collapsed in front of the officer.

"GODDAMN IT."

Son of a bitch. Ken punched the side of the opened window Grace had escaped from. He had seen her turn and look back at him when he yelled, but he didn't want to attract more attention by running after her. Besides, Grace had enough of a head start that he wouldn't be able to catch her.

If he hadn't stopped for something to eat and to get the rest of the materials he needed, this wouldn't have happened. He wrongly assumed the shot he gave Grace would keep her out for at least twelve hours.

Ken scanned the room looking for anything he left behind. He had been so psyched contemplating what he was going to do to Grace when he returned. Now, as adrenaline left his body, he was drained and furious.

He picked up the remains of the ties, and the duct tape, wiped down the doorknob and anything else he might have touched. He closed the door, pulled his cap low on his forehead, and walked out avoiding the camera aimed half-assed at the parking lot.

Few people were walking around in this seedy neighborhood, especially in the daytime, and no one was looking at him. He walked over a block to get to his parked car.

The sidewalk was devoid of people when Ken opened the door and got into his car. He couldn't believe Grace had gotten away. Rubbing his forehead, he fumed. *Bitch. When he got his hands on Grace again, all bets were off. Maybe he would have a little fun with her before he killed her.*

He purposely chose the most run-down, out-of-the-way motel he could find. No one would question noises coming from the room. What he wanted was to have his way with her, so she understood just who was in control. Initially, he only wanted to scare her. But he missed Rachel and wanted this over so he could go back to D.C. So, killing Grace, it was. He would make her death look like a suicide. He had already typed out a note using the pen and pad he had stolen from her condo. In it, she blamed herself for shoddy reporting, the senator's ruination and Jean's death. Even after death, her reputation would be tarnished.

Damn. His strategy was foiled. He needed to up his game. He needed another plan. Grace would suffer greatly for this little stunt of hers when he got her the next time. Think.

Hmmm. Yes. That would work. Plan B was looking up. Ken smiled to himself and drove away.

FRANTIC TO SEE GRACE, Sam arrived at the same time the ambulance pulled into Black Pointe General Hospital. Tears were flowing as she watched the medics remove the stretcher with Grace on it, bloody and weak. Her friend, the kindest gentlest person she knew, didn't deserve this.

She followed the medics as they wheeled Grace into the emergency room and transferred her to a bed. The nurses immediately checked her vitals and wounds. Sam watched as they cut Grace's shredded dress off and covered her.

Looking at Grace's swollen, red lips, Sam wanted to reach out and kill the kidnapper. *Bastard duct-taped her.* She took in Grace's raw, bloody wrists, and she wanted to beat the shit out of the person who did this to her. Grace's feet were swollen, cut and bleeding. Sam didn't know how Grace managed to walk on them. The pain must have been unbearable. *The bastard was going to die when she caught up with him.*

The doctor had been in and looked Grace over, checking out the bump on the back of her head. The nurses had wiped most of the blood off Grace's body and bandaged her, and the orderlies moved Grace up to a room. Hailey and Laura rushed in just as the nurse put an IV in Grace's arm to sedate her. Anne would come over after school. Sam filled them in as best she could.

A shadow filled the doorway. The women looked up to see Luke standing there breathing heavily. He saw Grace lying on the bed and stifled a groan.

"My God. What happened?"

What happened? What happened, shit for brains was that you didn't believe my friend. Sam wanted to kick his ass for being an ass. Hailey and Laura barely said hello. But, for some reason, Grace was in love with the douchebag even though he kicked her to the curb.

"Don't know. Grace hasn't said anything yet. They've given her something to sleep and for the pain which she wouldn't have, had you done your job and taken her seriously."

IT WAS SEVERAL HOURS LATER, and Luke hadn't moved from Grace's side. Walking into the room with her friends there had been difficult. They had looked at him as if he had two heads and hardly said a word to him. Displeasure with him radiated from their bodies. Thankfully, Hailey and Laura had just left with Sam to get coffee, and the atmosphere in the room lifted measurably.

So why was he here? Damned if he knew. If his friend

Wyatt hadn't recognized Grace's name and called the ambulance for her, if he hadn't called Luke to tell him what had happened, he never would have known. He didn't think Sam would have been that charitable and called him.

He had broken it off with Grace thinking she had lied to him. He missed her terribly and wondered if he had made a mistake. Hell no. He knew he made a mistake. The past couple of weeks without her had been agony. Ben was pissed at him. Hell, even Paul was upset that he broke up with her.

Luke winced at Grace's bandaged wrists and feet and the bruises that had formed on her body. He wanted to kill the son of a bitch who hurt her. Grace looked so fragile lying there all bandaged up. He was in awe of her ingenuity and strength. Not many kidnapped persons knew how to break their ties and escape.

When he found the bastard who did this, well, the bastard would be wishing he was in hell.

He rested his hand lightly on Grace's. "Sweetheart, I am so sorry this happened to you. I promise I'm going to put this guy behind bars as soon as we find him. That is, after I beat the shit out of him."

LUKE WATCHED as Grace woke up slowly and moaned. She glanced around but didn't appear to recognize where she was. The panic in her eyes reflected the horror she had been through—the kidnapping, the zip ties, the duct tape.

He place his hand on her arm. She turned her head slowly.

"Hey."

"Um."

"Sweetheart, your mouth was duct-taped, and your lips are swollen, so don't try to talk."

Grace mumbled something, then settled down and fell back to sleep.

Sam and Grace's other girlfriends had been in and out of the room still giving him the stink eye. They asked him what happened. But he couldn't tell them any more than what Wyatt had told him which was that Grace had run out of the woods, bloody, hysterical and collapsed in front of him. They had gasped. Horror and then pity crossed their faces. That changed to anger and pissed off which was directed at him. He promised them that he and Ben planned to turn over every stone to find out who did this to Grace and why.

Grace was going to be OK. She had to be. Her body would take time to heal but it would. He planned to be there to help her. There was only one small problem, and he would take care of that.

Grace was waking up and trying to talk. Luke couldn't hear her well, so he leaned in. "What is it, sweetheart? Tell me."

She took a shallow breath and whispered, "Well, detective, do you believe me now?"

Then she closed her eyes and fell back asleep.

CHAPTER THIRTY-TWO

Grace's friends had finally left. Thank God. If there was a special hell for exes, Luke knew he was in it. He had a lot of fence-mending to do.

Sam walked into the room with two coffees and handed Luke a cup then sat down on the other side of Grace's bed and glared at him. He had a feeling he was about to get an ass-kicking.

She looked him up and down. "Hmm, a fine predicament we find ourselves in, wouldn't you say?"

LUKE LOOKED LIKE SHIT. Sam took in the dark circles under his eyes and something else. Guilt? Maybe. *How to handle this?* Grace loved the asswipe sitting by her side holding her hand.

Grace had been kicked around like a football in D.C. She knew Grace should get on with her life, but Grace had to make that decision. Luke kicking her out of the house and not believing her was a low blow. He hadn't been in D.C. She had. Her friend had been dealt a devasting one-two-three punch. Intervening with the D.C. police had gotten Sam nowhere. She hadn't been able to get a straight story from anyone.

Sam took great pleasure in mentally beating the shit out of all of them especially asswipe number one, James Moore. Grace's ex-husband.

And Luke, *what to do about him*? Grace loved him. But Sam knew Grace wouldn't stay with someone who didn't believe in her or have her back.

"I'm going to tell you a story about the lies and betrayal Grace endured in D.C. from her work, from her so-called friends, and her prick ex-husband. How the D.C. police hadn't believed her and called her a liar. How she had been kicked around and pointed at like she was a leper."

Sam took a deep breath. "You will not interrupt me. When I finish, if you still believe she lied to you, leave. And never show your face around us again because I will rip your dick from your body and feed it to the sharks."

Then for emphasis, she glowered at him. "I will destroy you."

"Understood?"

LUKE PUT his hands up in defeat. "Got it. You'll rip my dick off. Destroy me." *Whoa. Harsh.* Luke didn't think Sam cared that he was a detective and she was threatening him. He was glad Sam was Grace's friend and protecting her.

Shooting daggers at him, Sam shook her head. "I happen to know Grace loves you. I don't know why because you're a total dick."

Luke looked chastised. "Tell me something I don't know."

Sam nodded. "Just making sure you understand what

happens if my friend gets hurt again by you. I don't care if you're a cop or not."

An hour later, Grace was still asleep, and Sam had filled him in on what happened in D.C. He felt like a heel.

She described how Grace had researched Washington society and outed a couple of crooked politicians before she was scammed on the Senator Irish story.

Listening to Sam tell the story he realized that there were too many coincidences in the Irish story. Luke didn't believe in coincidences. Someone had been out to get Grace but why? Paul probably didn't hear that part of the story. He did say most of what he heard was rumors.

Lots of questions filled his mind while he listened to Sam. He stared at Grace's battered body—wanted to hurl. To have so many bad things happen to her and yet, she continued forward. She was braver than she gave herself credit for.

But, why hadn't the D.C. police believed her? It was impossible for all those things to happen and for someone not to leave a trail.

He had finally tracked down the detective who investigated her case. The detective had nothing good to say about Grace and nothing new to add. Strange. Was someone in the department on the take? Possibly. Wouldn't be the first time.

Did the senator have help from someone in the department to squash evidence? Possible. The police may not have found fingerprints, but they should have gotten phone records, bank records—actually done some investigation. Something was off. Indeed, a lot of somethings were off.

Sam asserted by the time she got the call to come to D.C., Grace was a basket case. Sam offered to help and bring her team up to investigate, but Grace stopped her. Grace also hadn't wanted her family involved, so she never mentioned her problems to them. She wanted to get out of D.C, and Sam had helped her do that. They packed up her things and drove back to Black Pointe.

Luke thought about his friends and family and how lucky he and Grace were to both have people who watched their backs no matter what. Except he hadn't been watching hers. Failure.

Grace was going to have him watching her back from now on whether she liked it or not. Being away from her he realized he loved her even though he had never mentioned love to her. Luke thought Grace had the same feelings. But he had been an ass before they got to talking about love.

He felt they complemented each other. They were perfect in bed, and he smiled to himself remembering all the sex they had that last week they were together. She was loyal and caring, smart and funny. He wanted her in his life to love, cherish and keep safe. Especially safe, and by God, he was going to do just that.

Sam had to leave for an appointment, but Luke had one more important item to discuss. Apparently, he said the right thing, and she signed off on it. Now all he had to do was to get Grace on board.

CHAPTER THIRTY-THREE

Luke sat by Grace's bed. She was still sleeping but moving her arms and moaning. It sounded like Grace was fending off someone and calling for help. A nightmare fueled by a nightmare. He was furious. Furious at the asshole who attacked her. Angry at himself for being a strait-laced, uptight, rigid ass. Furious he hadn't believed her.

Grace was going to be released the next day, and by God, he would be there to pick her up and make things right. Right now, he had a stalker to find, and Grace's friends had promised to come back to stay with her before he had to leave.

Grace slowly opened her eyes and blinked. Piercing shafts of bright light coming through the window hurt her eyes. Wiggling around, she took stock of her aches and pains. Not too bad. The stay in the hospital and medications had helped. The IV was out, and Sam would be there in an hour to bring her home. Sam told her she had installed more security at her condo. So much more, it sounded like if a mouse sneezed, it would set off the alarm.

Stretching, then very carefully putting her feet on the ground to stand, she shuffled to the bathroom. Everything hurt. By the time she got to the sink, she wanted to sit down and cry. Looking in the mirror scared her. She looked like hell—swollen lips, dried blood scattered around her head, scratches, bruises, and bandages everywhere.

Sam had brought her a toothbrush, toothpaste, a hairbrush, and a change of clothes. Doing ordinary things like brushing her teeth made her feel almost human. She moved slowly and removed the hospital gown, changing into sweatpants and a comfy top. Underwear and a shower would have to wait. She was gathering her things when she heard footsteps. She peeked out and saw Luke walking into the room.

"What are you doing here?" Of all the people she expected to see, Luke was last in line. In fact, he wasn't even on her radar.

"I'm driving you home." He had the audacity to smirk.

"Oh no, you're not." Grace picked up her toiletries and hobbled back to the room. "Sam will be here any second. She's driving me home."

"No, she isn't. Nor are your friends. I am." He took out a bag and started packing her toiletries. "Plus, I'm not driving you to your home. I'm bringing you back to my place. You'll be safe there."

Grace snorted. "Safe from who? You? That hasn't worked for me so far."

OUCH. He deserved that. Luke sat down on the bed. "Grace, I'm sorry. I was wrong about you, about us. So very wrong. I made a mistake not listening and believing in you, but I'm listening now." Grace cocked her head, lifted an eyebrow, her arms tight around her body. Disbelief. He had a lot of explaining to do.

"Last night, I had a long talk with Sam. She told me your story, and I believe you both. I'm ashamed to admit I didn't have faith in you. The more I think about it, there are too many coincidences not adding up. I intend to follow up on them and make this right for you, for us. If there is an us." Grace shrunk back making herself as small as possible. Her face reddened. Luke wasn't sure he was convincing her.

He took Grace's hand. "I told Sam how I felt about you. She told me what she would do to me if I ever hurt you again. I promised her that would never happen."

He shuddered. "I gotta tell you, Sam is one scary woman."

"Damn straight." Grace leaned over and pulled on a pair of slippers. "However, I'm not in a place to be very forgiving. So, Sam might forgive you. My friends might forgive you, but I'm not there yet. Maybe I never will be."

Luke sighed. "I know, honey, I know. There is a long list of things I'm sorry for. I'm so sorry I didn't believe you. I'm sorry I didn't have your back. I'm sorry I didn't trust you. But I intend to make it up to you every day. Please think about giving me, us, another chance."

COULD SHE TRUST LUKE? She had let her guard down with him before, became vulnerable and let him in. Look where that got her. But she loved him.

Her whole life had been about redemption, justice and second chances. Did he deserve that too? She wasn't sure. Taking a deep breath and against her better judgment, she nodded.

But she was going to have a little "come to Jesus" talk with Sam. Sam should have informed her that Luke was picking her up and taking her to his home.

Although if she had known, perhaps sneaking out of the hospital would have been a good idea and safer for her heart.

CHAPTER THIRTY-FOUR

Grace had been at Luke's for two weeks. Overall, her body had healed well, except for her mind.

She jumped at every little noise. She didn't go out alone after dark, and if she went to events or interviews, Luke, Ben or another friend went with her. Steve had insisted that she take more time off, but she needed to stay busy. The isolation and fear couldn't go on. It had taken her too long to feel in control. This scaredy-cat routine had to stop except she didn't know how to stop it.

Also, she didn't know what was happening with her case. Had the police any luck finding the stalker? Had they solved Jean's murder yet? Was she still a suspect?

The door opened, and Luke came in shaking rain from his hair. "It's coming down so hard I could hardly see the road."

Grace was pacing. Nothing gave her peace anymore. Staying at Luke's made her feel secure, but she had to step up and take control of her life.

"Babe, what's wrong? Did something happen?" He went over and hugged her while guiding her to the sofa.

She shook her head, taking a moment to answer. "Luke, I

can't live like this. I can't go anywhere without being afraid. I'm constantly looking over my shoulder. I hate asking people to go with me everywhere. That's not the way I want to live my life, afraid of my own shadow. I've worked too hard to overcome these feelings." She took a big gulp. "And I've been afraid to ask how my case was coming along."

SHIT, he felt like a heel. He was guilty of being negligent in not keeping her up to date on her case. He kissed her forehead. "You've been cleared. I'm so sorry I didn't tell you sooner. Richard and Diane are also cleared. But we don't have any more information on who kidnapped you. He's clever. I'll give you that. No fingerprints, no clues left behind, nothing to identify him. But we're on it, and it's a matter of time before he screws up."

Grace nodded, tears running down her cheeks.

Luke's heart was breaking. Grace was right. She had come so far, and to be frightened again wasn't fair. He clasped his hands in front of his face. He knew what he had to do. He had been thinking about it since Grace came out of the hospital.

"I'm taking you to the range tomorrow. Plus, I'm going to ask Pete to give you self-defense lessons. You need basic skills to defend yourself and get your confidence back."

Grace's eyes widened. "I've never held a gun before. I don't know if I could kill somebody."

"Honey, I'm not asking you to kill anyone, just learn to handle a gun so you can protect yourself." Luke could kick himself. He wanted Grace to feel safe not panic even more. But if she were empowered to protect herself, it would be a huge step in her recovery.

Sighing, Grace looked down at her hands. "I can't believe

my life has come to this—learning to shoot, physical self-defense. There was a time when I believed words were strong enough to take care of problems."

Luke reached over and raised Grace's face toward him. "Grace, words are powerful, and writing is what you're good at. But there is nothing wrong with knowing how to defend yourself. It's a wild, wild west out there. Everyone needs to be prepared to defend themselves. Especially if the police aren't around."

NODDING, she relaxed. Luke's hands were warm and felt like home on her face. She looked into his eyes, and those baby blues weren't babies anymore. There was grown-up male heat there, probably the same heat reflected in her eyes.

Not waiting for Luke to get closer, she clasped his face and kissed him softly. He was surprised but didn't pull away.

"Grace," he said, pulling her even closer. "I hope this means you want me, honey. Because I'm going crazy here with need for you."

They had been sleeping in Luke's bed because she was afraid. Just sleeping, not having sex. She hadn't been ready for sex. When she had woken up in the guest room screaming the first night she stayed here, Luke had carried her into his bed and held her tightly until she fell asleep.

Grace could tell Luke was holding back. Holding back for her—his face a fusion of want, indecisiveness, and lust. She kissed him again putting more desire into it and then he took over. The heat in his eyes was now on his lips. Hot, hot heat. His tongue sought refuge in her mouth. She opened for him and entwined her tongue around his in that age-old dance of love. He kissed like a man dying for a drink of water. His passion was overwhelming. When he slipped his hands under her shirt and pulled her bra up to caress her nipples, she lost it. She had been too long without sex, without Luke inside her and she wanted. Him. Now.

"Luke," she groaned, "please take me now."

Laughing, Luke pulled away. "Oh no, honey. I've been waiting for you, and I want to spend hours getting reacquainted with your beautiful body."

"Aaagh. Please, I can't wait." She was hot. She was on fire. She was not above begging.

Luke stood up and held out his hand. "Honey, I want to take you bent over this table, and that one and that one but tonight, we're making love in my, our, bed."

She placed her hand in his and followed him down the hall.

CHAPTER THIRTY-FIVE

Grace never felt so beaten and weak in her entire life but in a positive way. She and Pete had been working out for a week, and the only thing she had to show for it were aches, bruises, and more bruises.

Luckily for her, Luke kissed each new and old bruise every night. There was something to be said for having your boo-boos kissed. Of course, he kissed other things too. Thinking about the other things he kissed distracted her enough that Pete was able to attack her from behind and throw her to the ground.

"Oooooff." Grace huffed.

Pete gave her the mad face he was perfecting and growled. "Grace, you have to be aware of your surroundings all the time. We're trying to help you, but you need to pay attention, not think about lover boy over there." He held out his hand to help her up.

"Hey," Luke, the so-called lover boy, yelled. "You're jealous. Stop fooling around with my woman and get back to work."

Then smiling at her, Luke said: "Grace, honey, pay attention to the mean man."

Pete gave him the one-finger salute.

Conveniently, for them, Luke had turned an unused large living space into his home to a makeshift gym with weights and mats. Grace didn't think she would be doing quite as well if other people were watching her and mentally laughing at her.

Pete and Grace practiced another half hour, then Pete had to leave. As he was gathering his things, he patted her shoulder and told her she was coming along.

Luke had kept his promise to teach her to shoot. Finding the right-size gun was the first issue. She had small hands, and Luke's Glock 22 was a little too big and bulky. They decided on a Smith & Wesson 9mm. The first few times she aimed at the target, she shot a little wide. But with Luke standing behind her and holding her steady, she was getting better. She also completed the conceal and carry class and got her license. Thinking about having a gun on her person was disturbing but losing her life would be more so.

There had been no sign of her stalker. Grace hoped he moved on when he couldn't find her. She took different routes to work each day and kept Luke informed about her work schedule. Luke or one of his friends checked on her when they could. KnightGuard Security was flat-out busy. Sam hired new employees that were in training, so she didn't have anyone extra to watch Grace full time, but she helped when she could.

KEN WAS AGITATED. Sitting in the coffee shop across from Grace's office was boring. He came here every day with his computer, pretending to work.

He knew Grace went to the office most days. He saw her a few times when he went in to talk to Mary, but he didn't want to be conspicuous. It pleased him to sit at Mary's desk and watch Grace out of the corner of his eye. She always searched her desk before she sat down, and it delighted him to no end when she did. Mary didn't know much about Grace's schedule and wasn't a close friend, so she was no help in that respect. At least, she provided him with sexual entertainment.

He didn't dare go back to Grace's condo. He knew they had found the cameras and mics as well as the tracker on her emails. Ken also hadn't seen Grace's car recently, so he figured she was staying with someone. He had checked out her friends' places, but it didn't look like Grace was staying with them, so she had to be with the dick—a much better description than detective, he mused.

What could he do? He couldn't stay in this backwater town forever. He was low on funds, and Rachel was unhappy. At least Mary was satisfied with a good fucking. Plus, he didn't have to treat her to dinner. Thankfully, she was pleasing to the eye and loved cock. He could provide a hard cock in abundance, and just thinking about Grace and Mary got him hard. *Maybe Mary was up for some afternoon delight?*

He wanted to get back to D.C., back to Rachel, back to the energy, the making, and breaking of deals and lives. Back to what was left of his power base. Black Pointe was provincial. He had no power base here, and he didn't know the political players. He had no dirt on anyone here. He missed Rachel. Flying to D.C. several times to see her kept her satisfied but she was getting tired of waiting. She had always been there for him. Especially when she helped destroy Grace's reputation in D.C. However, he didn't think she would be happy knowing he was taking it to another level.

He was concerned about the job he interviewed for with that lobbyist firm. They weren't going to wait forever for him to return. It was a respectable position, enough to please even his status-conscious father; that is if he were still around. Not the same as working for a congressman or senator, but that bridge was crossed when Irish decided to off himself. *Stupid man. He couldn't wait it out or keep it in his pants. No bitch was worth dying for.*

CHAPTER THIRTY-SIX

Luke had just poured Grace a glass of wine in the kitchen when Sam walked in with Danny and Pete for dinner. She walked over and gave them all a hug. Ben had called earlier to say he couldn't make it; he was working another case and promised to touch base tomorrow. Tonight, they were going to talk strategy, and they were hoping to resolve this stalker issue once and for all with Sam's resources. Grace hadn't wanted to involve KnightGuard Security, but the police were at an impasse. Luke was trying to do everything possible to resolve this and move forward, but they had both agreed outside help was needed.

They all moved to the lanai with their drinks while Luke grilled steaks on the patio. The evening was chilly, and there was a slight mist over the river.

Grace scooched back into the soft pillow on the sofa and looked around at her friends who were talking and laughing. She was thankful for their help. The past couple of weeks living at Luke's had been restorative, and the benefits were awesome. He was a considerate lover and never failed to please her. By the noises he made when she went down on him and took control, she pleased him too.

But it wasn't just the sex. Luke was doing everything he could to prove to Grace that he believed her and had her back. He was not too proud to ask Sam for help. She had people, and resources and didn't mind going into gray areas his captain would shudder at.

Grace had a chance to reflect on all that happened with Luke and the fact they were in a good place right now. *Could it get any better than this?* OK, yes, there was that small fact her stalker was roaming around but still, the evening was perfect.

The group devoured the steaks and salad, then moved from the table to the fire pit to have coffee.

"Luke, Grace," Sam started, "Danny has some free time, and volunteered to spend it on your case."

Grace looked over at Danny and mouthed "thank you." He smiled back at her. "Anything for you, Grace. We all want to catch this bastard."

Luke spoke up. "We'd love the help, but I'm not sure what Danny is going to be able to do that we haven't been able to do already. We already have someone with Grace at night when she has an event. She's living here now. I have good security, and her office is aware of the stalker. This guy is smart. He doesn't call, so there are no phone records. He knows where the security cameras are, and he either gets innocent people to drop off the notes or does it himself. No one seems to know him. We have to wait to see what he does next."

"You're right Luke, but an extra pair of eyes won't hurt. Danny can monitor the street in front of Grace's office and follow her if needed. We're checking into everyone Grace ever dealt with in D.C. and here." Sam took a sip of wine. "I heard the police found the motel room where Grace was held."

Luke grimaced. "Yeah, it was wiped clean. They didn't find even a pinkie print. No one saw the guy. The security cameras were half-assed, and a couple not even working. The motel was a bust, and we still have no clue where he is holed up."

They discussed other ideas, but without the stalker making any contact, it was hard to put specific plans in place.

Another hour passed, and they firmed up a tentative strategy. Sam stood up, declaring it was getting late and she had a busy morning planned which started the goodbye train in motion.

Hugging her best friend goodbye, Grace promised to keep her up to date and to connect with Danny the next day.

Picking up the few dishes on the table, Grace walked into the kitchen and put them in the dishwasher. Warm arms surrounded her, and Luke nuzzled her neck. "You are the most courageous person I know. You're taking control of your life, getting involved in new work, not letting this creep get to you."

He whispered gently against her neck, "And having great sex with me."

Grace turned and smiled. "Just great?"

Luke put his hands on her face and pulled her closer. He tilted her head and gently, thoroughly kissed her cheeks, her eyebrows and her forehead. "No, it's been fantastic, amazing, incredible, magical."

"Enough!" she said and closed the gap between them, rubbing her hands down his chest, snaking down beneath his shorts to caress his rock-hard cock.

He groaned and pulled her even closer.

His insistent tongue separated her lips. She opened for him, and with the intensity, only lovers could understand, he kissed her with heart and soul. He tasted like coffee, sweet and hot.

He pulled slightly away and lavished kisses on her face.

She sniffed him. Inhaled his masculine, clean scent she would recognize anywhere even if she were blind.

Luke laughed. "Did you just sniff me?"

Grace smiled, sniffed him again and then kissed him lightly.

Turning the table, Luke showered her with bold, hard kisses and silky sweet kisses. His lips were soft and tender. Grace couldn't catch her breath, but she wanted this to go on forever. Then he stopped.

She missed his lips and kisses already. Luke ran his fingers up her arms and through her hair. Then he ran them down her side and caressed her backside. His eyes were dilated, liquid blue and shining with love. He smiled, his eyes crinkling. The corner of his mouth upturned; the dimple on his right cheek deepened.

He picked up her hand, brought it to his lips and kissed the back of it. "Grace, I need you."

He kissed her brows. Reaching down for her bottom, he lifted her to the counter. Laying her back, he pulled down the long skirt she was wearing. While he was down there, he nuzzled her mound through her panties.

"Oh yeah, baby, you're so wet."

Grace nodded and groaned. "Please."

Pulling down her lace panties, he spread her legs and used his tongue on her clit.

"Please," Grace moaned.

Luke lifted his head, licked his lips. "Ah, not yet. I have more exploring to do." He bent down to do just that. He licked and sucked and ran his hands under her bra, squeezing her nipples. Then repeated the process.

Grace didn't think she could handle any more of his "exploring." She sat up and grabbed his head and growled, "Now."

Luke laughed. Bending her over the table, he pulled a condom from his pocket, sheathed himself, and pulled her closer. Then plunged his cock into her folds.

Grace moaned. This was heaven. Nirvana. Ecstasy. Rapture. Paradise. Call it whatever.

IT WAS BORING as hell to protect someone from afar. Danny Knight sat in the corner window seat of Cool Beans, the coffee shop across from the newspaper's office. It had only been one day. There had been no action yesterday. And it looked like today was shaping up to be a repeat. He needed action. It was pouring cats and dogs out there. At least he was dry. It was still the rainy season in Florida.

From his vantage point, he could keep an eye on the patrons in the cafe as well as any lingerers outside who might have an interest in Grace. A bank of windows flanked the street, so practically any seat gave him a good view of Grace's office. Grace had mentioned that many of the journalists came here for meetings or to get coffee to go.

He looked around the lively café. There was a cacophony of noise, Baroque music playing in the background, whirring machines pumping out espressos and cappuccinos, and people talking and laughing. Most were shaking off rain as they came in. The whitewashed brick walls with the open shelves for cups and plates and homemade plank tables were modern enough to look chic and still gave a homey feel to the place. Looking around, he noticed half a dozen people intently studying their laptops. People were in and out of the shop with hot cups of coffee in their hands.

He watched Grace walk up to her building, shake her umbrella and enter. He loved Grace as a friend now although in middle school he had a crush on her. Since he was two years older than Grace, he was in high school and on to older girls when she moved away.

His mind wandered to a certain blond-haired brown-eyed BookShop owner. Hailey Marshall. He was in love with Hailey, not that she knew. She was funny, quiet, compassionate, smart. And so not into him. Rebuffed after trying for months to get her to see him as more than a casual date, Danny needed to find a way to move the relationship along. Lately, there was sadness about her, and he wanted to know who or what put it there.

Oh well. Right now he had to concentrate on Grace. His concern for Hailey would be on the back burner until they caught this creep, then he would find out what was putting the sadness in Hailey's eyes.

At least Grace was safe this morning. Danny would stay here until she left at noon for whatever appointments she had and then someone else would take over. Ben and Luke had been taking turns when they had free time. Sam tried to beef up security on her end, but KnightGuard Security was stretched thin until the new employees were trained.

He opened his laptop and settled in.

CHAPTER THIRTY-SEVEN

After a week of surveying the clientele at Cool Beans, Danny could recognize several regulars. A blond-haired, tattooed woman would come in at 9 a.m., order a blueberry scone and sit in a seat at the second table from the door. Weird, but he guessed it was her lucky table. Two other tables were occupied by businessmen also with laptops. A couple of male college-age students took refuge closer to the kitchen and stared at the pretty barista. One grandma with a toddler came in around 10 a.m. for hot chocolate. Another dark-haired man sat by the door, and he was there early almost every morning too. The tables by the bank of windows were sought after spots, and he had to get there early to claim his seat.

Doodling on the paper in front of him, Danny saw Grace exit her office building. He was about to call Luke when he noticed the dark-haired man sitting by the door hurriedly pack up and leave. The man stopped, looked for traffic and crossed the street in front of the newspaper. Shit, was this Grace's stalker? Could he get this lucky? He hoped so.

He closed his laptop, stood and got ready to dash out

when he saw the man stop and kiss a blond-haired woman on the sidewalk. Arm in arm, they walked in the opposite direction—*false alarm.*

Danny sat down again. It was going to be a long morning. He was drinking so much coffee he had a caffeine high going. He called Luke to tell him Grace had left, and Luke informed him they were on it.

UNDER ANY OTHER CIRCUMSTANCE, Ken would have loved the chic but homey Cool Beans. It reminded him of a little place in D.C. he and Rachel frequented. Today, though, he was tired of drinking way too much coffee and trying to determine Grace's schedule. Mary was no help.

Ken noticed Grace leaving the building. Not wanting to be too obvious, he didn't jump up and follow her. If she was walking, then she was coming back. He would wait a little while longer. Soon, though, she was bound to make a mistake.

He knew from the conversation he and Mary had with Grace the other day that she got her car back from the garage. The parking lot for the building was in the rear. No one saw him place his little present under her bumper. Again, avoiding security cameras was a piece of cake. Disguises were his new best idea. Ken was ecstatic. Putting the GPS on her car was probably the most brilliant idea he ever had.

So last night he was able to shadow her, following a few cars behind. The bitch never observed him tailing her to the cop's house. He would never have known it was the cop's house, but driving by, he noticed the truck he had seen Grace riding in.

Weird, what was she doing with the cop?

Going over several scenarios, Ken decided he wanted to make the cop suffer too. The cop believed he was so smart having Grace stay at his house. Well, as Yogi Bear said, he was "smarter than the average bear." Planning how he would kill them both made him smile. Should he kill the cop first? Or Grace?

IT WAS EARLY MONDAY. Same time, same place, almost the same patrons, and Danny had nothing. He was bored. Surveillance was a big part of the job, but he wanted some excitement.

He was about to take a sip of yet another cup of coffee when he noticed Grace leaving. The usual suspects were in their seats. All interested in whatever they were doing. No one seemed to be looking at Grace. Then one of the brown-haired men who was a regular packed up his laptop and walked out, strolling across the street. Was he going to follow Grace?

Danny readied himself to follow but stopped. Instead of trailing Grace, the man walked into the newspaper office. What was he doing in there? Did he work there? Danny didn't think so because the man hadn't gone over to the office any other time.

Danny didn't believe the stalker would have the audacity to walk into Grace's workplace. But who knew? There were a lot of strange ducks out there. At least the man hadn't followed Grace.

Ten minutes later Grace walked back to the newspaper. Danny saw the man and a woman coming out of the building and greet Grace at the front door. They stood there talking for about five minutes. Grace went in, and the couple left.

Another false alarm.

It was a brilliant idea. Walk into Grace's office to pick up Mary for a little R&R, and hope Grace would get back before they left. He saw Grace leave; she usually didn't go far or stay out of the office for long.

He called Mary, who was always up for sex. She told him to come up to the newsroom and meet her. The bitch liked to show him off like a prized pig. He planned on that. He sauntered up to Mary's desk, and she welcomed him with a big smile. She was finishing a police report and talking about the jogger murder case. He loved hearing the details and knowing the police were stumped.

Mary finished, closed her computer and stood to gather her purse. They stepped out the front door just as Grace was walking up. They stopped to talk to Grace for a few minutes. He loved this. The fact that Grace didn't particularly like him made him smile although she was too polite not to talk to him. The conversation segued into what Grace and Mary were working on and what events Grace was covering.

Perfect. Another perfect day.

CHAPTER THIRTY-EIGHT

Danny was still at Cool Beans every morning that Grace was in her office. He was on a hello basis with most of the regulars. The grandma who came in with her grandson for hot chocolate. The two writers who never stopped drinking espressos and typing. The young woman who worked at the clothing shop next door and was constantly checking her phone and there was Mary's boyfriend who stopped in a couple of times a week for coffee, then walked over to meet her. Weird guy. Sat there with his laptop, staring out the window watching for Mary. Wheezing and using an inhaler.

However, he still hadn't seen anything unusual. Everyone in the café seemed to have a legitimate reason to be there.

Danny was bored, and if he never drank another cup of coffee, it would be all right with him. Christ, even the smell of coffee was starting to turn his stomach. Danny wanted something, anything to happen. Although as surveillance went, sitting in an air-conditioned coffee shop while it was hot and steamy outside beat some of his other assignments' hands down.

Looking over at the newspaper building again, Danny

noticed the front door opening and Grace walking out with Mary. Out of the corner of his eye, he saw motion. Mary's boyfriend seemed to have perked up. Danny watched the boyfriend get up, throw his trash away and scurry across the street. Grace's interaction with the guy was curious too. Danny could tell she was uncomfortable around the guy, always seemed hesitant to stay and talk, then hurried on her way. Today was no different.

What was going on? The man's eyes were on Grace even when he was kissing Mary. Interesting.

Funny he hadn't caught that before. Danny took a few minutes to go over his copious notes of all the days, and hours the regulars stopped by for coffee. Now that he had a potential suspect, he noticed a pattern and realized the boyfriend was only in the coffee shop and met Mary when Grace was scheduled to be in the office.

Coincidence? Maybe. However, in Danny's experience, there were no coincidences. He decided to give it a week to double-check when the boyfriend came into the coffee shop. If he was right, this might be the opening they needed. He would call Grace later to ask about Mary's boyfriend.

CHAPTER THIRTY-NINE

Luke and Ben were chasing their tails. They had nothing new in Grace's case. They had checked and rechecked every lead they had. Richard Marsh and Diane Benoit had alibied. The police cleared Grace. They had no distinct fingerprints on most of the evidence that they collected from the crime scene. The couple of good prints they got where not in the system.

They were researching people Jean Mays knew or may have known in Black Pointe and D.C. They drew a blank on her too. She was too new to Black Pointe to have many friends except for Diane and Richard. It seemed like she was freelancing a bit. Some journalists knew Jean and weren't flattering in their description of her. They couldn't find any friends in D.C. to talk to or those they find, weren't friends and didn't want to talk about Jean—they were striking out everywhere.

Luke had a nagging feeling D.C. was still the key to this case. Jean had worked there; both Grace and the mysterious man worked there too. They were all journalists. Grace knew

Jean, albeit under a different name. Jean knew the unnamed man, but Grace didn't know who it was.

Diane had mentioned Jean was afraid of him. Why was Jean afraid of him? How were they all connected? Were they even connected? At some point, he believed he and Grace needed to make a trip up north and talk to people she had worked with.

Grace's car was back from the shop. Ever since her brakes failed, one thing or another had gone wrong with it. Annoying for Grace but he welcomed seeing her more. Taking on the investigative side of reporting seemed to excite her, and she got up each morning ready to go. Her confidence was back and her smile, wow, her smile. She had blossomed into the woman she must have been before all the problems she had in D.C.

Their relationship was solid, and he valued the time spent with Grace and their friends. Her friends were accepting him —slowly, but it was still better than nothing. It would take time, but they were coming around to the fact he was in the relationship to stay. His friends were more accepting, and he had been surprised when Ben acknowledged he liked her a lot.

The sex was decent too. *Hell no*. The sex was beyond decent; it was phenomenal and satisfying. The passionate, sexy side of Grace had taken him by surprise. She loved sex, loved making him come, loved having him go down on her. Watching her orgasm one or two times before they got to making love was awe-inspiring. She took everything he gave and returned it ten-fold.

God, he loved her. What he wanted more than anything was to catch this son of a bitch and keep Grace safe.

It was still the rainy season in Florida, and torrential showers had pummeled the city the last two days. He had driven Grace to work earlier. They had plans to meet Ben at Neptune's Navel down on a marina at Riverwalk. His friend Jake Summers owned the popular hot spot, and many of the cops hung out there. The bonus of the river view was usually appreciated, but with all the rain, it wouldn't matter today.

Luke pulled in front of Grace's building and called her on his cell to come out. Running out, Grace opened the car door shaking her umbrella before she placed it on the floor. Putting her seat belt on, she turned and gave him a big smile and kiss. Even though they had made love in the shower this morning, Luke was ready to skip meeting Ben, take Grace home and rub his body all over hers again. Unfortunately, he promised Ben they would meet. Sex would have to wait. Ben had been working on some other parts of the case and wanted to go over the details. Plus, the Navel was fun, and they needed some downtime.

"I haven't seen Ben in a while. It'll be good to get together with him," said Grace. Although Ben and Grace hadn't hit it off right away, they were tight now. "What do you think he wants to discuss?"

"Don't know. Ben said some new details on Jean's case have come up."

Luke was a careful driver. The rain hid a number of potholes in the road, so he was driving slowly to avoid them. Thankfully, the streets were nearly empty because of the storm.

He was surprised to look in his mirror and see a white SUV close to his bumper. "Asshole. Doesn't he see how hard it's raining, and realize the roads are slippery?"

He slowed down, put his flashers on, opened the window and motioned for the SUV to pass. No luck. Luke sped up. But the SUV kept up with him. *Odd.*

His hands started sweating, and he fought to keep them on the steering wheel. He looked again. The SUV was a huge hulk in his rear-view mirror, and it appeared to be aiming straight at them. *Damn. The rain brought out all the weirdos.*

Grace turned around. "Oh my God, Luke. I think he's going to hit us."

She no sooner said that when the SUV slammed into them. Grace screamed.

"Shit." Luke was pissed. He tried to move over, but the SUV seemed to be attached to his bumper. He couldn't see the driver's face. It looked like the asshole had a hat pulled low on his forehead. The sheeting rain made everything harder to see. It finally pulled away.

Luke slowed down, hoping to stop and gauge the damage to his truck.

Bam. The SUV's second strike was harder. It forced Luke's truck toward a cement barrier. He tried to steer away from it. He stomped on the brakes. But he couldn't stop. The SUV just kept pushing. He could hear his tires screeching, trying to find purchase on the wet pavement.

"Shit," he yelled. "Grace, hands in front of your face. Now. We're going to crash."

No sooner had he said that when Luke's truck was smashed into the barrier and it abruptly stopped. Steam hissed from the engine.

Their airbags had deployed. Luke took a deep breath, realized he was OK, then looked over at Grace. She looked dazed and had some cuts on her face and hands.

His heart was racing. He opened his door to give it to the asshole in the SUV. But the jerk had backed off and was now hightailing it down the street.

Luke was livid. Could this day get any worse? The heavy rain had made them late. Now some asshole had rear-ended them and drove away. He was going to have to call this in, wait for the police and file a report. They were lucky not to be hurt. However, the right side of his truck was mangled and crushed. He reached over to help Grace out from the driver's side.

"Baby, are you OK? Anything broken?"

Grace shook her head, water droplets spraying everywhere.

Grabbing his cell phone, he called 911. The cops arrived a few minutes before Ben. Since he didn't catch any numbers on the license plate, Luke could only tell the police it was a white SUV, probably with front-end damage.

The torrent of rain hadn't let up. Luke didn't think he could get wetter, but the rain was proving him wrong. He could barely see ten feet in front of him.

He glanced over at Grace and noticed she had taken her umbrella out. It was a little too late to stay dry. Her hair was stringy and hanging down her shoulders, and her clothes melded to her body. She was shivering, and Luke could see bruises forming on her face and hands. He was seriously going to hurt whoever the asshole was when he found him. Luke got out another rain jacket from the back seat and covered her shoulders. He motioned to Ben and told her to sit in Ben's car and warm up while he dealt with the police.

Luke had time to think while waiting for the tow truck. If he was a betting man, and he was, this attack was personal. There were no other cars on the road, and the SUV had aimed directly at them. This harassment was getting worse and had to stop—first Grace and now him. They had no idea who this creep was, but Luke suspected it was Grace's stalker and he was ramping up the harassment. And, he seemed to know a lot about them and their movements.

CHAPTER FORTY

Ken pulled his cock out of Mary, praying she wouldn't want to cuddle, and he could leave; however, that wasn't going to happen today. Mary was a cuddler. He suspected she was in love with him. Forcing a smile, he kissed her. And she enthusiastically kissed him back and got up to make him breakfast in bed. He didn't mind being waited on and oh Lord, he was hard again. Sex with Mary was so convenient.

He was going to have to break it off with her soon. His job here was almost finished. He couldn't wait to get back to D.C. and Rachel. *Ah, Rachel. He missed her so much.*

He lay on the bed, hands behind his head waiting for breakfast and another go at Mary. The previous day repeatedly replayed in his head. He had gotten such a rush when the stupid cop finally realized he was being pushed into the cement barrier.

Ken didn't want to kill them. Yet. He wanted to have a little fun and show the cop he couldn't control the situation. After driving the cop's truck into the barrier, he took off fast praying the cops wouldn't catch him before he could abandon the SUV. He had covered the license plate with tape, but it didn't matter since he had stolen the SUV from some stupid person who left the keys in it. *What was wrong with people today?*

His "Destroy Winslow Project" was almost over. He only needed to come up with a strategy to finish it. Seeing Grace's byline in the paper infuriated him. How dare she take up investigative reporting again? How many lives was she going to ruin before she was happy?

Smiling, he relished thinking about a little more harassment of Grace and the cop before he would take care of Grace Winslow permanently and get on with his life.

CHAPTER FORTY-ONE

Luke scratched his head, his hands sweating. He stared at Grace who was sitting on the sofa doing a crossword puzzle. She looked so peaceful. He knew she wasn't going to like what he was going to suggest.

Taking the plunge, he said, "Grace, we need to go to D.C."

It was a minute before she answered. Had she heard him? He opened his mouth to repeat what he said.

"No." She said emphatically. Grace put the puzzle down and swiped at her reddening face. She glared at him. He wasn't sure if he upset her or if she was afraid to go.

"Sweetheart." Luke sat down next to her and took her hand in his. "We all believe your problems in D.C. relate to your stalker, and that's where we'll get answers."

"I'm not going." Grace clasped her arms around her chest.

Oookay, this was going to be difficult.

Luke watched her fiddle with her necklace and twirled her hair. Then she smoothed down her pants. All the while looking everywhere but at him. *Classic delays*. He dove into the tempest again.

"I'm going anyway, but I would appreciate it if you would

come with me. You will have insight into situations I might not pick up on."

She looked at him with such sadness in her eyes, he almost took it back. But she needed to address the fear, and they had to resolve this harassment.

"Luke, I was pummeled there. I lost everything. I don't want to rehash my greatest failures again. I'm barely getting my life back."

He felt like he was banging his head against a wall.

"Grace, you are a lot stronger than you realize. Things are going well. Take a day or two and think about it, but I want to leave by the weekend. I need to book a flight and hotel." He wasn't above begging or kidnapping her and putting her on the plane. But he hoped Grace would come to this decision herself to go with him.

"Please, I would like you to come with me. I promise I won't let anybody hurt you."

Grace stood up and turned to him. "Luke, I know you're trying to help, but I left D.C. with nothing. No dignity, no reputation, no marriage, no job. Nothing. I've tried to make a good life here, but if we don't find this creep, I will have no problem moving again so he can't endanger those close to me or find me."

"Grace ..."

She put up her hand. "No. Let me think about this."

She got up from the couch, clenching and unclenching her hands, then looked at her watch. "Luke, I have to go. I'm meeting Sam at her place."

With that, she turned and stomped out.

Sam sat across from Grace and watched her friend twirl her wineglass. "You know Luke is right. This problem started in

D.C. Going there with a fresh mind and another person will make things clearer."

"I don't want to go."

"Sweetie, this problem isn't going away. You can't run from it. You can't hide. This creep will follow you wherever you go. You have to take a stand. You've built a great life here. You have people who will stand with you. Don't let this scumbag drag you any down again."

"I'm afraid. I'm mad as hell, and I want to beat the crap out of this creep," Grace admitted, "but I'm not sure I can or want to put myself through the embarrassment again."

"Grace, I understand, but you can't keep pushing down your emotions. You've been doing great since you took on more responsibility at work. You have a great relationship with Luke. It's time to get to the bottom of this and truly enjoy life again. Otherwise, the creep wins."

Sam tried to inject a little forcefulness into her voice without pissing Grace off. "You need to get some closure and empower yourself."

Grace rubbed her arms, "I don't want to go. It will be embarrassing to see all those people again."

"It'll be worse if this creep decides to kill you."

"There is that." Grace sighed heavily, "You and Luke are right. I'll think about going."

"That's all we can ask," Sam said. She was going to touch base with Luke again to come up with an argument that would convince Grace to go. Grace had to confront the past and put it behind her.

GRACE HAD to check on her condo, which had been empty for a couple of weeks. Luke was going to meet her there. Then they were going out to dinner and back to his house.

She rubbed her brow. The headache that had been haunting her for days was tightening around her forehead. Luke was going to want an answer from her, but he was going to be disappointed. Sam hadn't convinced her to go to D.C., and nothing Luke could add would persuade her to go.

Grace was only in the condo a short time before the doorbell rang. She opened the door just as Luke was pushing the bell again. He looked at her, anger emanated from him, and he kept running his hands through his hair. He was breathing heavily, and his face was flushed.

"Grace," he said, nearly growling as he came through the door. "I need to know the truth about D.C."

"Why?"

He pulled her into a hug. "Because I love you. Because I want you to be safe. Because you and I both know what's happening now is a continuation of something that happened in D.C. We need to figure out why you're being stalked and harassed. The harassment started after the exposé on the senator was published. Why? Was someone protecting the senator? Was something else going on?"

Grace took Luke's hand and sat down on the couch. She needed to pull herself together.

HE LOVED HER, but there were too many coincidences, betrayals, and deceptions. And they all started in D.C.

Going down once on that particular road with Becky was enough. He and Grace had to be honest and trust each other for their relationship to work. He had already made a huge mistake with Grace. Now it was her turn, to be honest, and trust him.

Luke sat across from her and crossed his legs. Paul had already told him enough for him to understand the deceit

Grace experienced. Sam had filled in more of the blanks, but he still needed to hear the whole truth from Grace. He would stand by her and love her, but he had to clear the slate today. Period.

Luke kept going back to the fact Jean was from D.C. The stalker knew Jean. Did Jean know the stalker? And who was this Rachel Lang who betrayed Grace? Why did she betray Grace? Jean, Rachel and this other unknown had to be connected.

None of it made sense. Why didn't Grace admit it and protect herself? Why would she keep what happened to her from him? It was going to stop tonight. It had to stop. They couldn't move forward with their relationship if they couldn't be honest or trust each other. Luke was going out on a limb here. Grace had to step up to the plate and trust him with her secrets.

"Um," Grace blew out a small breath. "This is so painful. I hate reliving the most embarrassing time of my life. I know Sam told you what she knew. And, to be honest, I do agree with you that this harassment started in D.C."

Over the next hour, Grace went through the highs of rising up the ranks from newbie to accepting the position of investigative reporter. She described the thrill of uncovering unethical behavior in Washington and receiving the accolades of her coworkers and boss made her life exciting and meaningful.

Then her downfall. Publishing what she hoped was an award-winning story exposing the senator and his dirty secrets. His fighting back. Her publisher asking for her notes. Rachel not producing most of her sources to corroborate Grace's investigation. The whistleblower had disappeared. Her publisher calling her in and firing her. The betrayal of her coworkers and the newspaper still hurt.

She described the methods the stalker used to drive her

crazy and how the police couldn't find any evidence. "The police told me they thought I just wanted to draw the attention away from my failure." Her voice broke. "The investigating detective dismissed obvious clues. Then I was blamed for the senator taking his life." She wiped a tear from her eye and shook her head. "It was almost the worst period in my life."

Luke knew most of Grace's story having heard it from Sam but hearing it from Grace's point of view was heartbreaking. He believed her. Having his brothers in blue not take her case seriously or worse, purposely ignoring the facts was embarrassing and made him angry.

Grace crossed and uncrossed her legs, fiddled with a pillow. He sensed there was more to her story. The silence continued for several minutes.

GRACE TRIED hard to keep herself calm. Getting agitated wasn't helping. She didn't want to confess the rest of it to Luke. If anything could rub her soul raw, that was it.

"You know I was married before." Her voice quaked. She swiped more tears. "We met in college and married after I graduated. We were so in love. He was on track to being nominated a state's attorney when the article blew apart, I believed him when he said he would stand by me."

"Boy, I was a fool. When I was fired from my job and not able to get another, his chances of getting the judgeship became slim to none. Having a wife whose reputation was ruined, especially in the political arena was a disaster to his career. The women I thought were my friends avoided me. Then James had me served divorce papers."

"The worst thing was," Grace stopped and inhaled deeply, "I had just found out I was pregnant. A couple of weeks later

I lost the baby. I guess I could blame it on stress, although it might have happened anyhow. It seemed like a punishment for ruining lives, mine included."

As if the confession couldn't get more embarrassing, she couldn't control the hot tears flowing down her cheeks.

"I felt I was a total failure at life and work. No one had my back. I was alone."

Grace couldn't stop the tears flowing. Her ex-husband's betrayal hurt the most. He promised to love her. His betrayal and lack of trust had sideswiped her. He hadn't believed in her and wouldn't stand up for her.

Luke pulled Grace onto his lap.

"Shhhh, it's OK sweetheart. Your ex gets the all-around prize for being an asshole. That was low. I'm sorry you had to go through everything alone." Wiping her tears with his thumb, Luke continued, "I'm so sorry you lost your baby."

Grace didn't think she could ever trust someone again, but somehow, she found Luke. Their relationship initially was built on lies and distrust. It had been broken and rebuilt. It was strong. They believed and trusted each other. She loved him. Luke had stepped up to the plate, had proven he trusted her and would watch her back no matter what. She knew he would accept her sad tale.

She got a tissue and blew her nose.

But Luke still hadn't convinced her to go back. "That's why it is important we go to D.C. It's the best way to get answers so we can end your pain and be happy."

"I'm sorry, but this doesn't change anything; I won't go back there. It would be just too humiliating."

Luke gave her a weak smile and pulled her into his arms and rested his head on hers. Grace knew the fight wasn't over, but she was too emotionally worn to worry about it right now.

Luke hadn't brought up the subject of going to D.C. in a couple of days. Grace appreciated it. But the more she thought about it, the more she knew she was compounding the problem. The answers were there. Everyone was trying to help her, and she was rejecting their help because of her fears and insecurities.

Grace was alone at Luke's house when the phone rang.

"Grace, sweetie, how are you?"

"Mom."

It was always a treat to talk to her mom. Grace settled in for a little girl talk. After pleasantries, Grace mentioned the stalker and how afraid she was to go back to D.C.

"Grace, you've never been one to run and hide." Her mom hesitated and said, "Hon, do you remember when you started the anti-bullying campaign in school and wrote the article for the newspaper?"

"Mom, that was a long time ago."

"Yes, but do you remember when some of your friends ignored you or called you names? Do you remember pleading with us to send you to another school, so you wouldn't be afraid or have to confront your friends?"

Grace nodded, not that her mother could see. "I remember. You and Dad told me I could transfer schools. However, if I did, I would never be able to look at myself in the mirror again because if I couldn't stand up for myself and my beliefs, no one else would."

"That's right, honey. The next day, you straightened your shoulders, looked us in the eye and told us it didn't matter what people said, they were wrong to bully, and you were going to stand up for what was right. You went to school, confronted your friends and convinced them to help you. You wrote that powerful piece on bullying that changed policy at the school. It took time, but it worked."

"Yes, I remember. It was a difficult time for me. Standing up and not running away was the right thing to do."

"Grace, it was true then and true now. This situation is the same. You know something happened to cause this stalker in D.C. to target you. People were wrong about you, then they betrayed your trust and bullied you into leaving. Now it's time to stand up for yourself." She hesitated. "I think you know what you have to do, right?"

Grace laughed. "Mom if I ever grow up, I want to be just like you."

"Oh Gracie, you are so much more than I am. I've never had to face the adversity you've dealt with," her mom said.

They spoke for a few more minutes about what was going on with her siblings and Dad.

"Mom, you're right about going back. I love you. Thanks for the pep talk."

Her mom told her she was the bravest person she knew, and it would work out. Grace hung up the phone and sighed. Her family was her strength. She could and would, do this. *After all, what was the worst thing that could happen?* Nothing that hadn't already been done.

Luke had come home earlier and was finishing some reports as she cooked dinner. They were sitting at the dinner table when Grace decided it was time to tell him. "Luke, you and Sam are right; we need to go to D.C. Let's get it done and over with."

CHAPTER FORTY-TWO

Faces had changed, but the *Washington Chronicle* newsroom looked the same. To Grace, the excitement of being in a newsroom never got old. There was still clutter everywhere. The noise of people typing on keyboards. The mumbles of people talking in the background. God, she had loved it here.

Grace spotted her old desk, and her hands started sweating. Crap. Why did she come back here? She should have just called.

Thankfully, she didn't encounter anyone she had worked with, and no one recognized her. The only person she hoped to see was Karen St. Clair, the woman who took her under her wing when she was a cub reporter. But Karen wasn't in the office yet. They had spoken once on the phone, but Grace had a few more questions for her. Her appointment with the new editor, Greg Farmer was scheduled for later, but Grace came early hoping to catch him in and get a head start on her investigation.

Walking down the narrow path through crowded desks, Grace felt like she was taking the walk of shame. *Stop! You have nothing to be ashamed of.* Grace sensed Luke's positive energy washing over her. He wanted to come with her, but she had insisted on doing this on her own.

Farmer's office was at the end of the room. Grace could see him at his desk and knocked on the glass door when she got there.

He looked up and waved her in. He squinted at her. Grace knew he couldn't place her. *Good.* Inhaling deeply and letting her breathe out slowly, she straightened her shoulders and walked in. "Mr. Farmer. I'm Grace Winslow. I have an appointment with you later, but I'm early. I wonder if I might speak with you now for a few minutes."

"Sure, come in. I have a couple of minutes before my next meeting."

He motioned to Grace to sit and asked what he could do for her. Grace didn't want to get into her old business; she just needed to find Mitch Donovan, her former editor, and Rachel Lang. Rachel never responded to her email, but Grace hoped Farmer knew where she was.

Getting right to the point, she asked, "I'm trying to find Mitch Donovan and Rachel Lang. Do you know where I can find them?"

"Why?" Farmer asked his eyes narrowing as he looked over at her. He had the nose of a reporter.

Hmm, this was not going to go as smoothly as she hoped.

"I used to work here with Mitch and Rachel. I wrote under the name Grace Winslow-Moore."

Farmer opened his mouth, closed it, opened it and said, "Aaah."

He looked intrigued. "I remember your name now. Your story was the talk of the town for quite a while. Good story. Too bad there were so many issues with it."

Ya think? Grace was not saying that aloud.

Farmer squinted his eyes and cocked his head. "Now

I understand why you're here. Well, Miss Grace Winslow-Moore, it appears this is going to be a little more interesting than I assumed when you made the appointment. So why are you trying to find Mitch and Rachel?"

"I have some questions for them that are rather important."

"Like what?"

"Well, it's personal."

Farmer steepled his hands, raised his brows and waited. Grace wanted to curl up and hide underneath his desk. *Could this be any more embarrassing?* His "aaah" said it all. But she came here to get answers, and she knew there would be some awkward moments. Feeling the strength of Luke and her friends, she continued. Grace knew she would have to give something up and told him the least amount he would be satisfied with.

"So, you think after all this time they will help you?"

"I hope so. Do you know where I can find either of them?" Grace wasn't above pleading with him, but they weren't at that point yet.

"Well, Donovan was let go a couple of years ago. It was no secret our former publisher had some connection to Senator Irish. Rachel stayed here for a while, but I found her reporting skills to be suspect. She wasn't honest with me, and I let her go a year and a half ago."

Grace sat still. Mitch? Let go a couple of years ago? Mitch and she were probably fired around the time. *What was going on?*

Farmer continued, "I believe Donovan is retired and living outside D.C. I'm not sure what Rachel is doing or if she is still around here."

Taking a chance, Grace asked Farmer if he knew Rachel's friends or who her boyfriend was.

"Don't know personally. There were rumors she was dating a guy in the senator's office, but that's all I know."

Farmer looked at his watch and stood. "I hope I helped. I'm going to be late for my meeting if I don't go. Sorry I couldn't help more."

Grace thanked him and left. As she was approaching the outside door, her former co-worker Karen St. Clair came rushing in and stopped short in front of her.

"Oh, my goodness. Grace Winslow-Moore in person." Karen gave her a tight hug. "How are you?"

Grace laughed. "It's just Grace Winslow now." It was good to see her old friend in person. "I'm fine. I was hoping to see you. Can you spare some time?"

"I would love too." Karen looked at her watch. "But I have an interview in a few. Can we catch up later?"

Damn, that was disappointing. Grace really wanted to pick Karen's brain. "That will be hard. I'm here with a friend, and we have appointments scheduled. Quick question though. Do you remember Rachel Lang's friend's name, the one who worked for Senator Irish?"

"Let me think." Karen took a moment. "I believe she was dating or engaged to him. He worked here for a while before I came on. I remembered after speaking to you that I'd heard he had been fired from the paper and then took a job in government. I can't remember his name though. I know he had a reputation as a sleaze ball and a truth-spinner. Rachel and Jan Lawson were eating up and spitting out people in Washington like watermelon seeds. I tried to stay away from all the drama." She threw up her hands in disgust. "I'm afraid that's all I know."

"Thanks, Karen. It's more than what I had. I'm sorry we can't catch up."

"Me too, I miss you. Keep in touch." Promising she would, Grace said goodbye. Wow. Grace knew she had to find

Rachel. She finally had the connection between Jan, um Jean, Rachel and the unnamed boyfriend. She was sure they held the key to her downfall and the stalker.

GRACE WAS able to find Mitch Donovan's address and phone number. It would have been nice to meet him in person, but she didn't have the energy or time to travel two hours to see him.

He answered on the second ring.

"Mitch, this is Grace Winslow, um, Winslow-Moore."

"Grace, of course." His voice sounded weary. "Long time no hear from you. How are you?"

"Been better. I don't want to keep you very long. Greg Farmer told me you retired. I've been having some problems in Florida with a stalker, and I'm hoping you can answer some questions for me."

"I'm so sorry to hear you're having problems. What do you want to know?"

"I heard you were let go from the paper the same time I was. I'm sorry if it was because of me."

Silence. "It wasn't because of you. It had been a long time coming. There were too many squirrelly things going on. You didn't know it at the time, but the senator was friends with the publisher of the paper, and Irish convinced him to fire you. I tried to stand up for you, and they fired me. I was glad to leave but hated not being able to talk to you about what was going on."

Grace rubbed her chest. This hurt to hear. It was her fault—everything was her fault. She bit her lip hoping the tears wouldn't fall. Failure, again.

Mitch didn't say anything for a minute. "Grace, you have to believe what happened wasn't your fault."

He stopped and then said, "Do you hear me? I was to blame. I knew what was going to happen if or when your story got published. I knew the relationships the senator had at the paper and around town."

"As for Rachel, I never trusted her but kept her on as a favor to the publisher although I still don't know what their relationship was. This problem was on me. I was the editor, and I had the experience and responsibility. The whole affair shouldn't have gone down the way it did. I'm sorry if it ruined your life."

Grace gulped. Not what she expected to hear. "Mitch, I don't know what to say. Thank you. I do blame myself."

"Don't be so hard on yourself. You were a good reporter. It was one hell of a story, and I was proud of it and you. Don't blame yourself."

It was good to hear she wasn't the cause of all the problems. Mitch had been a good friend and editor to her.

But she still had to find Rachel. "Before I forget, do you know where I can reach Rachel Lang? She seems to have disappeared. I had an email address for her, but she never responded."

"Sorry, kid. I haven't had any contact with her in a couple of years."

She thanked Mitch and hung up. Wow, after all the years of thinking everyone had blamed her and blaming herself, just maybe ...

CHAPTER FORTY-THREE

D.C. had an early cold snap. It was bone-chilling cold compared to Florida. Grace shivered and put her hands in her coat pockets. However, since they weren't going to be here for more than a couple of days, she could suck it up. Black Pointe got really cold a few weeks a year, so it wasn't as if she needed a coat enough to justify spending the money.

She was running late for lunch with Luke at the University Club and scurrying down the street. Not watching where she was going, she bumped into a man and dropped her purse. As they were both apologizing and leaned down to pick it up, the man's voice sounded familiar, and she looked over at him.

"James?"

The man looked at her, and she recognized a face she had kissed too many times so many moons ago.

"Oh my God! Grace! How are you? What are you doing here? I heard you left D.C. a while ago." James didn't seem all that surprised to see her. Although even if he were surprised, he would never let it show. Suave, that was James all right. Tall, good-looking in a boyish way. His sandy hair was a little shorter than it used to be. He had a few more pounds on his thin frame, but he still looked good. James was always well put together. Never a hair out of place. He believed in keeping up his appearance.

"I did leave, but I'm here for a couple of days getting information about a problem I'm having."

"Anything to do with what happened here?" James seemed genuinely concerned, but he was a political animal and could always put on a concerned look. Grace didn't read anything into it.

"It does. The person stalking me here has found out I live in Florida and is harassing me. I'm here to gather information. I believe it has something to do with the piece I wrote about Senator Irish."

James had the presence of mind to look sheepish as if he didn't know the story. "Any leads?"

"Not yet, but we only arrived last night."

"Who's 'we'?"

Grace thought about if she wanted to answer his question.

Nah. It was none of his business.

James glanced at his watch, "Look, Grace, I'm late to a meeting, but I'm glad to see you." He stopped and shook his head. "I've wanted to touch base with you for a while."

"Why?" Grace couldn't imagine why James would want to talk to her because she certainly hadn't wanted to talk to him.

"We ... I ..." James hesitated. "I ended things badly with you. I was so focused on my career and worried about my reputation; I wasn't fair to you. I'm an assistant DA now. I have a wife and child I love dearly. I sometimes think about how badly I treated you especially when it turned out you were right about Senator Irish. He was scum. I didn't believe in you at the time, and I should have." James looked apologetic. "I should have done a lot of things differently. I want to say I'm sorry and I hope someday you can forgive me."

Grace stood there stunned. That was not the conversation she imagined she would ever have with James. Her imaginary conversation with him always involved physical pain, then more physical pain.

"Thanks. I guess. It took me a while to get over how betrayed I felt by you in particular, and by everyone else. It hurt a lot. Except for this stalker, I'm in a better place, have a new man in my life who watches my back and loves me unconditionally. My friends are supportive of me, and I have a career I love with a boss who trusts my judgment," she said rather vehemently.

Grace could see James was taken aback by her verbal assault. Did he think his too late apology was going to get him off the hook for betraying her?

He managed a little smile anyway and said, "Ouch. I guess I deserve that. I am sorry and happy for you that things are getting better. I'm sorry you didn't get the justice you deserved here."

He looked at his watch again. "I have to go. But for the record, the more I live in and learn about Washington, the more I realized that you didn't stand a chance here. Irish was out to crucify you. There were rumors he had connections everywhere especially at the police department and that he was connected at the newspaper too."

He stepped forward as if he was going to hug her but stopped instead and said goodbye. She watched James walk away, and after finally being able to tell him off, Grace felt vindicated.

The cold was starting to freeze her earlobes, so she hurried into the club.

Whoa! What did James say? Irish had connections everywhere, especially at the police department. Mitch already told her Irish was connected to the publisher at the newspaper. Did Irish have something on the publisher?

Didn't Farmer say the same thing? What the hell was up with that?

LUKE ARRIVED a few minutes early to lunch. Grace had texted him earlier that she made reservations at the University Club and would meet him here. His tie felt like a noose around his neck. But a tie and jacket were required here. "Business casual," the Club called it.

He followed the hostess who led him through a sea of white-clothed tables filled mostly with men in suits. The muted background hum of voices and clink of silverware were the only noises Luke heard. He took in the cherry paneled walls and heavy damask drapes, pretty but not his style—no dart throwing, beer-swilling here.

This was Grace's world. At least how he had imagined it. He didn't know why he assumed that because Grace was nothing but down to earth. But she had an understated elegance that would be at home in this environment.

The hostess pulled out a chair for him at the reserved corner table; Luke sat with his back to the wall, able to look at the rest of the restaurant. A waiter appeared out of nowhere to pour water and take his drink order.

Nothing to do but wait. By the time Luke's single barrel bourbon came, he saw Grace maneuvering around the tables following the hostess. She looked sophisticated with her hair up in a messy bun. A bun he wanted to let down while he had his way with her. *Stop thinking about sex.* She wore a long sleeve pink sweater tucked into a slim skirt. Black heels accented her long legs. *God, she looks beautiful. Sophisticated. She belongs here*. She fit right in with this crowd. Luke noticed more than a couple of men sneaking looks at Grace, and he wanted to walk over and *hold that thought.*

Not cool to punch the lights out on every man who ogled Grace.

He stood as she leaned over to kiss him. "Hi, sorry I'm late."

She sat down. "Had to call Mitch. At least, I was able to get what I needed from him. I can't believe he wanted to talk to me after all that happened."

"What did he say?" Luke asked. He had wanted to be with Grace when she spoke with her former editor, Mitch Donovan. Grace had thought Mitch would be more relaxed if she called instead of showing up with Luke. Besides, Luke thought if he had a moment alone with good ol' Mitch, he wasn't sure he could stop himself from hurting him. He needed to stop thinking like that. There were too many people who had hurt Grace, and he wanted to take pleasure in hurting all of them.

"Let's order first, and then I'll tell you." They placed their orders and Luke settled down waiting for Grace to collect her thoughts.

"Pretty spiffy place, did you come here often?"

Grace laughed. "God no. This is where my stepfather stays when he's in D.C. He does a lot of business here, but this club is so not my style."

Luke couldn't help feeling a little relieved. Grace looked at ease here, and he knew she grew up in this world, but the only thing he could offer her was a step-down from all this. He hoped she could be happy with that.

Enjoying another glass of wine after they placed their order, Grace looked at Luke and knew it was time to talk.

He listened as she repeated everything she had learned. This whole story had the beginning of a novel.

Her eyes filled with tears and he wanted to hold her in his arms, but she kept talking. "I emailed Rachel Lang but never heard back. It doesn't make any sense why Rachel would want to hurt me. It seemed like she had a great career and had been with the paper for a long time. I learned Rachel was also friends with Jean Mays aka Jan Lawson. They were back-stabbers and working together they gathered gossip on a lot of politicians. I had heard some rumors but nothing first hand."

Luke laughed. "Sounds like the Washington political scene I imagined."

Watching Grace recount her story and getting more and more stressed, Luke put his hand over hers. Gently rubbing the back of her hand, he said, "I don't know anyone here, and I'm not sure who to trust, you should contact Sam and have her track down Rachel."

Grace hesitated and nodded. "Great idea. Sam's anxious to help, and she has great resources. I'll call her later. I'd also like to touch base with Senator Irish's widow. She might be able to connect some of the dots. It seems odd the Senator would commit suicide over taking kickbacks. Besides, when they retracted my story, there was no reason to kill himself. I never understood why. There would have been no reason for him to leave Congress unless he was expelled or resigned because of the scandal."

She shook her head. "I don't understand any of this."

Grace's eyelids were slowly shutting. Luke decided it was time to regroup at the hotel and perhaps take a nap. Hah! A nap. Riiight. Luke liked napping with Grace because there was very little napping involved.

Luke pulled out his wallet to pay the bill. Grace laid her hand over his. "Luke, we don't pay money here. The bill will be added to my father's account."

He started to protest, and Grace smiled. "Dad has to pay for meals each month whether he eats here or not. This is his way of saying thank you."

Luke struggled to find the right words, but nothing came out. He always paid if he was with a woman. Grace knew how strongly he felt about paying. They had this argument too many times. Finally, he conceded, "Okay, just this time. Thank your father for me. In the future, remember I always pay my way, and that includes paying for you."

THE NEXT AFTERNOON was warmer and dry. Grace and Luke decided to walk to the Watergate. The infamous Watergate. Infamous or not, it was still a prestigious building for politicians or in this case, a politician's widow to live.

They hadn't been sure if Senator Irish's widow would see them. Grace called, and Rosemary Walsh-Irish was hesitant at first, but Grace cajoled her into meeting them. She agreed to meet at 1 p.m.

As she and Luke walked toward the Watergate complex, Grace had forgotten how massive it was. She likened the complex rising out of the ground to monolithic gods eager to accept all those who entered.

Grace was not unfamiliar with the area especially after going to college, grad school and living here for a while. In fact, as a reporter, she had met informants here.

Entering the lobby, they walked up to the security desk, gave their names and said that Mrs. Irish was expecting them. Signing them in, the guard called up and then told them to go on up to the seventh floor.

Grace wasn't sure what to expect, but when the front door opened, the stunning, fiftyish woman with medium-length, grayish-white hair and sky-blue eyes was not it. Rosemary Irish extended a slim hand and shook hands with Luke and Grace.

"Come in."

She led them into the living room. "I have to say I don't know what I can tell you or add to whatever you're looking for. Warren has been dead for a while now, and I stay away from the political game."

She motioned for them to sit on a gray butter-soft leather sofa with a million-dollar view of the Potomac. In fact, Grace thought the condo was as stunning as Mrs. Irish. Formal but not stuffy. Whichever decorator Mrs. Irish had used, they had an eye for top-notch comfort and color.

They were sitting in one of two seating areas, this one done in cool grays. A dining table and chairs separated them from another seating area done in shades of beige which was more casual. Everywhere Grace looked, it was calm and peaceful. The balcony view overlooking the river was to die for.

"Mrs. Irish, my name is Grace Winslow. However, I was not upfront in telling you I was a reporter for the *Washington Chronicle* a couple of years ago using my married name, Grace Winslow-Moore."

Luke quickly turned his head and looked at her. Grace bet he didn't know that factoid.

Mrs. Irish was stunned. "You," she stammered.

Grace was sure they were going to be thrown out. "Yes."

Grace quickly continued. "I'm sorry I was the cause of much turmoil in your life. I was only doing my job. I never meant for the senator to commit suicide."

"Ms. Winslow, if I may." Mrs. Irish sat quietly for a moment. "Don't feel responsible for Warren's death. That was on him. He was in debt, which was why he was taking kickbacks. Plus, he was cheating on me, personal information you wouldn't know. He kept that part of his life very quiet. When I found out about the cheating, I told him I was divorcing him and cutting him off. You see, he didn't have any money. It's all my family money. He was frantic. He had gotten in over his head, and the mob was after him. His party was after him to resign. Congress wanted to kick him out. I guess he believed suicide was the only way out."

"Oh, my." Grace was speechless. She felt sorry for Mrs. Irish, but for all this time, she had been blaming herself for his death, and now she found out she hadn't been responsible. Maybe she'd been the catalyst for his demise but not the rest of it.

Explaining her stalker problem and that he'd found her again in Black Pointe, Grace asked Mrs. Irish if there was anyone on the senator's staff who might hold a grudge.

Mrs. Irish took a moment. "Not that I can think of. I believe everyone on staff got other jobs after Warren died. I don't keep up with any of them."

Grace couldn't think of anything else to ask her. She'd already received more information than she anticipated receiving when she made the appointment. Grace and Luke got up. Grace asked to use the restroom, and Mrs. Irish pointed to a small room off the living room.

Grace finished and walked down the hall, catching up to them. Luke and Mrs. Irish were waiting by the front door. She looked at the photographs of Senator Irish with groups of people, staffers, the president, and family.

"Was this his staff?" Luke pointed to one particular picture. There were a couple of women and several men standing around the senator and smiling.

"Yes. Warren was close to all of them. He employed young kids who majored in political science just out of college. They often lacked experience but made up for it with a lot of energy. I think his press secretary had a newspaper background. His chief of staff was the only one with real experience."

Grace thanked Mrs. Irish for her time and again apologized for any pain she caused. Mrs. Irish smiled wistfully.

"You know, with all that Warren was involved in, I loved him, and I still miss him."

"Whew, that was intense," said Grace as they took the elevator down to the lobby. "What a gracious woman. And to still love the philandering thief, wow."

"I know." Luke chuckled and grabbed her hand. "You gotta wonder about people sometimes. I'm surprised she still has pictures of his staff and reminders of his life on the wall. It has to be painful to look at them every day."

Grace thought about Mrs. Irish and her comments about her husband. "Maybe she misses the limelight, after all."

CHAPTER FORTY-FOUR

Luke walked into a tempest. The newsroom was beyond noisy. The last time he was here, it was nothing like this. Winding his way through the labyrinth of desks, Luke spotted Grace in a corner talking to a co-worker. He watched her get dressed this morning but seeing her standing there in a simple, pink-patterned sleeveless dress made his heart sing. *Gracious, beautiful, kissable, she was all that and more.*

She hadn't noticed him yet, so he took a minute to observe her. Then she turned toward him, and her smile lit up the room. Excusing herself, she walked in his direction. He couldn't help noticing several of the women staring at him. One licked her lips. *A little full of yourself, aren't you?* he thought. However, he only had eyes for Grace; she was the only woman he wanted to notice him.

"Hi. what brings you here?"

"Checking on you, wanted to see if you could get away for lunch."

She gave him the little half smile he loved, said to give her a minute. Grabbing her purse from her desk, she walked back to Luke.

"So, what's going on here? Everyone seems so excited."

"No, it's been a busy week, and we just finished a staff meeting. It's always crazy after a meeting."

As they were leaving, Grace's co-worker Mary walked in with a tall, dark-haired bearded man. Stopping to say hello, Mary introduced her friend, Ken to Luke. Making small talk for a few minutes, Luke asked Ken what he did for a living, and found out he was a journalist interviewing for a job at the paper. Ken kept sniffling and finally excused himself claiming allergies. He stepped away, took out an inhaler, inhaled deeply and walked back. Ken mentioned the wet, humid weather of Florida was aggravating his allergies. Luke wondered why he would want to work in a climate that was not good for him but kept that to himself.

There was something familiar about Ken, but Luke couldn't put his finger on what it was. Luke was ready to go. They said their goodbyes as he guided Grace out the door.

"I thought Italian would be good for a change. Is that alright?"

"Yum, my favorite."

Grace was thoughtful for a moment. "Does Mary's boyfriend seem odd to you?"

"Yeah. I keep thinking he looks familiar, but I know I've never met him. Weird he wants to work in Florida if his allergies are that bad."

"I know. For some reason, Ken creeps me out. I've met him with Mary a couple of times, and he always stares and smirks at me." Grace shivered. "You meet all kinds, don't you?

"Hon, in my field, you meet all kinds every day."

Arriving at the restaurant, they were shown to a table. The waiter came over and took their order. Luke looked around the small but comfortable restaurant. The smells coming from the kitchen were making his mouth water—

garlic, more garlic, and basil. A lively Italian tune played in the background.

Making small talk, Luke covered Grace's hands with his. He was always amazed at how small and delicate they were compared with his. Their food arrived. Luke and Grace had fun trying each other's dishes. He loved being with a woman who was a good eater, not one of those skinny rabbits who only ate lettuce.

At the back of his mind, he kept thinking about Ken. It was just a kernel of suspicion. He felt sure he had seen Ken before, and the way Ken kept leering at Grace irked him. It would come to him, it always did, but for now, he wanted to bask in the glory that was Grace. *Jesus! Bask in the glory that was Grace?* He rolled his eyes. Yeah, it was too corny even for him.

After finishing their meal, they each had an espresso. Luke paid and walked Grace back to her office.

"See you tonight." He gave her a chaste kiss.

"I'll be leaving early and can start dinner if you want."

Luke loved knowing Grace was in his home, in his bed. He wanted more than just living together but knew Grace wasn't ready. One of these days, though.

"Great, I can grill if you get everything else ready. Ben's joining us." Plans made, Grace walked through the double door and Luke headed toward his car.

The jogger's murder was on his mind. They hadn't found any suspects yet. The next-door neighbor and her boyfriend had alibied. Grace wasn't a suspect, so he and Ben had nothing and were looking at a potential cold case.

MEETING the cop had been so delicious. Ken couldn't believe his luck. They had shaken hands and after, the cop looked like he wanted to disinfect his hand.

Ken already knew he made Grace nervous. She always looked like she wanted to run in the other direction when she saw him. But she was too polite.

But what a great story this would make. Killer meets cop. Cop has no idea killer is standing in front of him imagining his death. Blah, blah, blah. Maybe he would write it when he got back to D.C. It was sure to be a bestseller. His strait-laced father would be turning in his grave if he knew what Ken was up to, the lengths he took to get a good story. He shuddered. This was delicious.

And Mary, lathering on about his getting a job here. Like he would ever stoop so low. He had the best in D.C. Although, good ole dad would probably have told him to suck it up and take the job. The old man had been impossible to live with after he won a Pulitzer for his story on crime. Always throwing it in his face. Telling him how to do his job. Always criticizing his work. Telling him what a disappointment he was. If dad only knew all the secrets and dirt he dug up on people, wouldn't he be surprised? He was the glad when his dad died. He would never have approved of his work at the *Chronicle* or with the senator.

GRACE WALKED BACK into her office. Mentally going over her day, she almost ran into Mary who was carrying a cup of coffee.

"Did you have a good lunch?" Mary's eyes lit up, "Man. Luke is easy on the eyes."

A vision of Ken leering at her made Grace swallow hard.

Grace was so not getting into Luke's good looks with Mary, "Yes, lunch was great."

"So, did you and Ken meet up for lunch?" Grace asked changing the subject.

"No. Ken stopped by to say hello, and then he had to run." Mary looked disappointed.

"I never asked but how did you meet him?"

"Oh. It was so romantic." Mary's face lit up. "I was running out of the office about three months ago, and we ran into each other. Literally. Ken helped me up and bought me a cup of coffee. We hit it off. You know he was a journalist, so we have that in common." Mary smiled.

"Oh. Who did Ken work for?" Grace didn't want to be too inquisitive, but Ken was too weird.

"I don't know who, but it was up north somewhere. I've arranged for him to interview with Steve." Mary winked at her "We don't talk too much about work if you know what I mean."

Grace wanted to gag. She didn't want to know about Mary's love life. She didn't want to see Ken at the office every day.

SOMETHING WAS NAGGING at the back of Luke's mind. Hitting the steering wheel with both hands, he let out a growl.

He needed to let off steam. So, he called Ben to meet him at the shooting range. Shooting at targets always relaxed him and maybe, what was troubling him would become more evident.

The target practice didn't help. Ben and he were competitive, but since he had been distracted, Ben had hit the bullseye more than he did.

"Looks like you're buying," Ben teased. It was a standing practice for them that the loser would buy the beer.

Luke gladly bought it.

Meeting Ken had been disturbing—he didn't like the guy. He didn't like the way he smirked at Grace. But, more importantly, the feeling that he had seen Ken before wasn't going away.

CHAPTER FORTY-FIVE

Grace was busy. It was a good busy, however. She was still covering events as well as writing a piece on the abuse of opioids in the area. She was grateful to Steve who had encouraged her to get back to the work she loved. It had been a leap of faith on both their parts. She was humbled that not only her editor but also her co-workers had her back—a vast change from D.C.

She wiped a few drops of sweat from her brow. The weather had turned hot and humid although it was almost the end of October and thankfully, no significant hurricanes had come through. Florida had lucked out this year.

Sam had called earlier to remind her that their friends were meeting for lunch at Salt & Sea. Luckily Laura had the day off and could join them instead of cooking for them.

Spotting the gang in their usual corner booth, Grace waved and walked over. After hugs and greetings all around, she sat down next to Anne.

"Grace, how are things working out with Luke? I hear you're a regular ninja warrior now." Anne smiled.

"Riiight. I can take on small children and out-of-control kittens," Grace replied. The women laughed.

"Seriously though, I'm so glad you are taking care of yourself. Have the police found the stalker yet?" Anne asked.

"Not yet. He hasn't left any prints or clues. Every time we spot him on camera, he's been camouflaged. It's frustrating. Although I haven't heard anything from him lately, so that's good news." She shrugged. "Maybe he packed up and went to stalk someone else, not that I would wish him on anyone. Or preferably, he'll do everyone a favor and drop dead."

They all picked up their wine glasses and toasted to the stalker dropping dead.

Since they all hadn't been together in a month, there was much catching up to do. Sam's business was booming. Anne's kindergarten class provided them with many laughs. The little ones were so cute and innocent. Laura's restaurant had hired additional employees for the season because the snowbirds were starting to come down. Hailey's bookstore was having a new author event that she was excited about. Also, she was hiring her first store manager so she could have some time for herself.

Grace was happy to see Hailey excited and her store doing well, but she was concerned about her friend. Hailey participated in the conversation and laughed, but there was sadness in her eyes. That was a one-on-one conversation for another day. Today was about laughing, talking, and reconnecting with her good friends.

Lunch was winding down. They were enjoying a cup of coffee and Grace was in the middle of a sentence when a bouquet of white stargazer lilies was placed in front of her. She looked up at the hostess, Maria, who smiled and told her someone dropped them off at the front for her.

Grace poked through the flowers. "Oh, they're lovely. But, there's no card. Do you know who they're from?" She immediately thought of Luke. It would be so unlike him to send flowers, but she was developing his romantic side.

"Oh gosh, I think there was a card. Let me go see," said Marie as she rushed back to the front desk.

Hailey leaned over to smell the flowers. "Honey, these lilies are gorgeous. You're so lucky." The rest of the girls nodded in agreement.

Maria came back with a pink envelope in her hand and tried to hand it to Grace.

One look. *No! Not today! Not here!*

Grace froze. Her heart was pounding. Sweat started dripping down her face, and she was gasping for breath.

She reached out for the note, but her arm fell short. She didn't want to touch it.

"Don't touch it." Sam stopped her arm, picked up a napkin and grabbed the note with it. "I'm calling Luke right now."

LUKE AND BEN rushed over from the station. Seeing Grace look pale and uncontrollably shaking broke Luke's heart. The bastard had to be stopped. He hated that the beautiful flowers had been used for such evil intent. They still hadn't identified the stalker. The bastard was clever; Luke had to give him that. But Luke and Ben were still confident the stalker would make a mistake and they would find him. But before they arrested him, Luke was going to beat the shit out of him. Sure, he was a detective and swore to uphold the law. But he was also a man looking out for the welfare of the woman he was involved with. This stalker had tortured Grace enough.

"Laura, can we go to your office?" Luke needed to move the group out of the restaurant into a quieter spot.

Laura nodded, and the group followed her to her office.

Grace started hyperventilating and sat down.

Luke reached out and touched Grace's arm. "Grace, honey, take a deep breath."

Sam was still holding the envelope by the napkin when Luke took it from her. "I'm going to open it. Laura, can you get security tapes for the past couple of hours?"

She nodded and rushed off to get them.

Luke carefully opened the envelope and cursed. "Son of a bitch."

"What does it say?"

Luke did not want to tell Grace what it said or show her the note, but she needed to know.

"The message says, 'You have good looking friends,' but what concerns me is what looks like dried blood on the corner." He turned the notecard so that Grace could look.

Big mistake. Grace took one look at the blood and passed out.

AFTER MUCH CONVINCING, Grace's friends left. Grace nursed a glass of wine in between putting her head between her legs.

Laura had pulled up the security tapes. They spotted a smiling young woman in jeans and a cutoff top holding the flowers and the pink envelope. She walked into the restaurant and stopped at the hostess desk about fifteen minutes after Grace arrived.

Looking over at the tape, Grace asked, "Is she my stalker?"

She couldn't believe this young woman would be harassing her. For one thing, the woman looked about twenty years old, and for another, Grace didn't recognize her.

"I don't think so," said Sam. "I bet she only delivered the

flowers. She's probably still in the area, and someone might recognize her. Laura, can you print a picture of her?"

Laura nodded, and the printer spat it out.

Sam reached for it. She said she was going to first ask around the restaurant and then try outside.

Luke bent down and took Grace's hand. "We are going to find this bastard and stop this. I promise you."

Grace was still shaky and sweating. "Not if I find him first," she said. "When I do, there might not be enough of him to arrest."

"That's my girl," Luke said.

AN HOUR LATER, Sam walked back into the restaurant with a young woman. It hadn't taken Sam long to find her. The woman had been drinking a bottle of water on a bench overlooking the river when Sam approached her asking about the note.

She said her name was Sarah.

"Sarah, tell me how you got the note and flowers."

"Well, I was studying when this youngish guy approached me holding the lilies. He said he wanted to leave a love note with the flowers for his fiancée and would she do him a favor and deliver the flowers to the front desk as a surprise? I thought the gesture was so romantic and gladly said yes."

Sarah gulped. "I'm not in trouble, am I?"

Sam patted her arm and told her no. Sam asked if Sarah could recognize the man.

"No, he had a hat and sunglasses on. Didn't his fiancée like the flowers?"

Sam told her it wasn't the romantic note the man said it was. Sarah was appalled and agreed to go back and talk with Luke and Ben.

As ideas went, it wasn't the greatest, but apparently, it worked. Ken sat on a bench half hidden by bushes. He was so tired of hiding in bushes. The girl couldn't see him, but he could see her and Grace's friend talking. He was sure the girl had delivered the note and seeing Grace's friend come out with a picture confirmed it. The bitch had been avoiding her usual spots lately, and her living with a cop had made his fun a little more difficult.

Following Grace today and realizing she was meeting her friends at Salt & Sea was a present he couldn't pass up. The cop had dropped her off at work this morning, then picked her up to bring her to the restaurant. It has been easy to follow his truck, park and grab a bench outside.

The chicken blood on the note was an inspiring idea. Ken knew he hadn't left any prints on the note and the chicken sure wasn't giving up any secrets. He had buried it deep in a dumpster. The idea had come to him several days ago and finding a live chicken wasn't difficult in this backwoods town. He merely told the farmer he wanted fresh eggs. How stupid was that? On the other hand, the farmer thought it was a great idea, back to nature, blah, blah, blah. The only back to nature scene he wanted was to leave this backwater town, go home to D.C. and have wild monkey sex with Rachel.

Ken was shaking with excitement and hoped her friends were as impressed with his ingenuity as he was. The cops were still chasing their tails, and soon, it would all be over for Grace.

CHAPTER FORTY-SIX

The Grace Project was taking too long. Ken knew where she worked, where she was living, where Grace was every day, and now she had bodyguards. He couldn't always see them, but he knew they were there.

It was getting more and more difficult to have any fun with Grace. Rachel was getting impatient; she missed him and wanted to move to Florida now.

He knew Rachel would be OK when he told her things didn't work out here. Rachel wasn't crazy about moving here; she loved D.C. She loved dishing out dirt on people on her blog and them not knowing it was her. In that respect, he and Rachel were alike. He liked to know everyone's dirty secrets too and boy, had they paid off when he was working for Senator Irish. He loved Rachel, wanted to make her happy.

Observing Grace at Luke's house was difficult. He had to hide in a neighbor's yard. It wasn't as close to the cop's house as he would have liked, but the telephoto lens on his camera handled the distance easily. The binoculars were an added bonus. Thankfully, the neighbor's house was closed up tight, surrounded by a fence and lots of bushes. He couldn't believe he was still hiding in bushes.

He assumed the inhabitants were seasonal and would be down soon. At least that's the information he got from the town assessor's office. *Gotta love public records.*

The only negative was his sniffling. The humid weather was getting to him big time, and his inhaler was getting lots of use. He wondered if he'd dropped the other one in Sexton Park. Had the cops found it? Bah, that was a lifetime ago, and he wasn't going to worry about it now. Concentrate on Grace.

He hadn't seen any cameras around the cop's property but guessed he had a good alarm system.

On the plus side, none of the neighbors had a dog. Big mistake. He was definitely getting a dog when he got home.

Grace seemed comfortable at the cop's house. He could smell the barbecue she and the cop grilled regularly, hear the laughter they shared. It pissed him off Grace was even laughing. Did she laugh when she took over his job at the *Chronicle* or when he lost his job with the senator because of her exposé? Probably not. What did she care? It was all about her.

Christ, he even heard the heavy petting when they believed they were alone. And that one night, oh Lord. The sliding glass door was partially open, and they were naked. Grace was on her knees shining her dick's dick. *Ha, that was a good one, the dick's dick.* Then the cop turned her around and fucked her from behind.

With all the moaning and groaning going on, he could have done away with both of them at that moment, and they wouldn't have known a thing. The cop was groaning and concentrating on Grace. Watching them, he couldn't help himself. He unzipped his fly, grabbed his dick and pumped away. Shit, they all came at the same time. *Goddamn, talk about group sex.* He hoped it was as good for them as it was for him.

The camera was on a tripod, no chance of it falling. Grace was easy on the eyes, and he wouldn't mind seeing more of her. Preferably naked, in front of him, on her knees, sucking away.

Enough of that. He needed to concentrate on finishing Grace off. Besides, no one compared to his Rachel on her knees making him happy.

The video camera was almost full, and he was going to edit it tonight and make a nice CD present for Grace. Boy, was she going to be surprised.

The moaning and groaning had turned him on, and he knew he was going to enjoy the remake of it. Ken supposed the cop and Grace probably wouldn't.

Less than a week, that's all he needed to finish off Grace. The fact that her name was now on investigative pieces in the newspaper angered him even more. She was getting recognition. He was getting a comedown job with the lobbyist and jerking himself off in the bushes.

Life wasn't fair.

IT WAS after midnight when Grace woke up. Her body felt uncomfortably warm. Luke was snoring lightly beside her, his hand around her waist. Ah, the source of the heat. Trying not to wake him, she gently moved his hand and got out of bed to make a cup of tea. She sat in the living room while her mind roamed through the whole mess that had become her life.

The incident at Salt & Sea had disturbed her even more than she let on. It was troubling enough to be the target. The fact that the stalker was targeting Luke was distressing too, but Luke was a cop and better able to handle the situation. What had unnerved her most of all was that the stalker was targeting her friends. They were innocents and had nothing to do with this. Whatever this was. She was afraid for them and needed to gather her thoughts about what to do next. This harassment and torture couldn't go on. If one of her friends were hurt because of her, she could never live with herself.

This situation needed to be resolved now. Sam got a hit on a Rachel Peterson, whom she believed was Rachel Lang, but Grace hadn't connected with Rachel yet. Her stomach was roiling from the unease. Her mind hurt. All of this was so far out of her realm of experience.

A gentle hand touched her shoulder, and she felt a soft kiss on her head. She turned toward Luke.

"Sweetheart, why aren't you in bed? Can't sleep?" Luke's hair was tousled, and he looked so sexy standing there with just pajama bottoms on.

"I'm OK. I slept enough, I guess." She heaved a heavy sigh. "I'm sick over the fact that this creep targeted my friends. I don't know what to do."

Luke swept a strand of hair from her face. "I know, but we'll keep you and them safe. I promise." Luke felt powerless. He kept telling Grace he would keep her safe, but he hadn't found the stalker yet. How was he supposed to keep her safe or take away her concerns?

"I didn't get in too late last night, but you were snoring away, and I didn't want to wake you."

Grace snorted. "I do not snore."

Luke smiled, sat down next to her and pulled her in close. "If you're up for it, there are developments in your case I'd like to tell you about. Plus, we know who the stalker is."

"Oh my God, you found him?"

Luke grimaced. "No. We haven't found him yet. Ben is working on that. His name is Ken Peterson, and he worked for Senator Irish. He also knows Rachel Lang and Jean Mays."

"Ken Peterson?" Grace was confused. "Ken Peterson? Who the hell is he?"

Grace mentally processed all the names she had contacted for her piece. She vaguely remembered that name. *Think*.

"Oh my God! I know that name. He was Senator Irish's communication director. We were never able to connect in person" Grace remembered she had made a couple of appointments with him, but he always begged off meeting. Now she knew why. "How did you find out it was him? What's his connection with Jean and Rachel?"

"Whoa, hon, one thing at a time." Luke grinned. He wiped the grin from his face and got serious. "The pictures hanging by the door at Mrs. Irish's condo of family and staff were the clue. You probably don't remember them. I saw him standing next to the senator, and thought he looked familiar. It took a while, but it finally came to me where I had seen him."

"I don't think I want to know this but where did you see him?" Grace closed her eyes. This sordid affair was getting worse. Had Ken been in Black Pointe all along spying on her?

"He's been here all along."

Grace moaned. She wanted to run from this room, from Luke's house and never stop. Her heart couldn't handle anymore. Her worst nightmare come true—her stalker was here. In her town. Spying on her. Probably spying on her this very second. She wanted to run to the window and peek out. See if she could spot him. She started to get up, but Luke put his arms around her and rubbed her back. "He grew a beard which is why I didn't recognize him immediately. And, he's dating your co-worker, Mary. I thought he seemed squirrelly when I first met him."

Grace covered her mouth. "Oh my God. This doesn't get any better, does it?" She felt the guy was creepy when she first met him and now to know he was the one stalking her ...?

And Mary? What did that say about Mary? Had she known? Was she part of this? Grace hoped not.

"Mary is in love with him. I bet he just picked her up to get to me. She's going to be devastated," said Grace.

"I don't understand any of this." She whispered. "Why would Ken Peterson be stalking me? I've never met him, never did anything to him. And what's his relationship with Rachel and Jean?"

"They knew each other in D.C. Sam sent me pictures of them all together. Sam believes Rachel and Ken are a couple. As for Jean, she was into getting dirt on people. Ken and Rachel were too. As you said, they were all working together. I have a call into a friend of Paul's in D.C. who might know more about them."

"What are you doing to find Ken?" she asked.

"Ben followed Ken's route from D.C. to Black Pointe. Originally, Ken used his real name and ID to make reservations for the plane, and he rented a car at the airport. But we haven't been able to find out where Ken is staying now. He returned the rental car he was using. He must be paying cash or using another ID to rent a car and staying at dives. Ben is checking all of them. We have an artist rendition of Ken with a beard and hope someone might recognize him."

Grace thought for a minute. "Luke, I don't understand any of this. Tomorrow first thing, I'll call Mary and see if she has a phone number or the place where Ken is staying. I won't tell her we know about Ken. Although, maybe he doesn't realize we know about him. Maybe he'll come by the office, and you'll get to arrest him."

Luke shook his head. "I doubt that. Ken is too clever and dangerous. By now he has to have figured out we know who he is and that we're looking for him."

"I want to be involved in this. It's my life, and he has already taken a part of it."

Luke picked up her hand and kissed it. "Absolutely. But my job is to keep you safe. Tomorrow we'll call Sam, Danny, and Ben over and map out a plan to catch this son of a bitch, once and for all."

BY THE TIME Grace got up the next morning, it was after nine. She stretched her sore muscles. She and Luke had not intended to make love, but cuddling didn't cut it last night. Luke had made long, slow love to her. It soothed her and Lord, how she loved this man. How he always knew how to make her feel so special, Grace didn't know, but she loved it.

Hearing voices in the kitchen, she put on her robe and walked toward the smell of coffee and bacon. Sam and Ben were there and said good morning. Luke came over to kiss her.

"We wanted to get an early start, and I didn't want to wake you. Danny will be here in a little while. Have a cup of coffee and sit." Luke gave her a mug and a big kiss.

"Thanks." Grace took the coffee. "Let me take a quick shower first and get dressed."

By the time Grace got dressed and walked back to the kitchen Danny had arrived and was eating breakfast.

"Hey. I was going to wait for you, but I'm starving," Danny said as he stuffed eggs into his mouth. Luke handed her a plate of eggs, toast, and bacon.

There was silence while they ate. Luke cleared the table, then returned with a cup of coffee and sat down. "We need to make a list of what we still need to do to resolve this case. Ken is escalating, and we need to stop him before someone gets killed."

Grace raised her hand. "Ah, would that someone be me?"

Luke shot her a dirty look. "Not on our watch, sweetheart."

Sam stood up. "Grace, no one's getting killed. Listen, I have a whiteboard in my car that I'll get which will make this process easier for us to see what's been done and hopefully fill in connections."

"I'll give Mary a call and see what information she has." Grace picked up the phone. "Should I tell her why I'm asking?"

Sam ran her fingers through her hair. "Well, this could go two ways. One: Mary will have information she will share. Good for us. Two: If Mary is in love with Ken, she might not be forthcoming with information. Bad for us." She exhaled a long breath. "I guess the only way to find out is to call."

Grace called the office and asked for Mary. Mary wasn't in yet, so Grace left a voicemail.

Sam groaned. "Damn, if Ken talks to her before we do, we will never catch him. Grace, do you think Mary is level-headed enough to give us the information?"

Thinking about that scenario, Grace shook her head. "Mary hasn't had a lot of men interested in her. I think fantasy will beat reality."

"Well, we can only ask and see what she says."

Several hours later, they all stared at the whiteboard.

"I don't see any clear answers up there," Ben said looking at the board.

Sam had been listening to everyone talk, but she suddenly had an idea. "Grace, do you remember anything more about your kidnapping?"

Grace thought for a moment. "No. I only remember waking up, untying myself, looking out at the parking lot, jumping out the window and running through the woods until I found that shopping center."

"What are you thinking, sis?" Danny asked.

"The motel is way outside of town. It's in an area with lots of strip clubs and low-end motels. Ken might have found a hidey-hole close by so he would be familiar with the area."

"You might be right," said Ben. "I asked around the motels within a couple of miles of city center but not in the outlying areas. I'll do that this afternoon,"

"Great. I'll continue digging information about Rachel, Ken, and Jean." Sam was jotting down notes as they spoke. "But, let's go back to your investigative piece on the senator. Why did you choose him? Who were your sources?"

"Let me think. It's been a while," answered Grace.

"A whistleblower called me, we met, and he gave me the lowdown. I was still new, so Mitch assigned Rachel to help. She found a couple of sources to contact. I had found some records of money being paid. Ken was the senator's press secretary."

She tapped her fingers on the table. "If I remember correctly, Ken didn't add anything important to the story. Now that I think about it, he had me running all over town talking to people who didn't have any information. He never got back to me in a timely matter, claimed he was too busy and didn't know what the whistleblower was talking about. The whistleblower disappeared right after the article came out and Rachel couldn't find her sources, so there was no one to corroborate the story, only the records I had which weren't enough to satisfy the publisher."

"What was the whistleblower's name?"

Grace thought for a minute. "I don't remember, but I have it in my notes on my computer. I'll send it to you."

"Great, I'll add his name to my research. If I can find him, we might get more answers."

Grace looked around at her friends and lover. “You all are the best. From the bottom of my heart, thank you for believing in me, and standing by me.”

Sam came over and hugged Grace. “Sweetie, you’d do the same for us. That’s what friends are for.”

“OK, then. I’ll call Mitch and Paul. They both work in publishing and might have some contacts who know Rachel, Jean, and Ken or know something connected to them,” Grace said.

“I’ll touch base with Diane Benoit and Richard Marsh again and see if they can think of anyone else Jean knew. Plus, they might remember something else,” commented Luke.

Grace looked at the whiteboard. It was sparse now, but she knew with them all combining their resources, they were going to catch Ken soon.

When it happened, Ken was going to feel some real pain. And that was a promise.

CHAPTER FORTY-SEVEN

Ken hated moving and changing motels every few days with each one dumpier than the next. Unfortunately, he couldn't register in a nicer one because they would ask for a credit card. The dives he was staying in didn't care who you were as long as you paid, especially if you paid in cash. Being in the area so long he was used to hearing the police sirens at all hours of the night, the moaning from rooms next to his, and the screaming in the parking lots. He was used to the unidentified stains on the carpeting. As for the sheets, well, he wasn't going there. Having Wi-Fi and a car made life tolerable.

He couldn't stop thinking about Rachel. He missed her so much and just wanted to hold her in his arms. Well, hold her and fuck her but instead, he was holding that bitch, Mary.

Today, it was time to change motels again. Yesterday while driving back to the latest dump, Ken noticed police cruisers stopping at the offices of some of the dives close by to where he was staying. They were getting closer, and he needed to find a room even farther out. He snorted. At the rate he was moving further away from the city, he'd end up in D.C. before too long. That would be laughable if it weren't so pathetic.

If that bastard Mitch hadn't given him his "pink slip" and replaced him with greenhorn Grace, he would have made a name for himself and maybe a Pulitzer by now. And showed dear ol' dad that he was just as good a writer. Working for the senator had been good for him financially. The stupid senator offing himself was the worst thing to happen to him after being canned from the paper. No one else liked his style of working. He sighed. That's what happened when you try to better yourself.

Smiling to himself, he took great pleasure in knowing Grace's time was getting short. He had the video footage he needed and had edited in a surprise package just for her. She was alone a lot of the time at the cop's house even though there was a police presence on the road. As if an unmarked car sitting at the edge of the property wasn't identifiable. They must think him stupid.

It was late afternoon when Mary called Grace back. They talked about nothing for a minute then Grace brought up Ken and asked if Mary had a phone number or any other information on him.

The silence was deafening. Sam would say this was option two—*bad for us*. Grace knew Mary wasn't going to give her any information.

"Why do you want his phone number?" Mary sounded suspicious. *What? Does she think I want to call him for a date?*

Grace took a chance and told her that the police thought he was her stalker and behind Jean Mays's murder.

Silence on the other end.

"I can't believe he would do such awful things. I know Ken. He is the sweetest, most thoughtful man I've ever been with, and he loves me."

"Mary, I know this is a lot to take in. The police are concerned Ken is unstable and will hurt me. Please, would you give me his phone number and where he is staying? If he's innocent, nothing will happen to him." Grace tried not to get angry or demand Mary tell them where Ken was. But she was frustrated. What was wrong with the woman? She had told Mary that Ken was stalking her and perhaps killed a woman and she was hesitant to give out his number.

Mary hemmed and hawed while Grace held her breath. Finally, Mary said, "I'm not happy about this, but I'll give you his phone number. I don't know where he is staying. He always comes to my house or the office. You're all going to find out he's innocent."

Mary gave Grace the phone number, and they hung up. Grace knew that this was going to affect their work relationship and friendship, but it affected her life more. *Living wins over friendship any time.*

Calling Luke, Grace gave him Ken's phone number and filled him in on what Mary had told her.

"Sweetheart, if he's innocent, I'll eat my hat. For Mary's sake, we'll try to keep her name out of this," said Luke.

Five minutes later Luke called Grace back and told her that it was the wrong phone number.

Grace checked her notes and repeated the number back to Luke. She had been very careful writing it down and reciting it back to Mary who had confirmed it.

Exasperated, Grace said, "Damn, I can't believe Mary purposely gave me the wrong number. I understand being in love but enabling a murderer and stalker? No way. What do we do now?"

"We take a deep breath. Mary used her cell phone so getting records will take time and be difficult to get. I bet she called him and gave him a heads up. I have security on you at home, and we can only hope he makes a stupid move," said Luke. "I'm so pissed. We are so close to this fucker, and as for Mary, well, I don't understand her protecting this slimewad."

S*HIT*, *this was all going to hell.* Ken was in a panic.

Mary had reached him just as he got into his room. Getting her to calm down took extra time Ken didn't have. He was surprised that the cops knew who he was. He told Mary he would come over later and explain that none of this was true. The police had the wrong guy. Telling her he loved her—*gag me with a spoon*—had pacified her. She had been hysterical, and he hoped he had calmed her down enough before she said anything stupid to the police.

Ken knew that wasn't happening though. The police were probably watching Mary's apartment. She had served her purpose, and that had been getting him close to Grace. As an added benefit, she was polishing his knob. Both jobs she performed very well. Now he needed to get another burner phone and to get rid of the one with the number Mary had.

Though he had planned on changing rooms again today, her call had thrown him for a loop. He needed to move again. He had to stop and think about this for a minute. His options were getting limited.

The police were getting closer. The detectives knew about him although Ken didn't know how because he had been careful.

He had to get the video to Grace, and he had to finish up and get back to Rachel.

First things first, he packed his things and wiped down all the surfaces in the crappy room. Keeping his head down, he walked out to the car throwing his bag in the trunk. *Think.* He needed to get out of Dodge and get out now. The GPS was still on Grace's car, thank God.

CHAPTER FORTY-EIGHT

It took a lot of digging and calling in of favors, but Sam was finally able to get the whistleblower's address. Owen Harrison and his family were living in the woods in New Hampshire. He had been one of Senator Irish's immediate staff when he blew the whistle on the senator's nefarious affairs. When Sam told him why she was calling, Harrison didn't want to talk to her. But at least he hadn't hung up. After explaining what was happening and that Ken Peterson was behind a murder and stalking Grace, he opened up.

"I hate that bastard. Peterson made my life miserable in D.C. and threatened to hurt my family if I didn't move or shut up. I chose to move and quite frankly, I'm glad to be away from the bullshit in Washington and know my family is safe." Owen could hardly keep the venom from his voice.

Owen's chin jutted out defiantly. Sam noticed the dark circles under his eyes and wondered if he had any peace since he left D.C. He kept rubbing a bald spot at the front of his head and looked twenty years older than thirty-five that Sam knew him to be.

"The senator was just as bad." Owen's face scrunched, his

hands clenching and unclenching. "I'm glad the bastard's dead. After I complained, a mobster type showed up at my wife's work one day and verbally accosted her. I could never prove the senator or Ken was behind it. My wife was, is still terrified. Whistleblowers are supposed to be protected. It works in theory but not in real life." Owen stopped, took a big breath and asked, "So what do you want to know?"

Sam asked him about Ken Peterson and if he knew Rachel Lang or Jean Mays aka Jan Lawson.

"You bet. Rachel and Ken are lovers. Ken couldn't stop talking about her when they were apart. Ken was taking kick-backs from the senator and doing his dirty work. He and Rachel both loved getting dirt on people. Jan, too. I avoided all three of them."

"Why didn't you say something to Grace about Rachel?" Sam asked.

"I never went to the office, so I didn't know Rachel was working on this. I can tell you most of Grace's exposé was true. Ken knew he couldn't stop the story, so he tried to cover his ass. I know he never mentioned that he was making plenty of money on side deals the senator was involved in. The senator had connections to many people in D.C., the newspaper's publisher, the police, any one of whom could squash the story or make Grace look bad. Grace didn't stand a chance."

He confirmed what Sam had suspected. "I'm still confused as to why Ken was upset about Grace writing that piece."

"Well, it wasn't just that one piece," Owen said. "It seems he blames Grace for replacing him at the paper." He shook his head. "Makes no sense to me. Although his father had been a big deal at the paper. Ken would occasionally mention that he never measured up and that his father always put him down. I think Ken needed to feel powerful. The man is crazy and blames everyone for his problems."

Sam and Owen spoke for a few more minutes. She had a clearer vision of what happened to Grace and how Ken, Rachel, and Jan were connected. She called Luke, and she repeated what she'd heard.

THE WIND WAS BLOWING HARD, whipping branches against the house. Grace jumped every time one hit a window. The thunder and lightning scared her into turning on all the lights. She disliked thunderstorms especially if she was by herself.

Luke had to work. So, it was comforting to know a cop was outside watching the house She wondered if she should run out with some coffee. *No*. Luke made her promise to stay in the house, telling her the cops were well equipped for watching houses.

She turned on the TV but found her mind wandering. Wondering what was happening. Where was Ken? How was Mary handling this? Did she even care that her boyfriend was trying to hurt Grace? When would this nightmare be over and when could she feel safe again?

There was nothing on TV keeping her attention, so she turned it off and picked up a book. Put it down. Sighed heavily. Grace realized there would be no peace and no answers to her questions tonight.

She got up to make a cup of tea. There was a light thump on the door. She looked at her watch. It was late, well maybe not that late. But who would be coming over this time of night? Maybe it was the cop needing to use the bathroom? It was a crappy night to pee in the bushes.

She peeked out the peephole but couldn't see anyone. Weird. She stood there for a moment questioning if she should open the door or not open the door. Finally, her curiosity got the best of her. She unarmed the alarm and opened it a crack.

"Who's there?"

No answer. There was no one there. It was probably the wind.

Opening the door wider, she took a tentative step out and glanced around. She could barely see the unmarked police car hidden behind the bushes. Outside of the occasional clap of thunder and trees swaying in the wind, nothing looked out of place. Turning to go back in, she looked down and saw a small brown box ties with a festive bow on the step.

Shit, this couldn't be happening.

Grace stared at the box, willing herself to pick it up. This had to be a bad dream. She looked around again. Picking it up with trembling hands, she quickly slammed the door, resetting the alarm. Her heart was pounding, and her palms were sweaty. Not good.

She didn't want to open the box. Setting it on the coffee table, she sat on the sofa staring at it, unrealistically hoping she would pass out and when she came to, would find out it was all just a nightmare. Right now, she would take a nightmare over reality anytime.

What to do? Call the cop over?

She didn't want to open the door again.

Should she call Luke? Luke was due home soon. Grace wasn't sure she wanted to disturb him if he were hot on Ken's trail. Although this could be important. Hell, she knew it was. Not calling Luke might be the biggest mistake of her life, but if Ken was here to kill her, she didn't want Luke here. She had to protect Luke. Ken only wanted her—she hoped.

Confident it was from Ken; she gingerly opened the package. A pink note fell out—no surprise there. Underneath was a CD. *What the hell?*

She wanted to look at it before calling Luke. Up until she opened the door and found the package, she felt safe but not now.

She opened the envelope, and the note said, "Peek a boo, I see you. You'll never be able to hide from me." She closed her eyes. This wasn't happening. She needed to see what was on the CD, although it wasn't going to be good. Holding back nausea, she got up to get her laptop and inserted the CD.

Nooooooo. That bastard. Ken must have been taping for days. How had he found out where she was staying? Where had he been hiding that she and Luke didn't see him? The bastard had overlaid some jaunty music to go along with the video. Oh God, their lovemaking, had been turned into a cruel joke. Grace clenched her stomach and fell back onto the cushion. Tears dripped down her cheeks, but she did nothing to stop their journey.

This harassment had to stop. She had to stop Ken. He was only after her. She was convinced that there would be no happy ending. Grace was sure Ken would get to her before Luke and Ben could find him.

Grace considered her options. Stay and let the fucker mess with her friends? With Luke? Continue to harass and then kill her? There were no good options.

This mess was on her shoulders. Grace made her decision. She had to leave. She was positive Ken would follow her wherever she went. At least he would be hunting her and not her friends. Luke would be furious, but this was her problem to solve. It was up to her to confront Ken and end this situation.

Tossing the CD and note onto the table, she hurried into their bedroom to pack a bag. Where could she go?

Think.

Ah, yes! She had just the place. Tossing clothes into her overnight bag, she sat on the bed and opened the side table drawer, adding one more item.

Somehow, she knew that Ken would follow her if she left. He was here already. She hoped the harassment would stop tonight. The only immediate problem was the cop guarding the house. She had to think about how to get past him.

Thankfully, she hadn't parked her car in the garage. At least one positive thing was going for her. It had started raining and was still thundering. She hoped the cop wouldn't hear her start her car. Perhaps if she got in it and didn't turn the headlights on, she might be able to get to the road without him seeing her. It was worth a chance. She picked up her bag and crept out the back door.

The fresh scent of nature as it was cleansed by rain usually relaxed her but not tonight.

She stayed close to the bushes. Raindrops slid down and over her eyes, forcing her to wipe them constantly. She crouched down until she got to the driveway. She inched her way to where her car was parked and unlocked the car. Click.

Shit, had the cop heard that? Hopefully not with all the rain and thunder. She slowly opened the door. Stopped. No footsteps. She jumped in and quietly closed the door. She shook her head like a dog, dispersing rain on the dash. She was clammy, and her clothes were sticking to her body—*perfect end to a hellish night.*

Her breathing was erratic, so she took a moment to inhale deeply, get herself under control. She would need that control and strength tonight. So far so good.

She turned the car on, left the lights off and slowly drove down the driveway—the windshield wipers squeaking as they swept water from her view. The rain came down harder, and so loud it competed with her heartbeat. *This nightmare is going to end tonight.*

CHAPTER FORTY-NINE

Grace was exhausted. She wanted nothing more than to feel safe for a little while and to know Luke and her friends were safe. Receiving the CD showed her just how safe she wasn't. She had been a fool thinking living at Luke's would deter Ken.

Sam and Luke could take care of themselves, but she worried about her girlfriends. Would they be next? The CD was explicit. Not only were she and Luke performing on it, but Ken had followed her friends going about their everyday business.

How had Ken found out where Luke lived? She had been diligent about taking different routes home, noticing cars around her, using all the tips Luke had given her.

She was disgusted by the fact Ken had chosen to record her and Luke when they were happy, innocent and at their most vulnerable. What was he thinking when he saw Luke and herself coming out of the house holding hands, kissing, looking happy? Ken had somehow captured their images as they got ready for bed. But, that scene of her going down on Luke and then making love with him had been the last straw.

She wasn't playing victim to a crazed voyeur and killer anymore. The harassment started with her and would end with her. She prayed she had made the right choice in leaving.

Luke was going to be mad and disappointed in her. Couldn't help that. Hopefully, he would forgive her. But she had to be alive for him to forgive her. She had to save herself, not put anyone else in danger. Ken only wanted her.

The rain had stopped. The drive along scenic Route A1A to her parents' place on the island usually relaxed her. But now she anxiously glanced behind her, praying she wouldn't see any headlights following her. Hopefully, she would come up with a better plan when she got to the house.

What did she ever do to Ken? The flower delivery at Salt & Sea had been one of his most brazen acts. Her friends had been frightened although they didn't say anything to her. Grace knew Ken wasn't afraid to kill, and he definitely wanted to kill her. *Rather extreme for his losing his job. I lost my entire life in D.C.*

The pity party over, Grace concentrated on the road. Another big dark storm cloud was rolling in over the horizon, and she wanted to get to the house before it started pouring.

She wanted to believe her parents' house was the safest place she could be until Luke or Sam figured out where Ken was.

Reaching the driveway, she stared at the unpretentious yellow stucco home. Rolling down the window, she could hear and smell the ocean. She and her three siblings had spent their childhood here, enjoying their waking hours' sea kayaking, swimming and just having fun. It had always been her safe place. Tonight would probably prove her wrong.

Not seeing lights in the houses on either side of her parents' house, she wondered if their old neighbors were around. She hoped not. She didn't want any of them getting hurt. She would check with her other neighbors' tomorrow.

But say what? "*Oh, by the way, a crazed stalker wants to murder me, perhaps you should leave town?*"

For now, she got out, punched the code into the keypad that opened the garage door, pulled in, and reactivated the alarm. Getting out of her car, she reached in back for her overnight bag and then deactivated the house alarm.

She carried her bag up to the second floor to the cozy room she had shared with her sister Jane. Not much had changed over the years. The seafoam-green room was the same as were the white coverlets on the twin beds. Beach pictures painted by her sister hung on the wall and the various shells they had found on the beach decorated the dressers. Her parents used the house mostly in the winter now that they lived up north.

She went downstairs to the main living space and turned on the heat to take the chill out of the air. Hurrying back to the car, she grabbed the food she brought from Luke's and put whatever needed to be cold in the refrigerator. She hadn't bought many supplies; her parents kept the pantry stocked. She was hopeful Luke could find Ken quickly. Plus, there was a store down the street open year-round, if she needed anything else.

Luke was going to be livid when he found her note. She didn't mention where she was going and didn't think he knew about this house. She didn't want him in harm's way.

Resetting the house alarm, she made herself a cup of tea, turned on the gas fireplace and settled in the study with a book, patting the gun in her pocket. She didn't know how long it would be before Ken would show up, but he would.

Her cell phone rang. She glanced at the number. It was Luke. Should she answer it? Maybe he had good news.

"Please tell me you found Ken?"

"Not yet, sweetheart. Soon, I promise. We're closing in. I'll be home soon; do you need anything from the store?"

Her heart was racing. Luke was going to be surprised ... no, pissed when he found out she wasn't home. She took the coward's way out and didn't mention that she wasn't at the house, that she left to save him and her friends. He would have made her promise not to leave the house. Promise not to engage Ken. *Not happening.*

Now she needed to regroup and plan her future. Hopefully, Luke would be in it, if he wasn't too angry about her taking off. If the Ken problem was resolved. If she was still alive.

LUKE GOT HOME and waved to Bob, who was on watch. Opening the door, he reset the alarm and called for Grace. No answer. She had specifically mentioned starting dinner. The house was quiet—too quiet. He checked every room, but Grace wasn't there. Where could she be? He checked the garage. Her car was gone. Had she run to the store without telling him? Had she told Bob? They were going to have a serious talk if that was the case.

He paced the living room. His mouth was parched. *Where was she?* He needed to talk to Bob but first walked into the kitchen to get some water, bring a bottle to Bob. Reaching for a water bottle, he saw a note. She left him a note?

With trembling hands, he picked it up and read it. Bile worked its way up his throat. *What the hell?* He was pissed. Beyond pissed.

How could Grace leave him a note telling him she wanted him safe, and the only way to do that was to leave him? He was a cop, for Christ's sake. He could protect her—he didn't need her protecting him.

They had some leads on Ken, and he expected to find the fucker before too long. He and Ben were so close to finding him. Just one more mistake. They thought they had a break when they found out Ken was staying in a shitty motel on the other side of town under an assumed name, but when they arrived, he had checked out. They were checking other dumps in the area. Ken must have rented another car under a false name because they found the rental he'd abandoned.

He needed to talk to Bob. He dialed Grace's cellphone, and it went straight to voicemail again. God, when he found her, she was getting a talking to. First, he needed to calm down. Getting angry wasn't helping him or Grace. Something must have happened for her to leave.

But as he looked down, he noticed a pink envelope crumbled by the coffee table. His heart was racing. How had that asshole found Grace? Did he take her? Was she terrified? Shit, he was terrified.

He picked up the envelope, and then spotted a CD. Taking the notecard out, he read "Peek a boo, I see you." This was not good. Not good at all. His laptop was on the table, so he sat down and inserted the CD into it.

Watching Grace go about her day with a smile on her face, watching her kiss him at the front door, and now knowing the bastard followed and recorded the two of them infuriated him. The lively background music made a mockery of a tender scene. The bedtime scene put him over the edge. And then there were scenes of her friends going about their ordinary business. Now he knew why she left.

Luke roared. That son of a bitch. This wasn't over. When he found Ken, he was going to beat the shit out of him and more.

Fuming, he ran out to confront Bob who was supposedly watching her. If Bob were asleep, there would be hell to pay. The storm was getting closer; Luke could feel the heavy moisture in the air. The thunder was quieting down, and he could hear the crickets chirping—a respite before the rain.

"Bob?"

Nothing.

He didn't see any movement in the car. He pulled his gun out and slowly approached Bob's door not wanting to get accidentally shot. He shivered. Shuffling closer, he called Bob's name again and knocked lightly on the open window with the butt of his gun but didn't get a reaction. A peek in the window showed Bob leaning over the steering wheel. Not moving. *Shit, shit, shit.*

He slowly opened the door, and Bob slid out. A quick scan didn't show any bullet wounds or blood. He felt for a pulse. Yes, he found one, but it was faint. Thank God. He dialed 911 and waited for the ambulance.

The ambulance was there in ten minutes. Once the medics loaded Bob on the gurney, Luke told them he would check back with the hospital shortly.

There was nothing he could do from home, and Luke decided to go back to the precinct. He was hoping something would come in that would help find this bastard. The storm was coming fast. Luke wanted to get there before it turned nasty. Feeling a despair as he never felt before, he called Ben, who said he would call right back.

He tried Grace. Voicemail again. Then dialed Sam to find out if Grace had called her.

Her phone rang twice, and Sam picked up. "Luke, what's going on?"

"Grace left."

"What? Left where?"

"She got a note and CD from Ken at the house. I don't know how he figured out where she was living, but he did. She's running scared thinking she can protect me, her friends by not being near us. I'm beyond worried.

"The cop watching the house is in the hospital doped out." He had to stop for a minute, his throat was tight, he was breathing heavy, and his heart was pounding, "Sam, I need to find her. Do you have any idea where she could have gone?"

A thought popped into his head, "Didn't you put a tracker on her phone for emergencies?"

"Yes, I did. Damn it all to hell. I'm going to kill that bastard when we find him," Sam spat out. "But first, I'm going to cut off his dick and then make him eat his balls and then ..."

He would have laughed at Sam ferociousness if he weren't so upset. Cutting off her verbal brutality, he said, "Not if I get to him first."

"I'll call you right back." Sam hung up.

The road was slick with rain now, and it was coming down in sheets. Luke tried to concentrate on driving, but he was frantic, and his mind kept wandering.

The phone rang. Hoping it was Sam, he answered. Ben was calling. "We got a break on Ken. He's registered at a motel close to Ramona Boulevard. Do you want to meet us there?"

"Shit yeah. Give me the address. I can be there in ten minutes."

He hung up. The phone rang again. It was Sam. "I tracked her phone. She's on the island at her parents' house."

"Her parents' house? What the fuck? I didn't know they still owned a house here. I knew she grew up in Black Pointe, but I assumed they sold their house when they moved to Boston."

"No. The house is in her stepfather's name, Goodwin, not Winslow. She never took his name."

"Shit." Luke banged his hand on the steering wheel. "I'm going to rip Grace a new one for not divulging that little tidbit."

"Luke, it probably wasn't on Grace's radar. Who knew this

was all going down like this? Besides you'll need to get in line. Where are you now?"

Luke told her and said that he was turning around toward the beach. He mentioned Ben had found out where Ken was staying, and that Ben was heading there to confront him.

"I'm going straight to Grace. Ben can handle Ken. Meet me at her parents' house." Sam promised to get there as soon as possible, and they hung up. Luke pulled over and turned toward the beach and Grace.

Luke's cell phone was ringing as he raced toward the beach.

"Luke, I just missed the fucker. The front desk said he checked out about an hour ago."

Luke gave Ben the address of Grace's parents' house..

"I'll be there as soon as possible," said Ben.

Would this nightmare ever end? Luke's breath was coming out in gasps. He was concentrating on the slick road, but his vision kept blurring. That's all he needed, to get in an accident on his way to save his woman.

He was terrified for Grace. Shit. He was terrified for himself. He said a quick prayer that he would arrive there in time.

CHAPTER FIFTY

So far, it had been too easy. Ken had tailed Grace toward the island. He stayed way back when Grace slid out of control on the slick road. *Foolish woman, driving so fast at night.* He guessed it scared her. When she stopped the car and let it idle by the side of the road for a few minutes, he pulled over so that she wouldn't see him.

He shadowed Grace to a large house by the ocean. He parked his car off the street in the bushes and watched her get out of her car, walk up to the keyless entry, enter the number and get back in her car.

By then he was already in place by a bush. When the garage door opened, he had just seconds to cozy up to the side of her car as she drove in. She wouldn't hear him over the motor running.

He was energized, alive. This was ending tonight. A movie couldn't have added more drama. The stupid woman leading the killer to a quiet out of the way spot. No one following her except the killer. Thunder, lightning, sheets of rain. Oh my. It made his heart quicken.

He had scrunched down on the opposite side of her car.

Grace's car hinges squeaked when she closed her door. A couple of beeps sounded as she deactivated the house alarm then the motor hummed as the garage door closed.

With him.

Inside.

Thump, thump. His heart was going a million miles an hour. Ken only prayed his asthma wouldn't act up. It was dusty in the garage, and he didn't have his inhaler. It was packed in his car ready for his trip back to D.C. and Rachel. Thinking of banging Rachel this weekend was keeping him motivated. First, he needed to finish the job. Well, Grace. Whatever. Tomato. Tomahto. It would be done tonight.

The sound of footsteps interrupted his thoughts of Rachel. Good. Grace was going inside. He warily peered around the front tire and saw light beckoning to him. He had seconds to sneak in. Silently he made his way to the doorway and scanned the interior of the house.

There. A closet. Ken tiptoed over and carefully opened the door, stepped inside, and crouched down behind coats, boots and other junk.

He heard Grace's footsteps heading back toward the garage, the slam of the door and the beeps of her punching in the alarm code. They were locked in together. Good.

That was close. It was a good thing it was cold out because the closet was cool. Any warmer and he would be unable to stop sneezing. Fool, why didn't he bring his inhaler?

Ken checked his watch. He would give Grace a little time to get comfy. Feel secure.

Grace's cell phone rang. He held his breath. Had the cop found out she left? He hoped not this soon. He needed more a little more time.

She didn't answer the call. Good. It seemed forever before Ken heard noises coming from what must be the kitchen.

The sound of a microwave. Shit, he was stifling in this hot closet. Would she ever settle down?

It had been silent for a good half hour, that was long enough for Grace to get settled. Slowly twisting the doorknob and glancing around, he saw the kitchen down the hall. Gingerly, he unfolded himself from the closet and crab-walked behind the center island. He took a chance and popped up. No one in the kitchen. Perfect.

Standing, he looked around the pristine kitchen, taking in the white cabinets and the cool blue on the walls. It had the beach feel Rachel would love.

Focus. He needed to focus.

A fully loaded knife rack was right in front of him. Thank you, Jesus. He chose a filet knife. Perfect. His hand caressed the sharp edges. Gotta love a family who knew how to take care of its knives. Much better than using his hands which he'd initially planned to do.

Now, where was the star of the show?

Taking his shoes off, he walked barefoot through the kitchen, the dining room, and the living room. The bedrooms were probably upstairs. The house was spacious and nice, gotta give her that. Walking down the long hallway from the living room to what looked like a den, Ken glanced at family portraits on the walls. Nice family. Happy family. Guess they'll miss her. His dad never had any family photos around. Well, that wasn't true. There was that one big picture on the wall of his dad receiving his Pulitzer. Shoving it in his face. No wonder his mom left—egotistical bastard.

There was a soft light on in the den. Grace had turned on the gas fireplace, and he saw her sitting in a chair, covered with a shawl, asleep. Ken sat down on the sofa and looked at Grace. Pretty woman, not his kind of pretty but still pretty.

Here was the woman who'd replaced him at the newspaper, ruining his chance of getting ahead, destroying his cash cow when she wrote that exposé on the senator. It was all her fault. Things had finally been going his way. Power and money. He worked so hard to show his father that he had been wrong about him. He had gotten ahead, in spite, of what his father thought of him. He had promised Rachel the moon, and a house that they could settle down in, have a family, and by God, he was going to fulfill that promise.

He stroked the knife in his hand. Sharp. *Yes!* He stared at the small drops of blood from his finger, then sucked them. He had stroked the knife a little too hard.

A buzzing startled him. He looked around but calmed down when he realized it was Grace's cell phone. She didn't wake up. He stared at her sleeping peacefully for a few minutes.

Time to party. He murmured, "Grrrace."

She didn't wake up.

"Grrrace, wake up."

Still sleeping.

Walking over to her, he ran the tip of the knife across her throat. No blood yet but there would be.

"Grrrace, time to die," he purred.

Still sleeping. Damn, she needed to be awake to complete the game.

GRACE WAS SLEEPY. So sleepy. The adrenaline had burned off. The soothing tea and warm fire had finally relaxed her. She would call Luke and Sam in a few minutes to tell them she was safe. She debated whether to let them know where she was.

Grace was sure Ken was close. When he found her, she would shoot him—no doubt in her mind. Finish him, or he would finish her.

She still didn't understand why he'd targeted her. Lots of people lost their jobs. The man was probably a little left of crazy to take it to this extreme. It didn't matter. He was escalating his efforts, and she knew it wasn't going to end well for her if she didn't take charge.

She pulled the shawl tighter around her shoulders. If she could close her eyes for a minute, it would give her time to think about her next steps, Luke and how to deal with the fallout of running. In retrospect, leaving Luke's house wasn't the smartest idea she had, but Grace had been frantic when she got the CD.

Just a few minutes to rest. That was all she needed.

Her eyelids were so heavy. It couldn't hurt to close them for just a minute. Could it? She was confident the answers would come, but first ...

She closed her eyes.

The dream was disturbing. All hell had broken loose. Luke was angry and walked away from her. Sam was pissed. Everyone had deserted her. Betrayed again.

Not a good dream at all. And what was going on with the pain across her throat? And the hot breath near her ear? Grace opened her eyes.

Oh, shit.

She glanced sideways. Ken smiled. A great big Howdy Doody smile.

THUMPITY, THUMPITY, THUMP. Her heart pounded hard in her chest. Could Ken hear it? She couldn't control the shaking in her hands. She was paralyzed by fear.

She watched him sit down across from her, shake his head and grin. Holding a knife like a lover. She knew this was the end.

There was a buzzing noise. Her phone. But where was it?

There.

She put her hand out to get it.

"Tsk, tsk," he whispered.

He shook his finger. "Don't touch it."

What to do?

Her hand touched cold steel under the shawl. Thank God, she brought her gun. Could she? Could she fire and aim to kill him?

No time for doubt.

Carefully, she grasped the handle. Slowly, she turned the barrel aiming at Ken, hoping he wouldn't notice the movement under her shawl.

He was sitting there still grinning.

Gently, Grace placed her finger on the trigger.

Then he was lunging at her.

She pulled the trigger. The sound echoed in the room. It deafened her, but she could still hear Ken roar. She thought she'd hit him, but Ken continued lunging at her. The knife glistening in his hand.

He tried to knock the gun out of her hand, but she threw her shawl over his head, pushed him and ran. He was thrashing about trying to uncover his face with one hand while brandishing the knife in the other.

Grace took off running toward the stairs. She raced up them, still holding the gun.

Running into her parents' bedroom.

Locking the door.

She pushed a chair under the knob and activated the panic alarm. She ran into the huge master bathroom, latching the door behind her. She could hear Ken screaming "You're dead, bitch!" over the ear-splitting screech of the alarm.

Thankful she still had the gun, but she realized she didn't have her phone with her—nothing to do about it now, though.

She tried not to panic. She took deep gulps of air. The coppery smell of her blood was making her sick

The bastard had wounded her. She looked at the huge gash on her arm oozing blood and felt faint. It didn't hurt now, but she knew when the adrenaline wore off, it would hurt like a bitch—providing she was still alive.

Hearing faint thuds, she knew Ken was trying to break down the bedroom door. She prayed the police would get to her before Ken did. But if not, well...

She hunkered down in the tub and pointed the gun towards the door. Her hands shook uncontrollably. She frantically glanced around the bathroom—there was nothing else in the room to use.

A giant crash had Grace slinking down farther in the tub.

Any second now Ken would come crashing through the bathroom door and Grace prayed for strength.

Screaming "Bitch!" Ken burst through the bathroom door. His right arm was bleeding heavily. He held it close to his side —useless. His eyes were wild. His face red and blotchy. He sliced wildly through the air with the knife.

Whoosh.

"You're going to die tonight, bitch." Spittle flew from his lips.

Whoosh, whoosh.

Grace stood up, aimed the gun at him. Her hands were trembling and sweaty. Her finger slipped off the trigger. *Shit. Try again.* She pulled the trigger. The noise reverberated in the small room. Her ears hurt.

He yelped. Had she grazed his side? Thought she had. Couldn't tell.

Shit. Ken kept coming. He was in a murderous frenzy. His face contorted in a deadly rage. His lips pulled back in a death grimace. His eyes were wide open and wild.

"Die, bitch."

She aimed again. But Ken was too fast. He tried to knock the gun from her hand with the knife. She pulled the trigger.

Click. Click?

The gun had jammed.

Ken smirked. Slithered up to her like a snake with a mouse in its sight.

He was poised to strike again. His arm up, the knife gleaming, a maniacal smile on his face. "Gotcha now, bitch."

A voice shouted at her to get down.

Get down? Grace put up her arm to protect herself. The knife rocketed down. At the same time, she saw a flying body hit Ken, shoving him to the floor.

Pain. *I'm dead.* The last thought she had before darkness overtook her.

CHAPTER FIFTY-ONE

Hearing the sweetest angel voice ever calling her name, Grace opened her eyes. Luke. Thank God. It was Luke's voice calling her.

Luke was standing by Ken who he had knocked out on the floor.

Luke leaned over to her. "Grace, sweetheart, are you all right? Are you hurt?"

She closed her eyes. It was too hard to talk.

He ran his hands over her body. "Shit, there's blood everywhere."

Grace recoiled at the gruesome scene in front of her. Luke was bleeding from the shoulder. Ken was moaning, holding his side as blood oozed between his fingers. He was trying to stand up. There was blood splatter everywhere.

Luke turned, grabbed Ken by the hair and knocked his head into the sink. Ken screamed.

Watching Luke none too gently handcuff Ken, she tried to answer him but only manage a squeak.

Ken was standing now and still bleeding profusely from his arm, yelling for the police.

Luke shook his head. "Shut up, shit-for-brains. I am the police, and you're under arrest."

Grace gingerly stood up in the tub, testing her legs which felt like noodles. She reached out to the wall for support. Blood was dripping down her arm, and she couldn't stop her body from violently trembling. She needed Luke's arm around her, but he was fending off Ken who kept butting him with his body.

Luke slammed Ken again.

The alarm was still shrilly blasting, piercing her eardrums. She couldn't stand the noise anymore. She carefully stepped out of the tub, scooted around Luke and Ken and turned it off.

Silence.

Thank God. Silence. Well, except for Ken who was now on the floor crying.

Two cops, guns drawn plowed into the bedroom followed by Sam, Danny, and Ben.

Noise, pandemonium, chaos.

Everyone was yelling.

Grace put her hands over her ears and turned away. Tears ran down her face, and she couldn't stop the sobs. Sam had her. Holding her while the police sorted everything out.

Sam moved away. Strong arms enveloped her, and soft kisses caressed her neck. Luke turned her around. "Baby don't ever scare me like that again. I love you; I told you we would handle this and protect you."

Grace couldn't stop sobbing, and Luke led her out into the hall. She hugged him close, feeling his strength soothe her, and nodded.

LUKE HELD Grace while she sobbed, reflecting on how little time he had to get to her.

He had pulled into Grace's driveway and noticed a black sedan parked in the bushes.

Oh, my God am I too late? Sam had given him the keyless code to the garage, and he pressed it, running in with his gun drawn.

He was forced to break the door to the house open, his hands were sweating, and his heart was pounding so hard he feared Ken would hear it before he got to him. Where was Grace?

Thankfully he heard the ruckus and breaking of wood over the alarm and was able to follow the noise upstairs and observe the drama in the bathroom. He had milliseconds after Grace's gun jammed to tackle the bastard who was lunging at her.

He had never been so frightened in his life.

Watching the woman he loved facing a mad killer was something he never wanted to see again. However, she looked like a warrior standing up in the tub with her gun locked and loaded. That was the memory he wanted to keep.

EPILOGUE

They looked like a couple of boxers who lost a good fight. Grace's right arm was in a sling and healing. Luke's left shoulder was bundled up in bandages, and they both had bruises all over their bodies. But they were alive and free, unlike Ken who would be spending the rest of his days in jail for murder and attempted murder.

Grace's parents' home was still cordoned off. Friends were arriving with food, drinks, and good cheer. Sam had decided the weekend would be a perfect time to throw a party to celebrate Grace's promotion. Grace hadn't been sure, but after talking it over with Sam, they had decided Grace's memories of the house shouldn't be negative ones. Her parents were due to arrive the next day and would stay at her condo. She and Luke were felt so blessed to be alive.

The sun was setting. The moon was rising over the ocean. A big red moon. The Blood Moon. Dusk. Peaceful time. Grace stared out at the whitecaps pushing their way toward shore. Ebb and flow. Love and hate. The ocean was like life, you never knew what was going to happen, but something always would, and life would continue on.

Luke gently touched her arm, "Penny for your thoughts."

Grace smiled. "Not thinking much."

But she had been. Ken had confessed to killing Jean, the other jogger and tormenting Grace. He gave them Rachel's information, and they had contacted her. Rachel was upset Ken was arrested for taking his hatred of Grace to the next level. However, they couldn't get any more information from her.

Luke was still mad at her for taking off to her parents' house. However horrific the experience had been, she had gained the confidence to stand up for herself. Was she sorry? No. She loved Luke, and if she could keep him safe, she would do it again.

LUKE GLANCED OVER AT GRACE. She had said she wasn't thinking about anything. In his experience, women often said "nothing," but, in reality, they were. Her experience was going to take a while to get over, and he would watch Grace closely in case she needed his help. He was so angry with her and yet so proud. He still couldn't believe she had gone to the house to save him. *Him!* He was happy the shooting lessons had paid off. Grace would be dead now if she hadn't had them.

Luke took a minute to thank his lucky stars and plan a time when he and Grace would have a stern lecture about saving him. If she wouldn't agree with him, he thought he would just put her over his knee and redden her very fine ass until she did. God, why did that thought pop into his head? He was getting hard just thinking about it. Even though it was dark, if he had to get up, they would be able to hang a flag on Mr. Cool.

Grace glanced at him and then down. Her eyes widened, and she started to smile. "Don't say a word," he threatened.

Sam came over and sat in the sand in front of them. "I don't think I can handle anything like this ever again," she said. "That took ten years off my life."

Ten years? That's all? Luke thought it was a lifetime but still, he was grateful for Sam's help.

"So, what's next, Grace?" Sam glanced over at him. A small smile on her lips. "Is it true you were offered your job back in D.C.? Are you going to take it?"

Luke stopped breathing. His stomach contents threatened to back up. Grace hadn't mentioned anything to him about moving back to D.C. That was the job she wanted—wasn't it? Working in the big city? The excitement? Writing about the movers and shakers? Her career would take off. Would he stand in the way or let her go? Could he start over in D.C.? He nervously fingered the box in his pocket. Too soon. Grace needed to find her way first.

LUKE HAD TURNED PALE. He slumped in his seat and went completely still, a blank look on his face. Grace wasn't sure he was even breathing. She hadn't mentioned to him that she had been given an apology and offered her old job back with a substantial raise. It hadn't taken her more than a nanosecond to refuse it. Too many betrayals and bad memories. Her future was here with the man she loved.

Grace gave him a small smile and rubbed his hand. "No. I love it here. The newspaper is going to keep me on as an investigative reporter. Nancy Frey isn't coming back. Her mother needs her."

She heard Luke exhale softly.

Grace then glared at Sam who wouldn't stop smirking at Luke. *The little witch!* Sam winked at her. She guessed Sam finally got Luke back for abandoning Grace. Oh yeah, payback's a bitch and with her friend Sam, Luke was lucky that was all she did.

"Besides," Grace said as she glanced at Luke. "The love of my life is here."

She saw love shining back at her.

Book 2 of KnightGuard Security, *Evidence of Murder,* tells Ben and Marlee's story. Turn the page for a preview.

As always, reviews are nice. If you enjoy the book, please leave a review.

Follow me on:

Twitter: @lsferrariwrites
Facebook: @lilaferrariauthor
Instagram: @lsferrariwrites
Pinterest: @lsferrariwrites
Goodreads: @lilaferrariwrites
Bookbub: @lilaferrariwrites

For more information on books by Lila Ferrari, visit her website at www.lilaferrariwrites.com, where you can subscribe to her newsletter to get updates on releases, fun facts and enter giveaways.

Preview of

EVIDENCE OF MURDER

ROBERT GILLIGAN hummed along with the car radio after a long night and day of crazy, fantastic sex with the love of his life, Amber. They fucked like bunnies in heat on every surface of the fancy hotel room overlooking the ocean. He would have liked to continue all weekend, but Amber had to leave early to go home to change for "a thing." He hated "things," and women seemed to have a lot of those. However, it was a shower for her best friend, so here he was—satiated but frustrated. He could never get enough of Amber.

As he headed home, an accident on the highway detoured him through downtown Lakedale. Plenty of time to rehash the best weekend of his life so far.

Thinking about Amber got him hard again. *Damn.* Another cold shower and a date with his hand. Not the first time, not the last.

A honking horn brought him back to reality and the realization he was driving past the commercial area where his accounting firm, which was providing him with the lifestyle he always wanted, was located. So different from his childhood where new clothes and food were in short supply Not that anyone would ever know that part of his history.

His money now was all in offshore accounts. Knowing how to manipulate the books was the gift that kept on giving —to him. He'd planned ten years for this moment, and in a few more years, it would be him and Amber on an island wearing nothing at all unless they wanted to.

He saw lights on in the front office and frowned. The office was closed on the weekend. Did the cleaning people forget to turn them off?

The blinds were half-open, and someone was walking around. Robert slowed down for a closer look. Was that Jim? What the hell was Jim doing here on a Saturday night during their slow season when there was no reason for anyone to be here?

He turned his headlights off and pulled around to the backside of the building where security cameras didn't have a good angle. He parked here when he didn't want people to know when he came into the office to monitor accounts. Even though he could work at home, the office was more accessible. Just couldn't be too careful. How fortunate it was that his building was in a nearly deserted office park.

Now that he thought about it, Jim and that bitch Marlee Burns had been acting somewhat squirrelly lately.

Marlee asked him something about one of his accounts a while ago—the one from which he made personal withdrawals. What a laugh—personal withdrawals. She shouldn't know anything about that account, except she took a call from someone at their firm questioning a withdrawal when he was away from the office. She asked him about it. Him. As if he would ever tell her anything.

Would she have talked to Jim about it? He knew she didn't mention it to Amber or she would have told him, but then Marlee didn't tell Amber everything. Marlee was outspoken and nosy, and she wasn't one to let things go, even though he told her a couple of times that he would look into it. Furthermore, Jim was her boss, and rumor was they were dating, so maybe she did tell him. Stupid move. His future happiness was not going to be derailed by those two.

He got his gun from the glove box and tucked it behind his back. Gently closing his car door, he swiped at the sweat dripping down his forehead. The heat and humidity of Florida were a constant, even in the fall. He let himself in the back door and stopped when he heard murmuring. He inched closer. Jim was talking to a woman.

"Marlee, I think I found some discrepancies in this account. Figuring it out will take a minute. Would you mind getting us some coffee?"

"Sure thing."

Marlee. Of course, it was her. In his business, as always. Robert couldn't believe his ears. Damn if she wasn't the bane of his existence.

Footsteps moved away and toward the kitchen. Time to find out what the hell was going on. He snuck up behind Jim, who was looking intently at his computer and writing something down.

"What the hell are you doing?" Robert kept his voice low.

Jim jumped and turned, his eyes wide and afraid. He tried to cover up what he was looking at, but Robert saw one of his client accounts open, exposing all his little secrets.

Again, he asked, "What are you doing?"

"N-noth-nothing." Jim's eyes darted over to the computer. "Just had some work to catch up on."

"Liar." Robert pushed him aside and looked at the computer screen. "You have no right to look into any of my accounts."

Jim's eyes narrowed, and his chin came up defiantly. "I have every right if you're embezzling."

"You need to prove that."

"Oh, but I can." Jim got cocky. "I've been following the breadcrumbs for a while, and I'm going to the police with my evidence." He leaned back in his chair, folded his arms and smirked.

The blood rushed to Robert's face. "Calling the police

isn't happening. I've worked too hard to get where I am. My future isn't going to be ruined by shit like you."

He grabbed Jim by the collar. "You son of a bitch, what do you have?"

Jim's body twitched as he struggled to get away. He gagged. "I have everything I need on a thumb drive that will send you to jail," he spat out.

"Not happening." Robert held on to Jim's collar and reached behind his back to pull out his gun.

Jim's eyes widened in disbelief. He twisted to get out of Robert's hold, but Robert held on tight. Jim gulped. It was the last thing he did before Robert pulled the trigger. Jim went down. Robert hadn't killed him. Yet. He needed that thumb drive.

A high-pitched scream assaulted his eardrums. Damn, he'd forgotten about Marlee.

He turned and saw her running out of the break room, throwing the coffee cups she was holding onto the floor, coffee splashing everywhere.

"Marlee," he yelled. "Come back here. It isn't what you think."

But she didn't turn back, just kept running. Robert started after her but tripped over Jim's prone body. Marlee was too fast. She got to her car and fishtailed out of the parking lot before he could get out the front door.

Damn it all to hell. What a way to finish a weekend of fucking. Getting fucked.

What to do? The better question was, what would that stupid bitch do? Go to the police. Riiight. Like he hadn't mentioned so many times that his cousin was chief of police. Go home? Hopefully. Marlee rented the small renovated garage behind Amber's house. She also confided in Amber quite frequently. A bonus for him. Maybe tonight he would get lucky again.

He dialed Amber on the off chance she was still at home. She was and agreed to what he asked.

He hung up and walked back to deal with Jim and decide what to tell the police, if anything. He needed to be smart and think this through.

Learn more at lilaferrariwrites.com.

BOOKS BY LILA FERRARI

KNIGHTGUARD SECURITY SERIES

Each book in the series is a stand-alone and can be read in any order. Reviews are greatly appreciated.

Evidence of Betrayal — Book 1 (Luke and Grace's story)

Evidence of Murder — Book 2 (Ben and Marlee's story)

Evidence of Lies — Book 3 (Pete and Julie's story)

Evidence of Deceit — Book 4 (Joe and Claire's story)

Evidence of Revenge — Book 5 (Sam and Mark's story)

Evidence of Secrets — Book 6 (Hank and Laura's story) - available soon

Evidence of Evil — Book 7 (Logan and Maddie's story) — available in 2022

NEW SERIES

SEALs of Distinction – Book 1 available in 2022

Haywood Lake Mysteries — Book 1 available in 2022

ABOUT THE AUTHOR

I've been writing forever. Poems, plays, short stories, cookbooks, grants, newsletters, newspaper articles and now full-length novels.

Growing up in New England where summers are sweet but winters are long and cold has given me lots of opportunity to expand my creativity.

I have enjoyed: basket weaving, spinning wool, quilting, canning, teaching cooking and traveling.

I have been a recipe tester, sailor, farmer, shepherd, cattlewoman, chick herder and Master Gardener.

Like many women, I have worked full-time, raised two children, and helped my husband's career. Finally, I get to make my dream come true. After all, dreams never die, and new doors open every day.

Today, I live in sunny Florida with my husband enjoying paradise. In addition to writing novels, I recently took up birding and photography. My photos have done well in local contests.

My stories are about courage, redemption and second chances. Everyone deserves them, don't you agree?

Made in the USA
Columbia, SC
07 February 2022

54836763R00207